KILLING
TIME

KILLING TIME

RICHARD HOLLAND

Matador
9 Priory Business Park,
Wistow Road, Kibworth Beauchamp,
Leicestershire. LE8 0RX
Tel: 0116 279 2299
Email: books@troubador.co.uk
Web: www.troubador.co.uk/matador
Twitter: @matadorbooks

ISBN 978 1800461 383

British Library Cataloguing in Publication Data.
A catalogue record for this book is available from the British Library.

Printed and bound in Great Britain by 4edge Limited
Typeset in 11pt Adobe Garamond Pro by Troubador Publishing Ltd, Leicester, UK

Matador is an imprint of Troubador Publishing Ltd

For Nicky, Alex, Dominic, Wellie & Bernie

CHAPTER 1

Murder isn't appreciated like it should be. Not a common assault in the street that goes wrong, a botched mugging, or a burglary that gets out of hand. Or one of those clumsy ten a penny stabbings that litter the news in London. One after another. A procession of endless crime. Anybody can stoop to that, allow their emotions to run riot in the heat of the moment and lose it.

Anybody can become a murderer, but it takes a level of finesse to do it well. To be classy.

There's nothing respectable about simple thuggery, but when it's planned and considered, that's when it can be beautiful. Poetic. The details make a murder, when you know it's coming. What it is that's coming, who it's coming to, and when. Especially when they are blissfully unaware. Ignorant. That's the thrill, not in the chase, but in the knowledge and the planning of the event, and the delicious and excruciating details.

Society can't nod to it because it's wrong, or perceived to be wrong, but everything can be so well planned and so well executed that it can be exceptional. Perfection, even. Literature, architecture, music. Murder. There'll never be a Grammy or an Oscar for it, and that's a shame, because high quality crime can be admired by those of us in the right circles.

So what if your idol is one of the Kray's or Charles Manson? Everybody needs a hobby.

*

William Reynolds is an ageing man of deteriorating standards. He doesn't present well and clearly hasn't looked after himself. Baggy old clothes, a slight arch to his back and greying hair that looks to be combed regularly, if not washed. Slick, black and grey, swept backwards like an old school gangster. He wishes. He's in his late sixties but looks a good few years older, with haggard skin and dark bags hanging under his eyes. Features that aren't there simply because he's tired. Visible effects of a long and full life that has taken its toll, and that he wears heavily.

His teeth have a worn look, a yellow tinge that only nicotine can provide. He's either been smoking for decades, or is one of the modern types who has quit, but still smokes the odd one in the garage when he feels like it. He may have quit, or tried to, but he looks like he still enjoys a smoke. I've never understood those who quit after forty years of smoking Marlboro's. The damage is done, the lungs and body are well beyond any form of repair. Maybe he could just use one of those electronic things that seem so popular now, fashionable even, although I'm struggling to see him vaping.

He moves well enough for a man of his age, but his days of running for a bus are well behind him. He walks freely but with a gentle edge to the movement, and probably has a stick in the house somewhere, just in case.

William has not weathered well, and life has not been kind to his body. But I know that already. I know his routines. I know when he wanders out to the local Londis to buy a paper, milk or a lottery ticket. I know when he waters his garden later in the autumn evening like you're meant to, and when there's not a hosepipe ban in play.

Routine is great. We all live by it. Monday to Friday alarm. Meetings, commutes, Friday night post-work drinks with friends at that same pub. Dentist once a year, all that shit. We all like it to some degree too, as boring as it is. We all revert to type and fall back into that groove. The rat race.

But that makes us predictable. It makes *him* predictable, and it also makes him susceptible. There he is, pottering around with his plants, chirping away to some birds or his watering can, planning a cup of tea and a few biscuits, or whatever old people do, but he'll be dead within a few hours. He has no idea. No idea at all.

My knowledge of his routine and his health will all contribute to what's about to happen to him, which is why I'm *buzzing* inside. The perfectionist in me is breathing hard and controlling my emotions, so this evening will not be rushed. That would be wasteful, and a human life should not be wasted. It should be valued, used well and lived virtuously, but the simple fact is that some just need taking. Some lives just need extinguishing, and in this case slowly, but I have standards and they will be upheld. Besides, William Reynolds is barely the cream of the crop, and he will get what's coming to him.

The evening is well settled. It's late August and the day has been good, but a chill has settled in and the sun stopped offering any warmth a couple of hours ago, least of all to a pensioner.

Daylight has faded and there is dampness in the air with a cool breeze. It's quiet.

My car is parked a few streets away so as not to be too obvious. This road is tight, and any unrecognisable car parked in the street on a night like tonight would stand out like a sore thumb. The neighbourhood watch brigade wouldn't miss that trick, especially with what's about to happen. Give the old bastards something to talk about.

I'm dressed in black with a dark hoodie. My attire shouldn't set me apart but I'm not a resident, and am conscious that any human contact could be fatal, could even mean I'd need to silence more than one pensioner tonight. But I've made provision for that.

My approach to the house is deft, and releases a slow, nervous energy. The street is quiet. Nicely silent. The area is semi-respectable as William earned a wage, held down a job and worked for much of his adult life. The parts that he could anyway. He'd also married well and had a family, but he's a widow so is home alone tonight, as he is every night. Has been for years now.

There isn't a soul to be seen. Perfect. Everybody safely in and tucked up. Nobody out. No dog walkers. No witnesses. There isn't a gate to navigate; the posts and hinges are there but the gate is long gone. There's a crazy paving type path with a few plant pots scattered about. He's made a bit of effort and seems to be keeping things nice.

There's no gravel to crunch, no security lights. Nothing that could make too much noise, alert a neighbour, or William himself, to somebody being outside. The things that could easily give the game away before it's started, make a hard job harder. But it's that danger that excites you, makes your heart skip a beat, like an affair or a drug. Wrong but so very right. The itch that needs scratching.

He's in there and the back door is unlocked, the TV is on and he's still up. Killing the evening. Killing time.

The handle to the door is old, worn steel that is bitterly cold to the touch, even through the glove. The opaque glass is pitted and bobbled. The bottle green paint is tidy enough but crusted at the edges; paint that has seen decades since it was anything near to being fresh. With a gentle push the handle goes down. It isn't locked. It rarely is; he's got comfortable and complacent. With barely a sound it opens freely. No squeaky hinges, no reverberation.

I slip inside.

The early steps into his house are like walking on the moon. Foreign ground. Slowly, one at a time. My motion is careful and exaggerated. I'm on his turf now. I'm no longer a pedestrian who could plead ignorance if challenged. I'm inside the house and there's no going back.

There are several rooms and divisions to an old-fashioned property with an equally old-fashioned layout. There's a lean-to leading into a small kitchen, a little recess in the wall that looks like he's using it as a pantry, and a hallway. The kitchen still has a Belfast sink on metal legs with a big curved tap, but this isn't a restoration or some high-end installation. The kitchen is as modern as William, with melamine sides and worn lino floors. There's a small dining table and a solitary wooden chair.

I can see him. There's less than ten yards between us, and William hasn't flinched. He's just sitting there, motionless. I can see the back of his head slumped into his chair; an old brown leather armchair that fits him like a glove, the deep and worn crinkles mirroring his own battered complexion.

My momentum is helping me to glide forwards, my confidence is growing, but I slow myself down to avoid any careless mistakes. I have no intention of rushing this and missing out.

I continue to move carefully forwards. The rucksack I'm wearing is making the simple task of walking much harder. It's essential though. It contains the necessary kit, the tools for the job.

The distance between us is closing and he's completely motionless. It's still just another evening for him.

My hands are gloved but well practised. Dexterity is key; the ability to handle and manipulate will all play a part in what I'm about to do. What I'm about to commit.

So agonisingly close, the sensation of adrenaline is really starting to ripple. A bead of sweat forms on the nape of my neck and I can feel my heart rate climbing, pulsating through my body.

The TV is on. An old set. No flat screen. I'm in the same room now. It's so tempting to rush forwards. To panic and not enjoy these last few steps. To lose them. It would be easy just to beat him round the head, to rush the start and regret wasting it; even easier for the anger to explode, to lose control, but I'm forcibly holding it back.

He's still unaware, still pissing another evening away. QI is on, an old episode. Stephen Fry is wearing a purple blazer and talking about bees. David Mitchell laughs and William seems to enjoy the gag.

Focus. He deserves better. He deserves my attention, and he's yards from getting it.

I start to sense him sensing me. The adrenaline spikes in my veins. He knows. He fucking knows. But he can't move, he's rooted to the spot. Too scared to react, too cowardly to move, or just plain terrified. I'm not sure which, but my enjoyment of the moment rocks through me.

This is delicious. This is the moment I'll remember. Savour. The precious seconds where he knows I'm behind him. The fear is radiating out of him now. Pouring. I can practically smell it. He has absolutely no power left. He's fucked and he knows it, and he can't move. The fear has paralysed him. An old man crippled in the moment. The last few steps don't need to be quiet. He isn't moving and I march forward with a real arrogance as I finally get within touching distance.

There is no reaction, no verbal exchanges, no burst of energy to call on as the final yard provides the first physical contact between us. The night is young.

CHAPTER 2

DCI Rob Rhone sat back in his office chair, a large black leather chair with chrome fittings. It sprang back as he rocked on it, thinking about the reports on his desk. The number of sexual assaults in and around Victoria Park had been increasing, and pressure was mounting for the force to provide a solution; to improve the optics. Rob was battling with his superiors who wanted a visible presence, night patrols and uniformed officers on the grounds. Rob hadn't disagreed but was of the view that that would move the assaults, not reduce them. Having ten assaults happen in the streets or alleyways around the parks may change the way the newspapers reported it, but Rob wanted people to be convicted. Not moved.

He sat, wearing dark blue trousers with a crisp white shirt and brown shoes. Smart, but these days a tie only came out for certain occasions. Today wasn't one of them. The suit jacket hung from the back of his door, now that the heating had done a sufficient job of warming the office.

Rob ran his hand through his mousy brown hair, realising it was due a cut as he did so, and then ran his fingers through his short stubble. Subconscious acts. He read the report summary again and flicked a biro through the fingers of his left hand as he processed the detail, before pushing his wire rim glasses back up his nose.

Rob Rhone is an experienced police officer, the type who can silently look you up and down without moving his eyes and measure you up, making you feel deeply uncomfortable in the process.

He'd earned his stripes in a world where DNA profiling, CCTV, automatic number plate recognition and cyber crime were relatively new concepts, and could all give a black and white result. Policing had evolved, it was different, and Rob had seen people skills decline as a result. Instinct is less prevalent in modern policing because it isn't needed to the same extent as it was in days gone by. Arrest a suspect, let the lab boys, CCTV or mobile data either prove they did it or exonerate them, and away you go. Easy justice.

The ability to read a human being, know what they're thinking, why they're thinking it and what drives them. That's policing. Knowing why people do the things they do, why people commit unthinkable, inexplicable atrocities against one another on a seemingly daily basis. City stabbings and endless, relentless drug crime.

Sitting in a room with a murderer or a rapist can be difficult. Can be emotionally draining, but Rob almost seemed comfortable talking to them. It's hard to listen to a murderer, to allow them to speak, to explain – *try* to explain.

Rob could use silence and allow it to sit in a room. Allow it to fester. The awkwardness was lost on a man of his nature, but people would often talk and say way more than they ever meant to in his presence.

Those skills extended to those in his charge too. He could be a difficult man to work for. Hard and reliable, but difficult. He demanded loyalty and expected the highest of standards in return. He was consistent, and could occasionally be blunt, be abrupt without knowing it, or leave a pause when you asked him a question and really wanted an answer. But he cared. He cared about the people under his wing, a rarity in today's disloyal and self-important world.

He could read you. He knew when you weren't 100%, when you were off your game, when you'd had a late one, a row with your spouse or a weekend you'd rather forget.

It's an instinct and an ability, to look somebody square in the eye and *know*. To be able to get deep into their psyche. Rob had traits and beliefs borne from nineties policing, and had come of age as DNA profiling and the digital world had boomed, and was something of a hybrid as a result. He'd been regularly promoted as a standout officer, and had reached the position of DCI in his early forties, an achievement he was happy with.

Rob had held senior roles in the force for a period of time, and like in any operation, and in any business, you need a good team of people around you. Strong people. He'd made the steps through his career, achieved the promotions, but to be a good DCI or DS you need to be exceptionally focused and hard-working, sacrifice things you may not want to. Golf. Nights out with friends. A marriage or two.

Rob was divorced, having married in his early twenties, but was a proud father to two boys, who were both now settled well into secondary school and growing up quickly. He was a bachelor again and more than happy with that arrangement. He was free of the complications and commitments that a marriage or relationship can bring. The hassle.

Rob had been successful in the force, had made the necessary transitions as the culture and expectations shifted. He'd developed the range of skills needed as the rungs got higher. And on the rung he was currently perched, he needed every one of the skills he had used to get there, but he also needed to be a manager. A co-ordinator. Policeman or not, this is 2019 and things need to be done a certain way, and Rob was more than at home with that notion.

Any future career moves are less clear, even in his own mind. Ambitious, but a policeman, not a politician. Another step up the ladder into an assistant chief constable role and the transition is seismic. Away from the real action, the coal-face. He's comfortable in the role and in his life, living in the moment whilst harbouring an undisclosed view that murderers and rapists are easier to predict and work with than politicians.

CHAPTER 3

"Go on then, who wants a coffee?" offered DC Jennifer James. "I made one earlier but waiting for you tossers to make one's like waiting for Christmas."

Jen was full of charisma, stacked with personality and brimming with sass, which made her a popular and highly respected character around the station. Her bounding energy made her a fantastic detective, and she'd been deservedly promoted to her current rank at a younger age than her recent predecessors would have expected. She would no doubt feature in Leicestershire's policing hierarchy of the future, should her determination and vigour continue.

She launched from her chair, standing tall and waited for a response.

"I'm waiting!"

She stood, a broad smile across her face, her foot tapping impatiently. A tall figure, wearing a knee-length black and white print dress, and a black Gucci belt with a gold GG logo to the centre. Black tights and flat black shoes completed her attire. The dress framed her perfectly, shaping her figure and falling off the curvaceousness of her body in all the right places.

Her mid-length brown hair spilled over her shoulders, usually tied but loose today and flowing beautifully. It could be red again next week, or black, or purple. Smart, classy and professional. Tomorrow she could be wearing jeans, a top and a scarf, but she'd still look the part and carry herself perfectly. Effervescent femininity and a 'no shit' persona rolled beautifully into one. Modern and relevant.

The only quality that could hold her back was her wicked sense of humour, and ability to deliver a cutting one-liner. Funny to most but occasionally inappropriate in the greater scheme of things, especially if you were on the receiving end.

Rob and his DS; Nicky Green, had recruited Jen from a dead-end role she was holding in Lutterworth, a small but affluent town south of Leicester. She was treading water, and they both knew immediately that she was ready for greater responsibility. Something bigger. She had the strength of character needed in the city, as well as some tough traits that she'd need to take on a DS role and the politics and responsibility it entails.

"Good on you, Jen," shouted DS Nicky Green. "No sugar. You know me, trying to be good."

Nicky is fifteen years or so older than Jen, and married. No eternity ring yet though, something she griped about periodically. She'd married her husband just over five years ago, before Jen had joined the team. A well dressed, attractive and confident blonde, bespectacled and usually with a designer handbag on her arm, Nicky is a solid police officer of great experience and Rob's dependable right-hand woman.

Having been on the force for nineteen years, Nicky is one of those who has seen it all, and has experienced the good, the bad and the ugly, which had forged a warm persona, but a tough core that could be intolerant. Nicky didn't suffer fools.

She'd started in uniform as a young woman, and worked hard and consistently over the last two decades to earn promotions, resulting in her current role as detective sergeant.

Her promotions had taken longer than Jen's, for no other reason than the hierarchy of the nineties seemed to prefer middle-aged men in beige suits for DS. A real boys' club. It was a time when the station resembled a crap version of *Life on Mars*, only without the charisma. Or the Audi. Nicky was multi-skilled, knew everybody and was a go-to character for all manner of issues, of both a professional and personal nature. If you needed information, a snout or a journalist, marriage guidance, gift ideas or your phone unblocking, Nicky was your girl. A genuine all-rounder and part of everything good about life in the station.

The relationship between the two women forged quickly. It was rock solid as a friendship, and extremely respectful on a professional basis, with both women highly proficient in a work environment. Despite their ambitions and rank, the two were perfectly matched socially, and were very capable of polishing off several bottles of wine or a bottle of gin on the wrong weekend, or even on the wrong weekday evening.

Rob enjoyed the occasional drink with them after work. It was always enjoyable and made the team stronger. On more than one occasion he'd had to make his excuses and disappear into the night, knowing full well the girls would still be going strong several hours later, by which point the volume would be fever pitch and the level of the humour would have fallen off a cliff.

The office and team had evolved greatly under his leadership. He'd sacked a couple of fuck-wits who felt and acted like they owned the place, regardless of rank. "Managed them out" was the HR slant, but the net effect was much the same. It takes longer than it used to to get rid of somebody, even if they need to be got rid of, but long service doesn't entitle you to treat people like shit any more than the next person. The sackings changed the mood of the office, and everybody felt it. It shook some, made others change their tune and made many others breathe a sigh of relief. Positive sackings, real old school.

It had also created an opportunity. A reshuffle, which was sufficient enough to show all the right people that this team was equipped to represent the city, and was fit to serve. It gave Rob a female DS and female DC for the first time in the force's history, a fact he was proud of. It was also something of an irrelevance, as Nicky and Jen were the best officers for the job by a country mile, but sadly these things still look good in 21st century Britain to some parties. The brass.

Rob knew he had real strength in Nicky as his DS, and equally he knew that Jen was a perfect fit for her role as a senior DC. All three had exceptional qualities, were perfectly congruent as an operating unit and were becoming the envy of other sections of the force, something Rob enjoyed a great deal.

The kettle had barely finished boiling when the call came in. A frantic mess of a call from a neighbour who thought they'd seen or heard something 'off', or might have seen somebody in a cul-de-sac full of old people who usually go to bed by 9pm. Maybe even Nicky and Jen were expecting a broken window or a small-time burglary, but that wasn't what they got.

The two women looked at one another. Jen sighed, swayed her head to one side, then took a large gulp of her still red hot tea, knowing it would be a while before the next one. She slid her mug across her desk and launched herself to her feet, grabbing her jacket on the way out of the door.

CHAPTER 4

Jen and Nicky arrived at the house first, having travelled together in Nicky's Mondeo. Rob had wanted to make some calls and hung back in the office to finish up. Speak to the new pathologist en route. Nicky had taken a call from a contact who knew she was heading to the scene and had prepped her with an outline of what to expect, which had allowed her and Jen to grab their own sterile coveralls from the station before leaving. Always a better option than borrowing on site if possible. Somehow the white paper of the station stock prevented the stench from settling too deeply into their clothes. They'd suit up on arrival and wouldn't have to wait, or borrow a set from forensics where the quality and sizes were variable.

Uniform had arrived quickly following the call, and had immediately escalated the incident, which in turn had filtered to Rob's team. The obligatory police barrier was already hanging between lampposts and blowing well. The wind was stronger now and the blue and white plastic tape was rippling loudly in the air. It was dark, and the night had deteriorated considerably. The interior lights and blues on the patrol cars lit up the end of the road like a nightclub, strobing their way into the night sky.

A number of officers were busying themselves in the street, having set up the initial site cordon, with some looking visibly relieved that Nicky and Jen had arrived. Another couple of uniforms in bright hi-vis jackets stood by the side entrance of the house, guarding it. Jen recognised one as PC Emma Sharpe as she walked up the pathway towards the door. They'd done some courses and spent some time together a couple of years back. Health and Safety or First Aid. Advanced Driving maybe.

Inaudible noise was coming from the radios attached to the jackets of the officers wearing them, velcroed to their upper chests. Pale looks were being exchanged between some younger officers who had already stepped inside the house. There were few words. Nicky and Jen exchanged a look. No words. They walked the last few yards up to the house and flashed warrant cards, introducing themselves as the ranking officers; a formality, as most of those already at the scene knew who they both were.

An officer gestured the two in via the side door of the house, stepping aside to invite them through. Jen and Emma exchanged glances and mouthed "Hi" – as an oblivious Nicky carried on her path, through the open back door and into the lean-to of the bungalow.

Uniformed officers continued to section off parts of the garden, knowing that the forensic work would be painstaking and every detail must be upheld now, and fully preserved. The golden hour. The forensic team had already started to arrive in the background. Lamps and equipment that would be needed well into the night, and through into tomorrow were being unloaded from a medium sized white Volkswagen van.

Forensics had parked another two of their vans adjacent to a patrol car and a '68 plate VW Tiguan, no doubt belonging to one of the retired residents, who were either tucked up tight and oblivious to what was happening, or curtain twitching right now. Not one of them had left their house and made it to the police line. The night was too cold for venturing outside. This was the wrong demographic for being nosy at this time of night, and there'd be no Facebook live coverage of this scene.

Some conversations were happening quietly as the officers on site continued to take care of the scene, with several of the early forensics crew starting to make their way in to the house.

Rob had arrived and parked away from the rest of the cars. Nicky and Jen had signed the site register, which had been hastily set up, and were already fully adorned in their white paper suits and blue slip-on shoe covers. Even with her own preferred suit and extra thick face mask, Jen hated it. Felt scuzzy and unclean, even before going in.

It felt even scuzzier afterwards.

The face masks were futile; the stench of death was thick in the air. Hanging. Like something you could never explain, just something you got used to. Knew.

Blood. Faeces. Death.

Vile unmistakable smells, often mixed and totally overwhelming in the atmosphere of any crime scene. The smell of death's ability to corrupt the airwaves is unparalleled, but it still has a spectrum, and Jen and Nicky knew they were walking into a bloodbath.

CHAPTER 5

"Is anyone firing up the Dolce Gusto?"

DC Jack Bowery was a new appointment to the team in Leicester. A younger and greener officer, with a sharp suit and looks like a Next model. Cut shirts and chiselled jaw. A smooth operator who had glided through university and pissed the training at Hendon, before moving into a prized role with the Met. Highly intelligent but capable of showing an occasional lack of common sense, something becoming more typical of the Hendon graduates. But Jack was a razor-sharp talent and Rob had jumped at the opportunity to recruit him. New to his team but with a year's experience of central London policing under his belt, he had something to bring to the party.

He'd moved back home to be closer to his family in Market Harborough, as the Big Smoke wasn't all it was cracked up to be. Always an exciting prospect for an intelligent young graduate. 10% extra in your wage packet, the big city and bright lights. What they forget to mention is that you'll likely be living eight deep in a 'shared arrangement' with all manner of people. Nurses, bin men, bankers.

Jack had no issues with any walk of life, was a true metrosexual and was very capable of holding his own in company, but having to share a cramped communal lounge on his day off when all he wanted to do was eat binge food and watch Netflix had soon worn thin. As had the eye-watering amount of money he was handing over in rent each month for the privilege.

Watching a primary school teacher iron his shirts on a Sunday afternoon was not on his list of aspirational living, and he'd jumped at the chance to move on, the fifteen months' experience passing as more than acceptable on his CV.

Rob had taken a chance on him as an unknown, but something good was there and he felt that Jack was a better fit for the team even though he wasn't necessarily the best qualified for the job, or even the most impressive at the interview.

He'd also 'clicked' with both DS Green and DC James on a personal level, having made an impromptu 'guns' gesture with his fingers when saying hi for the first time, something neither had allowed him to forget, and that both imitated regularly. It was probably a nervous tic, but it had endeared him to Nicky and Jen, and both had very much taken him under their wing.

With no responses forthcoming, Jack made himself an espresso to have with an organic snack bar. It tied in with his lifestyle; one of excellent health and a razor sharp image. A lifestyle that also featured an expensive gym membership and a regular haircut, no doubt from an artisan barber offering slick fades and wet shaves.

He looked around the office, still adjusting to its layout, nature and quirks. Very different from the London office he'd left behind. One of stainless steel, glass and modern art.

Leicester's central police station had evolved over the last twenty years, which showed on the faces of some of the unfortunates who had been in the force long enough to have bounced around the walls for years. Some for decades. The long servers.

Sitting boldly at the top of Charles Street, bang in the city centre, and adjacent to the train station, is Lodge House, a high-rise concrete monstrosity which has been home to the constabulary for years during the glory days of Leicestershire policing. An era when John Lewis still had the tower and C&A proudly took up one end of the Haymarket, with the theatre at the other, knocking out award-winning productions.

The building sits on the London Road, a stark contradiction of the Victorian train station sitting proudly opposite. An architectural gem of a building representing the wealth of the city's industrial past. Carved sandstone with ornate features and solidly Victorian. Robust, honest and hardworking, and still magnificent, something Jack enjoyed seeing every time he left the office or drove towards it, especially if he came over Waterloo Way to the south. A beautiful sight, but her heyday, like those of the railways, is behind her.

Rumours had bounced around the old walls of the 'nick' for years about revamps, moves and new offices on the outskirts of town, but the recession, public spending and public confidence had all bumped shiny new offices for the Old Bill down the priority list for those at County Hall. *Public confidence,* always an easy 'out' for the bureaucrats looking to keep a firm hold of the purse strings. Jack wasn't one for rumours or gambling, but if he had a tenner to wage he'd back the force still being sat here in ten years' time. The last rumours seemed to have died down with the recession, and the ten years since the credit crunch had almost floated past in slow motion.

Decades' worth of sticking plasters had been applied to a building that hadn't been fit for purpose for years. Crumbling windows, narrow corridors and cables gaffer-taped to threadbare carpets and door frames. Not to mention the limited parking, blocked or locked fire escapes and other doors you wouldn't get a wheelchair through, should the tinderbox ever go up. Ironically criminal.

The city's population had topped 450,000, placing it in the top ten largest cities in the UK. Widely diverse by way of culture and heritage, and much the better for it. Richer. Leicester has embraced its diversity in a way other culturally mixed areas have struggled. Bradford. Tottenham. Brixton.

Half a mile away, the Highcross shopping centre presents a space age greeting to the heart of the city with its glass bridge spanning Vaughan Way and piercing the four storeys of a glass-walled John Lewis. It has a giant multiplex cinema sitting next to Nando's, and all the other chains you'd expect to find in a modern and cosmopolitan city.

The whole centre is massively different to how it was in the nineties. A few remnants of concrete multi-storey car parks still lingered, but on the whole the redevelopment had been wholesale. Although some of the shit nightclubs had survived like cockroaches, for another generation to enjoy, and to dance on their sticky floors.

The main investigative offices sat on the eighth floor of the building and had a window overlooking St. George's Way, back up towards the retail park, with a fleeting view of Mothercare, Wickes and Burger King. Jack thought Mothercare had long since shut up shop, but the sign with the logo still hung above it. The view up towards the kink in the road and Burleys Flyover was just about visible as the dank buildings at the bottom of Humberstone Gate blocked any further sights into the city.

One of the most pressing issues with the station was the train line. The London mainline practically ran underneath the building, and if it wasn't directly beneath, it seemed to be structurally attached. One of many design flaws and construction failures that nobody seemed to care about anymore. Despite the tower block design, it offered little protection from a diesel engine firing up her cylinders and dragging carriage loads of commuters to the capital, with a familiar rattle of block and glass commonplace around rush hour.

Jack sipped on his coffee just as a train departed for London. He exhaled, not yet used to the quirk of the building. Rob was oblivious to the noise, the years providing a numbness. He walked from his office and demanded the attention of his assembled team.

"Good morning all," he mustered. He'd had as much sleep as the rest of them. The room sat and listened. These situations were usually quiet, with the odd mutter or exchange amongst those present. A small team had been quickly assembled to investigate the murder and Nicky had drafted in those who were either directly required or who had played a role last night, even if just for the initial stages. Get a quick result and the team would stay small.

The introduction of a fresh crime was always intently listened to, but this was different. Even some of the monkeys in the room who normally sat flicking Blu Tack at each other could comprehend what was different, and felt the already palpable responsibility of the force to catch the killer. Rob's assessment of the crime was articulated well, but in this kind of situation not overtly necessary. Motivating a room of police officers to catch the killer of a brutally murdered pensioner was a soft sell. The vibe could be different when looking for someone who'd crocked a sex offender; then the levels of urgency could vary and the desire to find the culprit was not always as paramount as the hierarchy would report.

The room was beginning to process some of the early photographs, which had been taped to a whiteboard to one side of the incident room. A board that had seen its share of names, suspects and victims alike, and told stories of those no longer able to tell their own. The team sat, coffees in hand, notebooks to one side.

Rob acknowledged to the team the extent of what was the worst scene that many of the younger officers were ever likely to come across, regardless of the length of service left in front of them. It was the worst he'd seen. Worst he'd smelt too.

"I'll be working with the press liaison, and we'll also be making a formal statement before this leaks and the Mercury starts splashing headlines about the town. Jen, I need you running the info gathering, Make sure uniform do door to door thoroughly, then get them to do it again. Take Jack with you."

He switched his attention and turned his gaze towards Nicky.

"Nicky, I need you after the session to run through the next seventy-two hours, and we need to identify next of kin, brothers, cousins. We'll make contact and go break the news. We need to do it straight away; I want them to get the details from us."

There was still an element of shock in the room as Rob nodded to the woman who had appeared at the back of the room and gestured to his office as he started to walk. Nicky stood up to continue the brief and assign duties to the lower ranks as the tall brunette followed Rob to his office.

Rob had been delighted to learn that she was the new Chief Forensic Pathologist based out of the Leicester Royal Infirmary, conveniently only about twenty minutes away from the police station, unless either of the city's sports teams were at home. Football or rugby alone was enough to clog up the main roads like a smoker's lungs, and if they were both playing you may as well ditch the car and walk. Rob had been notified of the new pathologist's appointment, but until last night he hadn't had the pleasure of putting a face to the name.

She represented a new direction as a senior figure in the pathology team and was evidently still very young. Rob was used to pathologists and their ilk being balding fifty something men with a paunch, and thought 'divorcee' was in the job spec. In front of him stood a tall brunette, well dressed with a hint of makeup that simply enhanced an already attractive image. Not yet a face recognised by officers, seasoned or otherwise, but she carried herself with a level of authority. Confidence. Enough for some heads to have turned in the office.

She stood elegantly in a green raincoat with a waist tie, smart tailored trousers and black heels, looking enviably fresh considering where she'd spent most of last night. Her dark hair was up in a simple bun, and a balance of smart modern professional without overkill was being effortlessly struck. A new face and very personable, and a refreshing addition to the wider team, Rob had thought. She was certainly an improvement from her predecessor, who the team had christened as Rapey Dave.

"Dr Rebecca Ryan," was the simple introduction, along with an outstretched hand. Rob introduced himself, despite them both knowing who the other was after their initial meet several hours earlier, in the dead of night. It's always hard to shake hands with a pathologist at a crime scene though. Bad manners, surely.

"Early thoughts?" asked Rob.

"Savage beating," was the response, "but measured too. He was alive for a great deal of the ordeal, from the blood spatter and the images we have. He suffered, and he was made to suffer."

"Cause of death?" was the next question, forced out just before Rob took a bite from a Weetabix bar he'd dug out of his drawer, that had been stashed for such an instance.

"Hard to say. The autopsy will tell us the real story, but the injuries are so extensive it'll be hard to isolate a specific injury, I think. Significant blood loss, trauma. Both."

"And we think this is all within the last twelve hours or so?"

"Without question. It's likely he was assaulted at some point during the evening. It's possible there was a skirmish of some description until the killer overpowered our victim, but by the time he was cable tied to the chair and gaffer taped he was powerless."

"But the nature of this, the injuries – revenge, surely?"

"Hard to say. You'd think so, but the vic is nearing seventy, so not your average candidate for a revenge killing. Money? And that's your department anyway," quipped Rebecca withconfidence and a friendly smile as she stood up. "We'll be running a number of tests as a priority, and the autopsy will be going ahead in the next few hours. I'll call you as soon as we know anything."

"Thanks, Rebecca. I'll call you later for an update."

"Of course, I'll speak to you later," came the response, "And call me Becky."

CHAPTER 6

Rob sat back in his chair, took a sip of a lukewarm cup of tea and picked up a couple of scene photographs. The bar long gone, his groaning stomach still craving food.

Pictures of an old man slumped forward in a chair, hands bound at the wrists with heavy duty black cable ties over an oil green knitted cardigan. The grain of the fabric woven together with thick, dried blood.

So much blood.

The index finger of his left hand had been cut off, severed cleanly, and was lying on the coffee table as if part of a sick game. His face was low, his head hanging, and caked blood set thick in his hair making it look black. The limited light in the room had streaked across parts of his head, showing the blood as an iridescent shimmer of burgundy. Like red wine.

His feet were bare and his legs had been beaten, with bruising glowing on ageing skin almost immediately. His shins, the tops of his feet. Black and yellow circles were showing already where the skin had been hit with a blunt object again and again. Relentlessly.

Cut marks were visible through sliced clothing on seemingly random parts of his torso and upper arms. The torture of the cuts, blood oozing but placed well enough to avoid unconsciousness. That came later.

He had almost frozen, resigned to a miserable death long before the pain had stopped and the last breath had been drawn. The agony of it all. His face was unrecognisable. Beaten. Blackened. Twisted. Almost set in terror and bearing all the hallmarks of a brutal end. A vicious, painful end.

Every last ounce of skin was covered in blood, layered as the beating intensified and new blood trickled onto old. Laying thickly, like an old oil painting. Teeth were missing, but there were enough left for the records to confirm who this was. This was not a body for a relative to identify. Only time would tell whether those teeth were long gone, or removed last night, but Rob already had his suspicions of the latter, or some of them at least.

His head was leaning to one side, signs of trying to pull away from the pain but failing. The restraints doing their job and holding the victim firmly. The left side of his face had been butchered. The left ear was missing completely, and had been cut off quite proficiently at first glance and to Becky's trained eye. There was no apparent savagery to the cut, and it didn't look like it had been hacked at or removed crudely.

It had been sliced. Competently.

The blood was so overwhelming that it was simply too hard to tell, but it looked like the ear had been cut pre-mortem. It was evidently not still in the house.

Killers take many things. Locks of hair, keys, bangles. Ears was a new one, even to Rob.

He looked down at a man whose demise was unparalleled in terms of the level of violence, and with the extent of the injuries and the nature of the killing, Rob knew he had to catch the man responsible.

CHAPTER 7

It was lunchtime when Jen wandered out of Lodge House with her bag on her arm, heading nowhere in particular. One of the hardest parts of being based in the inner ring of the city with such a revitalised retail offering was the temptation, and an occasional lack of willpower. Wandering too far for lunch or just taking a smoke could result in an off-the-cuff purchase, a new pair of shoes or the next holiday. One of the travel agents on Rutland Street was always on hand to flog you a weekend in Rome, and had recently tried to sell Jack an 18-30 break in Magaluf the last time he walked past to buy a bagel.

Jen found herself wandering into the cultural quarter, away from the hustle and bustle and towards the cathedral, a location that often provided her some solace at lunchtime. A quaint spot to perch and watch the world go by, in a quiet corner of the city, which had become less quiet since King Richard III had been found. He'd been christened as the 'car park king', after a team of archaeologists from the uni had found him buried under a council car park in the middle of the city centre, five hundred years after his demise. Jen wasn't a historian or particularly interested in any form of royalty, but she liked the story and the notion. It had made the city a bit more interesting, Channel 4 had filmed a pretty decent documentary about it, and Benedict Cumberbatch had turned up for the service as the king was finally laid to rest. It was a nice place to spend a break. Could lend perspective.

Lunch itself could be challenging, or the opposite, depending on your culinary views. Surrounded by takeaways, cafes of all descriptions, street food and cultural offerings, food was highly accessible and saved on any form of effort, especially on a police officer's schedule. Even the notion of a lunch hour seemed absurd these days.

Nobody seemed to do packed lunches anymore, and Leicester has more than its fair share of bike boys and Deliveroo's zipping around with their turquoise green boxes strapped to their backs.

"Where have you been, Jen?" shouted Rob from his office, as she wandered back into the main office.

"I've had a Martin's Meats delivery," came the simple response, as she started to unpack her day's tucker from a brown paper bag.

"Of all the places to eat, Jenny, you go and buy that shit."

Jen was not a Jenny to anybody other than her mum, and she flipped a look as strong as you should to the senior investigating officer and the man who does your appraisal. Rob knew it and cheekily trotted it out every now and again, but to the rest of the world Jen was Jen, and if you used the alternative version, and you weren't Rob, you got seriously short shrift.

Rob had never liked Martin's Meats, a tiny old-fashioned little place sat up on Woodgate on the main A50, a busy inner city route that sweeps in past a Travis Perkins branch, and a derelict hosiery factory on the left-hand side. Some enterprising Europeans had set up a car wash in the remnants of the brickwork and seemed to be doing a tidy trade in an area of the city known locally as Frog Island.

He'd always thought it was one of those places where you seemed to get the same thing regardless of what you ordered, plus the meat there tasted like roadkill, or worse. He'd never had anything other than nasty. His 'go-to place' that side of town was Buck's Chippy. Proper takeaway food and the best lunchtime kebab meal he'd ever eaten. Mixed doner meat and chips with a mayo dressing for £3. His stomach rumbled slightly at the thought, and he wished he'd given Jen the money and his order before she left.

Rob still did pack up on a bad day, or preferred a few well used eateries dotted across the city centre for food, with Croques being his favourite. A tiny little sandwich shop tucked on Loseby Lane opposite an Irish pub. Gorgeous sandwiches and wraps, great value and great people. Rob's biggest gripe until recently was a refusal to take payment on cards, a wrong recently put right.

A cash-only business that wasn't a backstreet car garage or a builder, but small things annoy people, infuriate people, rile them, make them angry. People start fights for small things. People have killed for small things. Loose change, a push bike, a parking space.

Jen picked up what could have been a wrap, but might have been a naan bread, which was full of reddish meat of some description, and took a large bite. She chewed, and pondered what small things do make people kill, and what 'thing' the driver was behind the murder of William Reynolds. She flipped open a file with the provisional documents and a few images of the crime scene and contemplated hard, sucking back some lettuce that was protruding from her mouth as she continued to chew.

She flicked a look at PC Emma Sharpe, who had become involved in the investigation as part of the supporting uniform team following her attendance at William Reynold's bungalow. A number of others had been drafted in to support the information gathering, which was always a laborious and heavy part of any investigation, and always took significant resources.

Jen hadn't seen Emma properly for a good few years, but was pretty confident that she wouldn't be one of the uniforms needing the counselling that was already being offered to young and senior officers alike, and anyone else who had walked into William Reynold's house last night and witnessed his lifeless and battered corpse.

Jen thought about what would need to have happened to motivate somebody to kill in this way, and as the flavour of the meat flooded her tastebuds she wondered why the fuck she hadn't just gone to Croques and had a bacon and brie toastie.

CHAPTER 8

This is always an interesting period. The first murder went pretty much without a hitch and the police are looking for a murderer. Not a serial killer, or not yet at least. Even the next one will only make me a double murderer.

I wonder who decided that the definition of 'serial' should be three.

The story has broken and has been on the news channels for a good couple of hours now, and will no doubt appear on some of the regular channels, the radio and in the newspapers in due course. It's unlikely this will go viral anytime soon, but it will go big locally, and will be the talking point across the citys many cafes, factories and offices.

For a city of its size it's scarcely a criminal hub. The usual levels of drugs, robberies and pissed teenagers scrapping outside its many clubs, but a rap sheet of prolific murders it doesn't have. Colin Pitchfork is the most well-known. A double murderer who took the lives of two young girls in the eighties, but his notoriety derives from being the first man in Britain to be convicted using DNA evidence.

That was thirty-five years ago, and while Pitchfork is still rotting in a prison somewhere, albeit an open one by now, the city has achieved well in not becoming synonymous with high profile crime. Hungerford, Dunblaine, Soham.

That's all about to change, because the city has failed one of its own and protected others, and that's a wrong I will put right, have started to put right, and society will see that. It's why I'm so determined, so motivated.

I'm sitting in the window of a cafe sipping slowly on a cappuccino and munching on an iced bun, watching the world go by. Thinking. Thinking about Joe Davies. The injustice of Joe Davies. The fact that he's 'out', or was never properly 'in'. The fact that he's alive. Deciding on the when, the long overdue day when Joe Davies will meet his maker. He may have been looking over his shoulder, he knows what that feels like with the life he's led, or he may even know it's coming by now. Maybe he won't. He'll soon see what's happened to Bill Reynolds if he hasn't already, and may even put two and two together and get four. It'll allow the fear to start. The feeling of borrowed time.

It'll be trickier from here on in, as any murder is a simple one-off until the second one happens, and inevitably people start to look for the similarities. The connections. I'll need to act quickly after Joe is dispatched, as the police will know of a link, or be able to find one quickly. They'll look for the connection between the two victims, and maybe they'll find it. They should do. That, ironically, will depend on the competence of their predecessors, the accuracy of their records and the organisation of that shit-hole of a police station.

The good news for me is that that won't help Joe Davies any more than it helped William Reynolds. All being well he'll walk by shortly, on his way to the bookies. Standard Tuesday afternoon for a retired seventy-five year old. He'll have a paper under his arm and will stroll past without a care in the world, like an average old boy from any town. Old, retired, sweet, innocent. Except Joe Davies is only two of those things, old and retired, and that's only if you can ever retire from being a criminal.

To the world he's just an old man who should be left alone He's worked for some parts of his life; he even worked shifts, just like me. He's paid taxes and his stamp. Paid his way, and society likes that. Respects it. Views him as 'due'. He's due alright. Long overdue, and he'll get his comeuppance. They all will. Society is poor at judging, despite being well practised at it. It's something everybody does, but generally badly.

The dozen or so people in the cafe all now know of the murder. It was on Sky News ten minutes ago, and the couple next to me who are sharing a millionaire shortcake have just scrolled past it on the Leicester Mercury homepage on their iPhones.

Another couple are sitting close together, and are laughing and joking. Carefree. They're each wearing a wedding ring but I'm not sure they're married to each other. Maybe I'm wrong on that. Who knows? They've looked at me a couple of times and at no stage will they have considered me as the perpetrator of the murder being detailed on the large muted TV screen on the wall behind them.

But they have smirked at the greasy looking dude sitting outside the main window smoking a cigarette. Perched on a small, slightly rusted chair with a matching table, minding his own business. Dirty looking, dishevelled, balding and wearing an unflattering grey mac. Classic nonce. Only he probably isn't. He's as likely to be a retired civil servant down on his luck as a corrupt seventies' Scout leader who likes kids, but everybody thinks they know what a nonce *looks* like. Like they all look the same, wearing some kind of shiny badge. I'm not sure if murderers have a 'look' or carry themselves differently. Guess I'll find out. But society doesn't know what a paedophile looks like any more than a murderer or a terrorist.

So I'll hide in plain sight while all this is going on, and continue to plunder.

CHAPTER 9

Notifying Alan Reynolds should have been an easy job. The next of kin. Standard procedure. Never nice but a crucial formality in the process.

The only child of William and Margaret Reynolds, forty nine years old and a lifelong bachelor, Alan Reynolds isn't the average next of kin, if there is such a thing, and wouldn't be the easiest person to break bad news to. Relatives are rarely predictable in these cases, and grief and reaction can manifest and expose itself in all forms. Outbursts. Emotion. Grief in its most raw and unfiltered state. Tears, usually; disbelief, confusion and denial all being the standard fare.

Occasional and immediate anger, violence and a desire for vengeance had all been seen and suffered by an experienced team who had all given their fair share of bad news in recent years. There were too many car accidents, drug overdoses and club deaths to keep count of, but the memory of each was etched permanently into their memory banks. The knock on the door of an unsuspecting parent, child or spouse, especially those in the middle of the night, coupled with "Can I come in, please?" and "Would you like to sit down?", usually priming the bereaved relative of what was to come, as did the solemn and expressionless face.

It never gets easier.

A string of GBH & drug convictions for the deceased's relative meant that DC Jennifer James and DC Jack Bowery had drawn the short straw for today's task. Rob Rhone had the utmost respect for his two senior officers. He knew he had one of the best duo's on the force, and was well aware of how capable they both are of looking after themselves, as well as each other.

He also knew that he wasn't sending two unarmed female officers onto a shit-hole council estate to break bad news to a socially difficult and violent convict. Paradoxically in a modern and diverse world, and one of equality, that if Jack had his nose broken during an arrest, there would be a significant amount of paperwork for Rob to complete, which would detract heavily from his current workload. The level of piss-taking from the rest of the ranks would be equally sizable, with those lower down the pay scale never remotely sympathetic to a black eye or a kick in the balls to another officer, especially if it was caught on a body cam by one of the uniforms. First-hand evidence against the arrestee, and a great watch back in the station for everybody else.

The flip side to the gender balance only happens if the broken nose is found on the face of a female officer. Nobody laughs at that, and the shit-storm blows a whole lot stronger.

The second challenge to the morning mix was the address of the bereaved. Leicester's St. Matthew's estate sits on the outskirts of the inner city to the north east side, at the end of the busy Catherine Street. A grey council estate with classic 1970's housing; pebbledash appearance and brutalist design, surrounded on one side by factories, industry and a variety of bustling shops. Fridges on the streets, fruit and veg sellers and European retailers mixed together in a cosmopolitan, if slightly downtrodden thoroughfare.

Drug dealers, street crime, muggings and violence are commonplace on these streets. Gangs roam, trading drugs, goods, revenge attacks and fear. Hard currency in this far from salubrious square mile.

The estate sits around a mile from the sleek glass wall that represents the retail hub of the city centre and the capitalist mecca of the Highcross. Just around the bend of the A594, where Burleys' Flyover lifts you up and over, back towards the part of the city where the tourism board take their photographs. A world away from the life led by Alan Reynolds.

26 Taylor Road was set back from the main through road, just down from a woodyard, a scrapyard and an army recruitment barracks, and bang opposite the primary school. Rob had an issue living with the knowledge that people like Alan Reynolds lived near to schools. Petulant and unpredictable, violent and socially inept. As likely to kick off at nine in the morning as eleven at night, and equally likely to have had a drink at either end of the daily spectrum. Or worse. Something from one of the many teens peddling. Crack. Pills. Both.

Sarah's Law was introduced following Sarah Payne's senseless murder, and had helped a great deal of people, the police included. Society felt more comfortable knowing they could find out where the local paedophile lived, the local lynch mob especially, but for some reason living next door to someone with a conviction for glassing a fifty year-old woman just didn't seem as important. Residents were seemingly less bothered about having a dangerous and violent neighbour, just as long as they're considerate. As long as they keep the noise down.

Jack and Jen arrived at the house early in the morning. A hostile grey sky reflected the surroundings, and Jack took a good look around as he climbed from the car. His gaze was met by several locals who had probably already clocked them as Old Bill. Jack tucked his hands into his smart blue mac and walked towards the house with Jen a step behind him, her hair tied back, her appearance smart.

They looked like police.

A rousing knock on the door failed to be met with a response. Neither did a second rap along with a shout through the obscure glass of an old blue door. Jen was arching to get a view through a side window, where an old curtain and a tobacco-stained net blocked any decent view. Instinct told them their man was not at home.

Jen had spoken with a local team in the area on their way over. Given the apparent absence of the next of kin and his nature towards authority, a unit had arrived to both support and canvas. Jack saw PC Emma Sharpe climb out of a marked Vauxhall Astra, along with another uniformed officer who he didn't recognise. A second marked vehicle had also arrived in the street, and was being parked across the road from Jen's car.

All four officers stepped out and walked towards the house. The curtain twitching of the locals intensified.

Jack knew both officers from the second car; PC's Keith Wainwright and Bernie Copp. He'd met them both as part of his induction at the station, and as they were experienced PC's he had spent some time with them, as the station culture was significantly different to that in the capital. Bernie had been on the force for years. 'Coppy the Copper' was a gruff and slightly grumpy character, but had been through the ups and downs of both the force and the county, from the miners' riots in 1980's Coalville to football hooligans marching from the train station to Filbert Street, and latterly the King Power Stadium, during the violence-strewn football era of the early nineties. An unflappable persona, a well-respected character and one to be on shift with. Witty and dry, he'd grown up in Battersea with his parents, and, despite the years since, had held on to a 'Cockney geezer' front, having grown up in a pub, before fleeting careers as an auctioneer and the manager of a London nightclub. Always had a story, and great value they were too.

"So has he done it and fucked off, gov?" came the abrupt but characteristic question from Coppy. The question had occurred to a few of those assembled already.

The wider door knocking was underway, as Jen wanted to get a feel for where Alan Reynolds had been for the past few days, or whether he'd been noticeable in his absence. The initial grunts from local residents weren't exactly pouring glory on Reynolds, and they wouldn't be queuing up for character witness roles, should that need arise.

'Unemployed, loud and abusive when about, but not seen for a couple of days' was the broad gist from those who did bother to answer the door. Not considerate in the slightest.

"Do you think he's nervous and legged it, Jen?" came the question from Jack. Some of the officers had made their minds up; Alan Reynolds already knows about the death of his father, and this wasn't a notifying mission.

The look on Jen's face told the doubters that she disagreed strongly. She'd started to walk away from the main body of the estate into a quieter side road with garages. Observing subconsciously, and with transient noise coming from the school, she spoke her mind, arguing the toss with herself as she went.

"Why, though? Why kill your own father?"She stood with her hands in her pockets, rocking on her heels before continuing."Spouses regularly kill one another, it's as statistically likely as it gets. Any murder with a spouse involved generally involves ruling the surviving spouse out before widening the net. But a widowed pensioner isn't your average murder victim. And offsprings are much less likely to commit murder. Parricide is still rare in comparison."

Jack opened his mouth to say something but was cut off.

"Inheritance? But inherit what? And there was no absolute certainty that if William Reynolds was one of those miserly pensioners who had half a million squirrelled away that he'd be leaving it to an outlaw offspring. More likely to leave it to Cat's Protection or some other charity that pulled at his heartstrings, or those that still worked. So if he did kill his dad, why did he do it? And if it was him, don't you think we'd have found a bludgeoned body?"

"But we did, boss," came the fair challenge back from Jack, his brow furrowed.

"Yeah, but picture a foul-tempered and angry fifty year old losing his shit during an argument. Maybe he's smashed. Maybe he's high. And he's emotional. How does he kill?"

Jack pondered.

"Pick something up and batter him about the head? Or take a knife, although that would most likely be a frenzied knife attack."

Jen's point was dawning on Jack as he spoke.

"Agreed," stated Jen. "So we had the outline of a frenzied attack, but violence aside, we also found a body that had been made to suffer, and even with the brutality, it was *measured*. Calculated. Pre-empted. Alan Reynolds isn't a calculating mind, he's a capricious and social liability who'd struggle to speak to you in a coherent way. I think William Reynolds was killed by somebody he knew, or probably somebody he'd crossed, but I don't think that person was his son."

"So what do we do now?"

Jen rounded the team up and dispatched the uniformed officers. Too much visibility can also be a bad thing in a community. This wasn't Toxteth, the morning excitement was over, and this wasn't a drugs bust. Not today.

"We find him, Jack. He's either so wasted that he's disappeared and slept rough, or he's gone off grid for a few days, but as far as I'm concerned, we still need to tell him his dad's dead."

CHAPTER 10

Rob received a call from Becky Ryan, and shouted out of the open door to Nicky, telling her to finish her coffee. Nicky looked up to see that Rob had already grabbed his jacket from the back of his chair, which was now spinning on its wheels. He walked briskly out of his office and into the main office, where whiteboards and investigative material were being set up and early evidence was being displayed.

The stereotypical boards were already adorned with scene photographs and a victim photograph as well as an image of Alan Reynolds, which had been pinned and taped close to his dad. Lines drawn with old marker pens showed early relationships and links, scrawled in red and blue. There was a double-ended arrow between the two staring images and a large question mark above Alan's unflattering mug-shot.

"Where are you taking me, boss? Somewhere nice?"

"Yep, in one Nicky," came the reply. "Somewhere cool, calm and quiet. You'll love it!"

Nicky's eyes rolled back in her head as the realisation landed.

"We're going to the morgue, aren't we, gaffer?"

"Two from two Nicky, means you win a prize…"

Rob was a man of routine, so Nicky now at least knew how the next few hours of the day would pan out.

The day was cold but dry. Crisp. That meant Nicky was in for a walk, and she was not a massive fan of walking. Strolling, fine; wandering on a weekend, even better. Her and her husband had become 'parents' to a couple of miniature dachshunds a year or so ago; Harry and Marv after the villains in Home Alone, so the office banter was that she loved a 'short walk', but a moderate walk was her comfort zone and she was her own pacemaker.

Rob, however, was more of a power walker, and would be the one setting the pace.

William Reynolds' power-walking days were long gone. His current resting place was amongst the sterile surroundings of the hospital mortuary, within the bowels of the Leicester Royal Infirmary, just across town. It was close enough to the police station for most to consider walking it, before reaching for the car keys, but unfortunately for Nicky, Rob wasn't 'most'.

As a keen reader, she'd read Steve Jobs' autobiography, and had learned that he spent as much time walking as he did in the office, and had appointed more people and made more business decisions whilst on the hoof than he had in the boardroom. The beauty of fresh air, the invigoration of the outside world; affording increased blood flow that the majority of the working population often forget, or just neglect to treat themselves to.

Conversations happen when you walk that might not happen in a car. This was simply too short a journey on four wheels for anything salient to happen, but the ability to toss ideas and thoughts between you as the world whistles past is healthy, if not always appreciated.

Nicky fully understood the theory and the notion, but by the time they'd crossed New Walk and headed down towards Mandela Park she was starting to overheat, her glasses were steaming up and she'd realised she had the wrong shoes on. All things that Rob gave absolutely no thought to, or had no empathy for.

"This is a revenge killing Nicky, it has to be. Cold-blooded revenge. This is thought out, premeditated. He wasn't a random victim."

Rob was stating rather than asking, always willing to test a theory to its limits, especially in Nicky's valued and respected company. The aim being to try and break the theory in order to confirm or discredit the direction of the team. 'Constant evolution' was how he liked to coin it. The Japanese called it 'kaizen', or something like that. Rob was well into philosophy and theories, and loved to take new learning from anything and anywhere he could.

Nicky was less keen on philosophy. She just knew people were wankers and enjoyed catching criminals.

"It looks that way, just by the way in which he'd been treated," offered Nicky. She continued. "He's an old man with a quiet, withdrawn lifestyle, living in a boring retired street. There's no obvious monetary gain and robbery was never truly on the table. In all reality this was an execution, but just one of macabre proportions. Almost King Henry VIII type level."

Rob agreed. He had already started to look into execution as a modus operandi. Not a bullet to the head type execution, but an early delve into the city's past had thrown up some interesting events.

He'd spent the morning reading up, digging for inspiration. He'd found the case of twenty-one year old James Cook, who had been tried, convicted and executed for murder in the city in 1832, before his body was tarred and transported to Saffron Lane, at the top end of Aylestone Road, where it was displayed in a gibbet for all to see for a number of days. Rotting away.

Rob had found a number of instances of corpses being displayed, and had also learned that there was to this day a gibbet post at Bilstone, a small village way out in the sticks. He quite fancied the idea of going to find it one weekend with a long walk either side of it and a pub lunch at the end.

Although nonjudicial, he felt there was a ritual element to William Reynold's killing. The body had been left in a certain way in the chair, with the head slumped forward, restrained in death like an electric chair victim, the meaning lost, and something only privy to the killer. It was more 'Guy Fawkes' than 'shot at dawn', but the torture element was prominent, with the kill and subsequent death almost an anticlimax. A modern-day hung, drawn and quartered.

Rob had also looked fruitlessly at another link with the city. From the train station, the direct route to the city centre and the clock tower was along Gallowtree Gate, a name synonymous with execution, and public execution at that, and one he was surprised the council hadn't changed. Surely the last thing a commuter wanted was to walk along Gallowtree Gate each morning. Rob was always miffed that it hadn't been renamed something less provocative, and more – neutral. Progress Way had already been used, but something more modern would do. The spider's web of roads to the city centre were all gates: Church Gate, Belgrave Gate, Gallowtree Gate.

William Reynolds' corpse had been deliberately left; it had been presented to whoever found it, and presented to the police. Rob was not prepared to rule out an element that could link it to a judicial way of killing.

CHAPTER 11

Rob was delighted with the dialogue that only the walk could have generated, the time and fresh air affording an undisturbed and impromptu briefing. By the time they arrived at the LRI his head was buzzing with theories, links and ideas to check out as soon as he got back to the office. He started to scrawl notes in a small notebook he carried, which he'd follow up on later in the day. Nicky was desperate to find the nearest toilet, and scurried off as soon as they were buzzed into the morgue.

By the time she re-emerged, she looked relieved but still flustered. Her glasses, blurred with condensation sat proudly up on her head. Rob had already started to speak with Dr. Rebecca Ryan about the execution theory, what she thought and knew, and how it may tie in with an indication of motive, and the possible guilt or innocence of Alan Reynolds.

Rebecca smiled and acknowledged Nicky, whose reputation had preceded her, and the two shook hands, having never formally met but each knowing who the other was.

"Becky," was offered with a handshake.

"Nicky," came the response.

"I'll get you a glass of water," said Becky. Nicky was more than grateful for the gesture, and the opportunity to re-hydrate.

"So what do you know, Becky?" came the question from Rob, who'd already been offered a coffee by one of the junior pathologists.

"I know the cause of death remains unknown, regrettably. I know any small number of those injuries could have been fatal, and I know this was designed to be a prolonged attack."

"You know more than that though, otherwise I'd still be in Lodge House doing a city history class," came Rob's short response.

Swigging on the steaming black coffee handed to him, he asked, "So what don't I know?"

The three spoke with the beaten body of William Reynolds laying on a cold steel table behind them. He was covered modestly with a standard white sheet, and with the customary sewn-up 'Y' shaped incision visible across the chest, where Becky had skilfully dissected the body. Becky gestured to the body with her left hand as she spoke, but without looking directly at it.

"The injuries themselves, the nature and extent of the injuries, shows extreme violence and likely a lot of anger. This is a really personal murder."

Rob nodded in agreement, still supping at his coffee. "Go on."

"But each and every one of the inflicted injuries, each blow, each stab wound-"She paused, re-gathering her thoughts."Each stab wound on its own wouldn't have been fatal, and neither would any of the individual strikes to the torso. I believe that to be planned and very deliberate."

"So he wanted him to live, or be alive throughout?" asked Nicky.

"It looks that way. There are more than fifty wounds, fifty-three to be precise, where the body has been punctured or struck severely, but not one to any major organ, or any major artery. The body was beaten extensively whilst still conscious, and the bruising started to form whilst blood was still pumping, which shows in how the bruising eventually formed and became visible on the corpse. The beating was almost a sideshow though, and didn't directly contribute to the cause of death. The good news, if there is a crumb of it, is that no teeth were removed last night, so he didn't endure *that*, but there is one loose as a result of the attack, hence the blood that pooled in the mouth. The other missing molars are all down to age or lack of care, I'm afraid."

Becky ran her hands through her long black hair to the left side, adjusting and tightening it into a ponytail. She moved onto the most prominent elements of the murder, which had clear meaning and certainly weren't spur of the moment.

"The finger is an interesting element. It was cut pre-mortem, almost certainly with a scalpel, before being left for us. It's a very clean cut, and has been very skilfully done. This was not an amateur job, and was carried out by somebody with medical knowledge or a surgical ability. The combination of the injuries meant that any fight left in his body would have been minimal. The game was almost up, so to speak; he was a sitting duck in every which way."

Rob and Nicky were quiet, listening intently, soaking up the detail as Becky continued.

"It looks as if the removal of the ear was post-mortem. It's been as skilfully removed as the finger, if not more so, so seems more symbolic than torturous."

Becky looked at her audience, who were continuing to

soak up her description. She raised her hands subconsciously as she articulated her experience in the removal of body parts.

"It's not easy to remove a finger, or an ear. They're small but there's muscle, ligaments. It's gristly. You've got to want to do it."

Nicky was racking her brain, trying to recall a case where a victim had been dismembered. And why. Becky continued.

"To be clear, we won't be able to isolate a specific blow or wound that finally caused death. The knife wounds would have caused significant blood loss, and the blows to the head and body would potentially have led to bouts of unconsciousness throughout the attack. Given his age and physical status, it's likely the shock to his body and the overall trauma was enough to kill him. There's no evidence of cardiac arrest, but he wouldn't have survived this, and I'm not sure there's a pensioner who would have done."

"So is it not as savage as it looks, Becky? Am I missing something?" Nicky asked.

"No. It's savage, really savage, but maybe not brutal."

"How so?" asked Rob with a quizzical look, as the conversation took a turn he wasn't expecting. The three started to walk out of the main part of the mortuary, and away from the remains of William Reynolds.

"Well, there are a huge number of individual blows, but if you ignore the finger and the ear, which obviously have a sub-meaning within the overall attack, I'm saying that if *you'd* have been sat in that chair, DCI Rhone, you'd probably have survived the attack. You'd have lost a lot of blood, would have suffered unimaginable pain and would take a huge amount of recuperation, but to you it would probably only be a severe form of ABH. Attempted murder at most. It was only savage enough to kill a pensioner with failing health. Despite the blood, it wasn't just the battering we all saw when we first walked into that house. It was far more *measured* than that."

Rob and Nicky stopped to take a drink, to consider what they'd just heard. Rob was running each of the ideas around in his head about its potential meaning, rationale and how what he'd just heard could overlay with a two hundred year old murderer to find a modern day one.

"So the blows are plentiful but not individually forceful? Is that a choice the killer has made Becky?"

"It could be, it could be reflective if the killer is of a similar age and physical strength as the victim. In that case we'd expect the number of blows to be higher. But it could be a choice the killer has made to prolong suffering."

The conversation had caused them to crab slowly along a corridor as they spoke, and the group almost subconsciously found themselves walking into a side room with some chairs and a small table.

Nicky put her cup of water on the table and placed her handbag on a chair, taking the opportunity to sit down on a second chair. Rob followed suit but held his coffee. The same junior who'd made his coffee reappeared with Becky's tea, which Rob was surprised to see had arrived in a red Welsh Rugby Union mug. A large and proud red dragon against a bold white and green background.

"Didn't have you down as a rugby supporter, Becky."

"Books and covers, DCI Rhone."

Nicky was warmer now and at a temperature she was comfortable with. Her thoughts were gathering.

"This is real control, isn't it, Becky? *Real* control. What looks like a frenzied attack was carried out with precision and clarity. This guy is aware of how to inflict injury, where on the body to attack, how to cause maximum pain but prolong the suffering of the victim. Dare I say, he's good at what he does. This is somebody who knows what they're doing, hasn't rushed, hasn't panicked, and has carried out a competent and clinical assault. Almost like it was designed."

Nicky surmised accurately, and Rob nodded, in complete agreement. Becky nodded her agreement as she took a sip from a still steaming cup of tea. It was strong; looked like a builder's brew.

"Given the proficiency, Rob, it's possible this isn't the first kill, although from a modus operandi point of view it is. There's nothing like this on file, it's unique, but it's a 'good' kill, just very, very competent." The professional clinician in her almost admired the 'work' laying on her table back down the hallway.

"Could it be professional, Becky? Either a contract killer or a health professional?" asked Nicky as she glugged the last of her water, looking around to see if there was a cooler to top up the now empty cup.

"It could well be a professional, and even if it isn't, they're trained and highly competent," came the response. "There's enough knowledge to carry out the physical side of the attack, and the composure to complete the attack in the way that they have", which again came with a tone of admiration.

"Hitman seems unlikely; they prefer a clean kill. There is so much risk in this, so much time taken, it just seems too personal to be anything else."

"Kill again?" asked Rob, only it wasn't really a question.

CHAPTER 12

Rob stood staring out of the window of Lodge House, looking into the distance but unable to see it. The day was grey, in every way. Dank.

Rain was streaming down the windows of Rob's office, and had been since very early this morning. It was one of those days when you can't actually recall when it started to rain, but knew it wasn't stopping anytime soon.

The 'view' was obscured, and none of the remotely identifiable buildings of Leicester's skyline were visible through the murk. Rob raised his mug of coffee to his lips and took a sip, snapping out of the train of thought he was in, realising he wasn't actually looking out of the window anyway.

The senior investigating team were assembling in the main office and were readying themselves for a discussion and debate that was likely to last for a good few hours. Time well spent if the dialogue was positive and presented the team with clear direction. Rob walked out of his office to open proceedings.

"So from the top, then," came the loud instruction to kick things off.

He'd walked from his office into the open plan section of the briefing room where Jen, Nicky and Jack were sat, waiting to share the fruits of their labour from the last few days. The wider team had been assembled to support the investigation into the murder, and were sat ready to be updated with information gathered by the collective. To bring the pieces together. There was hunger in the room, and now was the right time to get the guys in the narrow channels up to speed with the bigger picture.

Rob had always enjoyed this element of policing, even as a young DC when he was sat amongst the assembled ranks. The opportunity to run through the snippets of information, rumours, the word on the street and the early witness statements. To share information between themselves, critique it, kick it about. Reflect.

As a junior officer, Rob had experienced a number of investigations where the opportunity to apprehend a suspect had been missed, despite the information that should have allowed an arrest being in the police domain. Information that had been missed, archived or not considered credible or relevant at the time of receiving it. Levi Bellfield's name had been given to the police on the evening Amelie Delagrange was murdered. It had been written on a police statement within twenty-four hours, but became lost amongst the plethora of witness statements, CCTV footage and other credible leads. Filed away and forgotten. Dormant until the truth revealed itself, and all became clear. The wood from the trees.

Rob was big on sharing. He was very open with his senior team and was a keen advocate in team sessions, where information could be assessed in microscopic detail. Any one person, however competent, could miss an individual piece of detail, or the meaning of it, but in these sessions the team could go through each part in context, and it was often the case that a member of the team saw a link or was able to relate one piece of the jigsaw with another. Fresh eyes.

Jack kicked in first. He'd only been involved in a few of these sessions but Rob knew the importance of establishing solid professional behaviours in junior officers, as he had once been.

Jack had been assigned to look at the early life and marriage of William Reynolds, to go digging and see what lurked in the closet that could hint at the reasons for his murder. The Why. And then the Who.

Any background checking was crucial. Crucial in building a picture and painting an outline of the life of an individual no longer able to speak for himself. The silent witness. In a case of this nature, when the victim was already drawing a pension, it was likely that the reasons for his death weren't found in his adolescence, which is why Rob had asked Jack to look into the earlier period of William Reynolds' life. It was good for his experience and development, but probably not critical if he misses something. Win win.

Rob was certain the reasons behind this killing were in the mid to latter stages of William's life, which is exactly why Jen and Nicky had been digging into those for the last seventy-two hours.

"Early life then, Jack, let's have it."

Jack stood up confidently, even though he was in front of his peers and a scattering of other officers who now numbered a dozen or more. The mood in the room shifted now it was game time. The chatter stopped.

Jack presented well and spoke articulately in describing the early life and childhood of William Reynolds.

"William was born at home in a terraced house in the inner city of Leicester, something very common for the proletariat of the 1960's. The house no longer exists and the area was lost to redevelopment in the late nineties. His father worked for Corah & Sons on St Margaret's Way, opposite the city's main bus station. Corah & Sons was a hosiery manufacturer, one of many, and a significant employer of the time."

This was a typical upbringing for William's generation, with half the city employed within the hosiery industry and the other half in engineering factories. Most of the buildings still stood, memories of better days when things were proudly manufactured in the UK, and in the city.

Jack touched upon William's school life. He had found that William was one of the rare ones who had made his way through both tiers of the education system, something his brother had failed to do, before leaving to start work aged sixteen. His parents had both been dead for many years, as well as his brother, who had succumbed to pneumonia several winters back, but whose health had been deteriorating for several years prior. William and Alan were the last of the Reynolds clan, a mantle Alan now held on his own. The last man standing.

Jack covered a pretty clear disciplinary record throughout William's school life, which impressed Rob, given the difficulty in sourcing complete or accurate records for this type of information, especially prior to digitalisation. Not all school records or the finer detail of an individual's school life were logged or readily available from that era. Digging through paperwork and into cracks still very much had a place in modern policing.

Rob acknowledged the findings and the picture it painted of William with a casual and approving nod, and gestured for Jack to sit back down with a "well done" as he did so.

Nicky stood to speak next, and although her and Jen had worked and researched together, Jen remained seated, happy to let Nicky speak and guide the team through what Rob suspected would form the nuts and bolts of the investigation over the coming forty-eight hours.

Nicky's piece followed on from Jack's, and picked up neatly from the period when he first started working. Rob liked it that way; he hated gaps, or any missed overlap. Felt it was sloppy policing. Jen and Nicky were well aware of Rob's stance on it and had co-ordinated well with Jack, making sure that there wasn't a missing link in between. A missing period could easily hide the motivation for a crime. All believed the motivator here lay in the last decades of William Reynold's life.

"William Reynolds had been married once, to Anna. A lengthy, if not always happy, marriage, and one which lasted a full thirty-five years, before her death in 2007. Anna succumbed to a cardiac arrest at home, which at no point was considered suspicious, and still isn't. Natural causes were recorded as the official cause of death."

Nicky paused, gauging the room before continuing.

"From what Jen has been looking into, we believe William has been single since he became a widow, and had become something of a recluse. No bingo, few hobbies, and he'd even given up his allotment a couple of years back. Alan Reynolds was their only son, which was something of a rarity at that time. We typically see families in the city during that period tend to be larger and with multiple siblings."

Jen chipped in, changing the direction slightly. She offered that she felt Alan had had a difficult time at school, with an inability to socialise, and with most other children having a number of siblings often attending the same school to afford them a layer of protection. A luxury not afforded to Alan Reynolds. Bullies are always prepared to find the 'weaker' characters in the school, regardless of generation, and Jen couldn't help but think that Alan would have fitted that mould nicely.

Life looked normal through William's twenties and early thirties, with nothing making him look anything other than distinctly average. Wife, child, job. All pointed to normal. He'd spent some time at Corah & Sons himself, following in his father's footsteps, again not something atypical of the time. He'd accrued a number of years' service, and was even promoted to foreman at one point, looking after a small team within his section.

Nothing showed an inability to interact; in fact, quite the opposite. Jen and Nicky had both seen many CVs with years of unemployment, multiple jobs, and sackings if you read between the very dotted lines. William's was respectable, generally.

The piece that was currently unclear to the team was at what point it went wrong, or even started to go wrong. William went from being a respected foreman to convicted criminal in a very short period of time, at which point it would have almost seemed uncharacteristic. The fish out of water, standing in the dock.

He'd managed to get himself two convictions for robbery, despite getting through the early period of his life without so much as getting caught shoplifting. Maybe he was just good at it, but it was far too early to have a great deal more than the stone cold facts. The convictions showed that William and a gang of four men had robbed a couple of local businesses of money and jewellery, and had used a good deal of violence and force within their MO. He'd been found guilty on charges relating to both robberies, along with the group of other men, and had spent some time at Her Majesty's pleasure as a result.

The bright news for Nicky and Jen was that he'd served his full sentence at Gartree prison in Leicestershire, which was straight up the A6 and on the outskirts of Market Harborough. It was a mere half an hour drive to continue the digging, which came as a relief, as a number of recent cases had seen Jen have to travel to prisons in Newcastle, Manchester and Stafford. Long drags. Long days.

Rob was clear that he wanted to know as much as possible about at what point, and where, William had met his four co-conspirators, and turned from being an employed father of one to a criminal. Both of the targeted businesses were in the inner city, in the days when people seemed to have no issue with shitting on their own doorstep, and seemingly felt nothing about stealing from under the noses of their friends and family. Neither of the businesses were still trading, and early enquiries had been unable to identify the business owners.

Nicky named the four other men from the gang, and wrote their names on a board behind her. It was nothing CSI; there was no sleek glass wall or white pens. Just an average-sized whiteboard, common in any classroom or office, with some squeaky markers. She wrote clearly in blue ink:

JOE DAVIES

CHARLES WORTH

PAUL HARRIS

DANIEL MORTIMER

She threw the pen onto the desk and continued.

"We don't currently have much other than their names, so

the next step is clearly finding out who played what role, who led it, and who had the nous and means to plan the robberies. We already have our suspicions that William was not the ringleader. If anything, we think he was a willing accomplice, or a foot soldier at best. So who found him, who recruited him and who got him involved in the criminal gang?"

Nicky looked up again, pausing to allow the room to think, to be clear on what needed to happen.

Jen agreed and added that other than on the police database, none of the four men had appeared in a simple Google search either. The internet was now a regular place to gain credible information, even if only to provide a link in a chain between two people who claimed not to know each other, or between partners in crime trying to hide their sins.

Facebook had played its fair share in taking down criminal gangs in recent times, most notably a group of drug dealers from the Highfields estate, who wanted to show the world their Range Rovers and gold chains despite their unemployment. Simple policing.

The issue in William's case was that most criminals who post their ill-gotten gains on social media don't have a bus pass slipped inside their wallet, and Jack had long established that William Reynolds did not have any kind of social media presence. His son, Alan, did however, and his online profile was visible, but there were no posts since about three birthdays ago.

That certainly wasn't the route he was using to communicate with his social circle, and he was barely an SMS convert either. Jack stood again to add that he felt that this wasn't an active criminal empire, or part of something bigger, but that he felt it had its dirty roots buried deep below the surface. All went against any theories of a sophisticated criminal gang from which William had gone rogue and needed to be silenced, even at his time of life.

Rob asked for a full brief on each of the four men and the team acknowledged. Jen and Nicky, as senior officers, would decide on who took what, and where to start post-brief. Jack would follow suit and pick up whatever was necessary. He enjoyed that, enjoyed getting to investigate whatever was assigned to him; he felt it was a better education than cherry-picking or being given the easy end of the wedge. It made him more flexible, more prepared to take on whatever, and whoever his peers would throw at him. It made him more trusted and less dispensable than someone who just keeps getting asked to make the tea, dig up the fluffy stuff and file paperwork.

Rob was happy and everyone seemed clear on what was needed.

"Go and make some calls, see who knows what, and be back in here at 2pm. I want to go through the offences and the gang in a lot more detail, so get the conviction and court transcripts out and we'll see what those men did, and were capable of doing."

The team started to chat amongst themselves, sharing their own thoughts, but Nicky could still see Rob's cogs spinning around. He was still visibly bothered about the motive behind the murder. The robberies and convictions happened a couple of decades ago, and William had more than served his time, been released and settled back into retirement. He had been drawing his pension. He had been released before he hit fifty, yet here he was lying on Becky's slab as a nearly seventy year old. More than twenty years had passed, and William had evidently been able to return to Civvy Street as seamlessly as he'd transformed into a convicted armed robber two decades previously.

"Why wait?" came the rhetorical question, the conversation now between Nicky and Rob, with Jen and Jack close enough to listen. "Why wait unless there's a missing pot of gold, or some information that only he knew? If he did know something, was it not salient until recently? But salient to who? Why would he sit on it until now, to the point that somebody would need him dead. To silence him? Or did he just know where the spoils are?"

Rob asked the last part with open hands and a simplistic angle. Most murders happen because one party has wronged another. Money, drugs, sex.

Rob lifted his gaze back to those in the room, who were now mostly standing before him, starting to disperse. He closed with a simple question.

"What changed that meant that William Reynolds had to die?"

CHAPTER 13

It was still raining heavily outside when the clock clicked over to 2pm in Lodge House. Rob had left the office, leaving Nicky, Jen and Jack to sort food in the interim, which had inevitably become a working lunch in readiness for the afternoon session.

Nicky had called out for a Nando's, who were now offering takeaway and were a stone's throw away from the station. It had quickly become a popular new lunch option. The three had placed their order, and had also taken an order from Bernie Copp, who was working on the case with a number of other uniformed officers. He'd placed an order for a double chicken wrap and some chips, before realising his lunch bill would relieve him of £15. He had left the office appalled, chuntering under his breath about how expensive it was, before returning twenty minutes later with a cheap bacon roll slathered in brown sauce from one of the local greasy spoons.

"£1.90," he proclaimed, while chewing on a strip of bacon. He continued to eat, and waved his cob triumphantly aloft. The others smiled, still waiting for their expensive alternative.

Jack had been working on a raft of court documents since the murder, and since William Reynolds' conviction had come to light. He'd learned the intricacies of acquiring such records with great speed in previous cases, and had cracked on, wanting to get the information in front of the team quickly. That said, gaining complete records was a skill in itself, and it still seemed easier to get hold of incomplete records than complete ones.

A dated and not fully integrated system made life difficult in certain circumstances, and details could be missed more easily than the force would ever publicly let on. Decades of IT bolt-ons to a system designed for 1980's policing were creaking. Functional, but creaking. "Project Momentum" was an IT project that had been launched, and would see a fully integrated and digitalised system live by 2021, which would be fully tied in with every one of the many national and international databases in existence.

Whatever perception the public had of the tools available to Rob and his team was certainly not matched by the reality. No Google-style function meant any errors in spelling, places or names meant that a file would not be retrieved, and whatever information held within it stayed put, waiting for another time.

Jack had been meticulous with his request; he had a triple-check method to make sure he acquired what was available. Missing anything would be criminal. PC Emma Sharpe had volunteered to help with the fetching and carrying of the numerous boxes. Having signed up for a marathon in the spring, she seemed more than happy running up and down the stairs with a payload.

"Each to their own," Jack thought, while checking each numbered document off against his own archive register. Many cracks.

Nicky, Jen and Jack had all been working studiously on the backgrounds of the gang members, and had continued to work along with a wider team of officers on unearthing what the lives of the five men were like during the 1980s. They were slowly building a picture of the four names written on the whiteboard behind them, as well as William Reynolds, to paint an image of each's characteristics, to bring them to life.

The door along the corridor slammed and the team started to clear away the remnants of their lunch, sweeping chip sleeves and peri-peri sauce wrappers into bins. Wiping their mouths like children. Rob marched through the door at speed, muttering a sequence of inaudible words under his breath without breaking stride. Jen made out "fucking miserable" as two of them, and all could see that the walk from the car park to the rear entrance was more than enough to have provided a soaking. Rob's shirt was wet, his glasses covered in large drops of fresh rain.

He threw his coat on a chair and looked for his mug, which was empty. He sighed audibly as Bernie grabbed it, and went off to make him a tea.

Jack moved first. He'd spent time on the court records, and had already shared the salient parts with Nicky and Jen. He'd taken ownership of that thread of enquiry and had done so proficiently. He stayed seated. There was less formality to this session but still an edge to the mood.

"March 8th, 1983. Four men storm into Stefan's Jewellers, a high-end and successful family jewellers on Belgrave Gate in the city. It was just before 11am, and there were a couple of customers browsing in the shop. Four men went in through the front door; they were all balaclava'd up, and the first two were armed with sawn-off shotguns. They went in brashly with guns in the air. No shots were fired but they were shouting, and one struck a male customer who hadn't complied with a request to lie down hard in the face with the butt of his gun. It broke his nose. The other members of staff were all threatened at gunpoint. The statements largely corroborate, and all detail being shouted at throughout the ordeal. Even once the women were on the floor, the two with guns continued to shout at them, loudly and aggressively. They were terrified."

Jack had the attention of those in the room and continued.

"One staff member appeared, or was pulled out from the rear part of the premises mid-raid. They didn't know he was there and they thought he was raising the alarm. He was beaten pretty badly, hit in the face numerous times. He didn't suffer any long-term injuries, but was badly shaken up and didn't go back to work once he'd recovered. The other members of staff recall being forced to the rear of the shop behind the counter, with the two other men smashing cabinets with steel bars, and filling holdalls with watches, rings and as many valuables as they could get. The other men didn't speak at any point, they just did the breaking and gathering."

Nicky interjected – "It's worth noting, Gov, that the court records only identify the responsibilities based on witness statements and on height/weight indicators. They identify the gunmen as Joe Davies and Charles Worth, and the breakers as Paul Harris and Daniel Mortimer. William Reynolds was always believed to be the getaway driver and never actually set foot inside. It's mostly speculation as there was obviously no CCTV, but it was consistent speculation, so it's largely accepted who was who. There seems little dispute that William was the lookout and driver."

Nicky nodded back at Jack to continue, and acknowledged his positive start to the briefing.

"They got access to the safe eventually by forcing a shotgun into the mouth of one of the employees while holding the head of one of the other employees against him. Told them they'd kill them both if they didn't open the safe. It was nasty stuff. They were very aggressive."

The looks between those in the room were not of shock. The occupation alone could numb the sense of it, but the disgust of hearing, and seeing what humanity could be capable of, and how this group of men went about their business, still triggered a powerful emotion. Sitting powerlessly; listening to how people inflict pain and fear onto others is always a difficult pill to swallow. The capabilities of man, at the wrong end of the scale.

"They obviously opened the safe. For a successful business, the safe was old. The employees knew the codes and thought they'd die if they didn't open it. It was a Tuesday morning anyway, so they knew that the weekend takings had been banked on the Monday. So the gang only actually got away with a few hundred quid in cash, which I imagine is much less than they'd have liked. The jewellery they got was worth a fortune though, north of £400,000 in today's money."

"That's a good haul," Rob chipped in, slurping on his steaming hot tea, feeling some warmth sink back into his body.

"If that's your gang and you've got that much in jewellery and cash, you'd be pleased with yourself. It'd drive you, spur you on." Jack added.

Rob could see where this was going. None of the team had been surprised by what they'd gone on to find out about the gang. Jack continued as eyes fell back on him.

"May 9th, 1983. They did it again. Court records show that four men burst into a jewellery store on Melton Road.

The shop was Laxmi Jewellers, another family-run business. It was just out on the edge of the city, bordering the Belgrave area, past Leicester College and situated bang in the middle of the Golden Mile."

"There must be forty jewellers on that stretch," asked Rob. "Well, there are now at least. Wonder how many there were in 1983, and why they chose Laxmi?"

Jack sat composed, content that he already had the bones of the answer in his head.

"They went in at 9.10am, just after opening on Monday morning, so there were no customers inside this time. Laxmi jewellers weren't as 'premium' as Stefan's, but they went at the staff members hard again. There were more of them this time. Staff members, that is. They hammered one with the butts of their rifles again, breaking his nose, and even then they still continued to give him a kicking. The two without guns were already smashing and grabbing, so the modus operandi was pretty identical. Crowbars were used as the tools for the job, and again they shit up the young staff members enough for them to crack the safe. There was no resistance at all and they also had the access to open it up. The key difference between this and the Stefan's raid was that they hit Laxmi on Monday morning. It was early and they hadn't done the bank run, so although they got away with a much smaller value of physical jewellery, they did get away with the cash takings from Friday, and all the takings from the weekend."

The room was quiet. Each of the team was picturing the raids in the early eighties. Men in dark clothing smashing glass cabinets, counter tops, and people. They were imagining how it must feel to be lying face down on a carpet with glass and shrapnel raining down around you, protecting your eyes and head with your hands and arms. How it must feel to be shouted at, intimidated and threatened, before being smashed with the butt of a rifle. A hard, glossy timber handle with the steel shaft housed within. Merciless.

Jack could see the contemplation on the faces of his peers. Silent thoughts.

"They got away with just over £20,000 in cash, which would be worth nearly £70,000 today. It's a smaller haul but I think they went after this because they knew there'd be more cash. They wanted cash rather than the goodies. Even with the value of jewels from Stefan's being so high, they'd then have to liquidate it, and that takes time."

Jen chipped in, agreeing with Jack's view.

"We can't see that any of the five had any kind of jewellery knowledge, specialism or contacts, so offloading any jewellery, however valuable for decent cash would have been hard for them. Time consuming too, as Jack said. It looks as if they focused on the watches they'd taken in the first raid. The brands were more well known, and selling a chunky watch in a pub, or through more generalist criminal contacts would have been easier than selling a pretty eternity ring. Especially as none of them knew what was worth twenty quid or twenty grand."

Jen looked back at Jack, who nodded, before adding more of their findings.

"The second robbery also looks to have been more directed at watches than grabbing every last gem. Laxmi was a watch specialist, but they obviously catered for the wider jewellery market. They actually left some pricey rings and chains this time, which looks deliberate, but took pretty much every last watch in the shop. I think they went a few miles out of town for this reason. I've nothing to validate it yet, but there were a lot of jewellers they could have targeted. There were dozens closer to the city centre than Laxmi, and higher end too, but they went a couple of miles out of the inner city so there had to be a reason. Maybe they made the decision, or somebody made the decision, to target *that* jeweller specifically."

"I agree," nodded Rob, approving of Jack sharing a hunch, something he was happy for his team to do.

"They didn't go to Laxmi off the cuff, they knew what they wanted for 'take two' and Laxmi must have fitted the bill."

"They'd learned," added Nicky. "The first robbery was big, possibly too big. Certainly bigger than they'd expected. But they couldn't do much with it. You can see their initial joy souring quickly when they were trying to sell a £10k necklace for fifty quid to dodgy Dave in a Humberstone pub. I think they'd have been happier with this haul; significant cash, as well as desirable stock they could shift quickly. It was *better* for them."

The logic made sense. William wasn't a bespoke jeweller with underworld contacts, and he wouldn't have been the middle man for the sale of the haul either. None of them were, that was the problem. A half a million quid haul sounds dreamy, especially for a rag and bone group of robbers, but you need to have the means to liquidate it.

Jen's phone buzzed and she lifted it from the desk, flipping it from its face-down position to glance at the screen, taking in the message. She waited for the moment to share the information she now had.

Rob clocked Jen and raised his eyebrows, the pause the invitation to share.

"Uniform have picked up Alan Reynolds, Gov. He's on his way back here now."

"Ok, great. You take him with Jack and we'll pick this back up, depending on what our man has to say. Nicky, keep digging at these men. We know what they did but not who they are, so we'll need to reconvene. There's a shitload of mileage in this and we're clearly only scratching at the fucking surface."

CHAPTER 14

Joe Davies has spent yet another day flitting between the bookies and a greasy spoon in the middle of town. From a fry up to Betfred and back again, with a tightly rolled up copy of the Racing Post tucked under his arm. He seems content, almost brazen, which I despise, but he's nicely oblivious to how his day is going to end. And his worthless piece of shit life.

His demeanor seems to have changed. Just in how he carries himself, how he appears when he walks down the street and back into the local pub when he fancies a pint in the afternoon, especially if he's had a win on one of the races. Horses or the dogs. He isn't picky and probably thinks he deserves it. Another self-entitled old man who Joe Public wouldn't look twice at. His plainness, his anonymity, is sickening. The sight of him offends me, makes me shiver, makes my blood run cold, but in twenty-four hours his cloak will be off and the world will know his name, even if only for a news cycle or two.

Joe has found himself a tidy little life at face value. Syston is a nice town about seven miles east of the city centre. A bustling little place rammed with shops, pubs and eateries, as well as all the usual suspects; Greggs, Subway. There's even a

Wetherspoons being built near one of the many high street banks. Nice drive in, good access, good schools. All the bullshit stuff estate agents usually blab on about, only this time it seems to be true.

I've been severely pissed off that Joe has wound up here since I found him. Annoyed that somebody like *him* has landed on his feet, found a nice place to enjoy the twilight of his life in a comfortable town, while the young couples from the area, those who actually went to school here, and grew up in the town, are shipping out in droves because they can't afford to stay. Having to go and find 'up and coming areas' or somewhere cheaper but with 'development potential'.

No hardship for Joe Davies though, no struggles. Nothing like Alan Reynolds has endured whilst living in St. Matthew's. The violence, street crime, early morning drug raids, daily muggings. Broken Britain in pictures. Some of the youths in Syston look more likely to carry your shopping home for you then hold you at knifepoint. What a difference seven miles can make.

This is much better than he deserves. He's a disgusting excuse for a human being and shouldn't be here; he's out of place. Well out of place. Even St. Matthew's would be too good for him. He deserves one thing and one thing only, and he deserves that slowly. Painfully. And he's going to get it. All of which makes this next part much more difficult. Harder to access, harder to go unnoticed. Harder to execute. Literally.

It's another evening job, so there's plenty of time to play with, to acclimatise. Time to wait. He'll be at home later. Another evening at home on his own, so again no spouse to deal with.

Tonight's challenges are gaining access without being seen, then carrying out the full sentence without being overheard.

This isn't a sparse area full of retired deaf people, and won't be an occasion to allow his full screams to ring out. That's annoying. I wanted to hear his pain. If I could have it as I want it, we'd be in a warehouse in the middle of nowhere, I'd make it last for days and he'd be trussed up and howling like the pig he is, begging for the end. But that would be far too risky, so I need to make do. If there is too much noise the neighbours will call the police before I've had the chance to enjoy the experience. His pain. His agony. All of it.

I'll wait, and I'll wait patiently. This has been a long time in the making and the police don't appear to be knocking at this door anytime soon. Tonight is important. Critical. William Reynolds was a starter for ten; mistakes could be afforded, techniques could be developed and an adequate kill was acceptable. But as it happened it went a lot better than expected.

Not tonight. Joe will get more but the situation is different. His custodial sentence should have been longer, indefinite, and I'm the only one in a position to inflict any form of justice on him, the only one prepared to.Full, uninterrupted justice. This one really matters.

The town is busy, so I should be able to get my car in and out relatively unnoticed It is easier to be innocuous to the naked eye, but there is a tonne of CCTV cameras around the middle of town. It's an old-fashioned place with the main roads converging in the middle, so Big Brother's gaze is far-reaching. I need to be smart, as those cameras will be gone through with a fine-tooth comb after tonight. Looking for something. Looking for somebody. I need to park close enough to blend in, and allow me to casually slip away once the job is done. I won't park in the actual street, that would be a mistake, but the town is busy enough that no one will notice another car on a side road. Plus no one's looking at me. No one's looking at Joe; not yet, at least. And when they do it'll be way too late for him.

There's no rain yet, but it's coming, according to the local news, and it's mild A nicer night for murder. Nobody likes getting wet, regardless of their occupation, although it can always help with washing away some of the trace evidence. Every cloud…

Joe's been around town all afternoon and is now well settled in the Fox and Hounds, one of two pubs flanking the middle of Syston. He'll have eaten and will have had a few pints too, so he'll be sluggish later. Worth the wait. He's older than William, only by a few years, but is physically in much better condition than his deceased friend. There will be more fight in this old dog.

I'm happy where I am too. I've found a nice little place about a quarter of a mile away. *Continental Cafe*, I think it's called. Just up the Melton Road over a bridge, and on the edge of a park. It's small but nice, with very friendly staff who are knocking out some decent coffee and an even better array of food. Plus the WiFi's quick. The building is on the end of a row. There's a weird looking double glazing/conservatory place next door that looks like a nineties throwback from when people actually had conservatories. I imagine they still employ beige looking men in pinstripe suits, who knock on your door and try to get you to part with five grand for a leaky conservatory, the kind that is always freezing cold in the winter and like an oven in the summer.

The other side is nice, a green space nestled between the cafe and the next building along, which is another nineties retro type place selling clothes. 'Keep it Casual', or something like that. I won't be buying anything. In the middle is an area that's been cleared and has a mix of block paving, raised sleeper flower beds and a couple of nice benches, still shiny black where the Hammerite has been well maintained. This is a nice area, they look after stuff. Wouldn't get any of this across town. Those benches would have been lifted and weighed in, and the rest would be covered in graffiti and dog shit. This place is far too good for Joe Davies.

It looks like the sort of space that only gets used on Remembrance Sunday, or when the Scouts or Boys' Brigade have a parade. Or for other commemorative days. I can just picture the mayor cutting a ribbon or shaking the hand of some noble local while the snappers from the Leicester Mercury take a picture.

I can't help but wonder if there is another reason for the clearing. A different reason for the flowers and the bench. Maybe it's a garden because the local councillors are green-fingered, really like plants or had too much cash sloshing around at the end of the last fiscal year. Or maybe it's because of something darker. My mind slides into a daydream; vivid pictures appear of the scenes outside 25 Cromwell Street, shortly after Fred and Rose West were arrested. Even the hardiest of estate agents would have struggled shifting that. 'A nice little do-er-upper' or 'conversion opportunity' just wouldn't have cut it. The bulldozers were outside revving their engines while the charge sheet was still wet, as they were at Ian Huntley's place. Get rid of it and the public will forget it ever happened.

Many will walk past a little memory garden or through a well-lit alleyway without ever thinking twice. Just another shortcut on just another street, not knowing or simply forgetting what happened on that quiet patch of ground. We're all cynics when it's all over the tabloids; 'should have seen it coming', and 'it never should have happened', but how many postmen, teachers and social workers got a glimpse of something darker, but carried on with their normal day, too oblivious or just too damn ignorant to be the whistleblower?

My mind snaps back into sharp focus as a trickle of rain starts to run down the window in front of me, and people begin to scurry for cover. It was forecast. Some shoppers scramble over the road into a Tesco Metro that is set back from the other shops, and is neatly tucked in behind a Royal British Legion and a pet shop. Are they still legal? Maybe this isn't such a good area.

The waitress offers me some more coffee but I've still got half a cup, and a pastry I haven't quite finished. Can't decide whether to have something substantial now, or wait until afterwards. I would need to wait until the adrenalin has died down, but if it gets too late there's always the risk of indigestion.

Stick to coffee. The caffeine that keeps me alert and awake, and buzzing enough to enjoy it. To heighten the experience of the evening's events. William Reynolds got what was coming to him, what he deserved. He'd been deserving of it for a couple of decades, but nobody noticed, nobody cared. I feel a spike of anger in my body, but let it ride through and over me without grimacing or reacting. My subconscious knows that any outburst from a stranger in a cafe just before an old man is murdered up the street will stand out like a sore thumb, and they'll be trawling the CCTV when somebody remembers somebody who lost their cool an hour or so beforehand. I'd be answering questions before I know it.

The sensation dies down, but not fully. It stays there. Riling me, but not enough to take a nice mouthful of a latte and not enjoy the taste. That anger needs saving, filing away for later. That needs bringing out when I'm in the house with him, and he's mine to take apart. The rage is welcome at that point, and if it rises up like it just has, it's going to be a very long and painful evening for Joe Davies. I smile to myself as I hold the coffee cup in both hands in front of my mouth, taking another sip and knowing that my moment is getting closer.

This evening will run its course, and the second stage of the plan will go ahead. The police are unaware, and although they have some pieces, they have crumbs. Crumbs on a table. They'll have names, they have a son, but nothing is connected. The second murder will change that. Really focus the investigation in on the links. One murder can always just happen, and the motive can be wide ranging. But two murders of the same ilk, that always starts to narrow things down, make it much tighter. Focus the mind. It's the only reason Joe's day of reckoning is today. I'd have preferred to get another clean kill under my belt before reaching him, just to hone things a bit more, but life isn't clean cut and his time has to be now. I cannot take the risk of him being found and protected.

So for now I'll enjoy my coffee, because time is still on my side, if only for another few hours.

There will be no stay of execution for Joe Davies this evening.

CHAPTER 15

It's dark when the time comes. The anticipation and desire has built nicely and I'm pumped. Ready to go. Ready to act. It's a short walk from here, just a few hundred yards to the house at most, I'm 'normally' dressed and there are a few people about. It's Friday night so it's to be expected. A varied mix of pub goers are out in force, along with those doing the early chip shop run. I'm not concerned. I'm able to walk past and seamlessly blend in. I cross a metal footbridge near a row of red brick terraced houses over a waterless brook and cut up towards a main crossroads, where the noise emanating from a pub reaches a crescendo. I walk past the open door, feeling the warmth from inside, grateful there are no smokers congregating outside, before turning right onto a quieter street. Barkby Road.

The noise dies down quickly as I walk away from the main road and up towards Joe's house; a modest two bed terrace that would suit a young couple down to the ground, a perfect first home. It'll have vacant possession tomorrow. Maybe one of them will buy it if I don't fuck Joe up too badly. But he deserves fucking up, and those old timber floorboards will have blood oozing through them before the night is out.

I squeeze my rucksack strap hard as some of the anger pulses through my left arm. I turn right again and there's nobody in the street. Perfect. His house is a terrace but there is a shared entry between his and his neighbours' house. His neighbours are a young couple who spoke to me several weeks ago when I first came across this place. Across Joe.

Number twelve. A modern uPVC door to the front, nice and secure no doubt, with no obvious way in. But Joe's been sloppy at the back. Careless, almost. There's nothing modern about that door. An old timber door with a large glass panel in it, probably not even double glazed. A brick would do the job, or any form of small tool could crack it, and I'd be in within seconds. But thankfully I know that won't be needed. There'll be no break-in tonight, and nothing so startling that would trigger an immediate response.

I've learned that Joe, of all people, has a cat, but he doesn't have a catflap, and I know that this is one door that will be both unlocked and with the key in the lock inside anyway. Fucking idiot.

The door to the rear opens into an extended galley style kitchen, typical of this type of property, with a small dining room to the left of the kitchen leading into a seperate lounge to the front, and a downstairs bathroom to the right. I set eyes on him from the darkness as he walks into the kitchen, and quickly crouch down beneath the kitchen window to stay deep in the shadows. Submerged. He drifts back into the front room, where the TV is on to keep him company. It's inaudible but the white light illuminates the wall between the darkness of the rooms.

The couple next door are in. I can hear their TV is on too, a film. Can't make out what they're watching but can picture them cuddled up on the sofa after a week at work, takeaway on their laps and feet up. Maybe he was on the chip shop run earlier, rolling out of 'Today's Catch' with their tea in a carrier bag. The curtains are closed and as long as the noise stays neutral, the evening is mine.

I wait patiently until I'm happy that Joe is settled in the lounge. I wait until he's finished going back and forth so that he won't disturb me getting in. He's sat down, comfy in his front room, I'm sure of it. I've waited long enough, I'm ready.

I stand up slowly, and move towards the back door, placing my gloved hand on the handle. I ease the old metal handle downwards, forcing the pressure gently through my arm. I feel the latch drop and start to push the door free from its frame. Just enough. Enough to slide in quickly and without making a noise. I push it back behind me but not fully closed.

Joe must have heard a noise, maybe felt a draught as the door opened and closed. He shouts "Doug!" and I stand still. Rooted to the spot. His fucking cat is called Doug.

He doesn't come, he doesn't look.

I've slid a cosh out of the side of my rucksack and am gripping it firmly. If he walks in now I'll need to attack him, overcome him quickly and get him trussed up. It would be a crying shame to start like that, though. There'll be plenty of time for blunt force.

I make some small steps as I move up the kitchen and to the threshold of the middle room, a small square-ish room with a drop-leaf dining table with a newspaper on it. Nothing on the front pages about William Reynolds. Shame. That would have given me a lot of pleasure, been a nice touch. There are two dining chairs, which surprises me. Joe is another widow and doesn't strike me as being somebody who shares his dinner table very often. The chairs are old-fashioned, a dark hardwood with a simple padded seat. Timber arms and solid legs. Ideal. He might be able to move it but by the time he's strapped to one of them he'll lose energy quickly. Like a fish out of water that I can play with. Tease.

I move through the middle room towards the open doorway, and hear a creak, a noise that sounds like he may be standing up. I can't see him yet. The door is offset so there's a wall between us, but not a great deal of distance. Three or four metres at most. I'm close to him now and itching for this to start. A flashback of my time with William Reynolds enters my head. A memory, a good one. This is the best bit. The bit where the fear starts for them, and builds until the realisation lands and to the point where they are stricken. Completely helpless, and mine to pass judgment on.

I wait.

Only a few more seconds and my body is bordering on ecstasy. I feel completely empowered, completely in control. Alive. I'm in his house but very much on my terms.

I wait another minute. A whole minute. It feels like an hour. Contemplating. Deciding whether to turn and walk through the door or to wait for him to come to me. The kitchen and the bathroom are downstairs, typical of an old terrace house, and he'll need one or the other before too long. A beer, maybe some chocolate from the fridge, a coffee or a loo break. A simple matter of time.

My patience pays off. He's definitely up and taking a few steps. And then a pause. Maybe looking for his glasses, or the cat. For Doug. I lean, pressing my back against the wall, and take a deep breath. Holding it in and waiting. Controlling my breathing.

He walks slowly through the door and into the dining room. We're in the same room, separated by nothing. It's dark and he doesn't bother to switch the light on. That would have helped. The light switch is on the adjacent wall to me and if he'd gone to it he would have had his back to me, less than two yards away. It would have made an ideal starting point, allowed a clean strike. He walks past me, within a few feet of me. He's oblivious, and continues to move diagonally towards the kitchen. He stops to yawn, arching his back with his hands.

This is my moment. He's vulnerable and the adrenaline compels me to move. I push my back gently away from the wall and my body moves upright, supporting my own weight with my feet rooted to the spot. I draw another slow, deep breath, and take a large step forward towards Joe. It's a good step, a light step.

I barely feel my own body weight transfer, and there's not a sound. He must be able to sense me behind him now though. Feel me. I resist the urge to strike even though it's ripping through my body. An inferno burning inside me. So close. He shapes as if he's about to move forward but stops again. He's within an arm's reach now, and with his back to me, but I wait. I'm enjoying this too much so my patience holds. He's taller than I recall and holds his posture. His head flickers slowly to one side, but without turning fully. I'm directly behind him and motionless.

He won't be able to see me in his peripheral vision yet, but I think he knows, or at least now suspects, that there are more bodies in the house than just his and Doug's. I control my breathing, slow it right down consciously, pursing my lips and exhaling slowly before sucking in a final long breath of air.

I should have attacked him by now. Maybe I've waited too long. Missed my opportunity. He could have been mine already. I admonish myself for my own arrogance; this could backfire. The line between rushing and waiting is wafer thin, but the first kill has given me the confidence to relish every last second of this. I lift my left leg and place it a few inches further forward. My right hand reaches into an open pocket on the side of the rucksack that is strapped tightly to my back, grabbing what I need and easing it outwards and away from my body.

Joe moves, starts to turn. Knowing but not wanting to accept what's happening, or what his instinct is now screaming for him to do. Another indecisive old man, not something I was expecting this time around. His head turns to the left, now knowing that he'll see something; somebody. His shoulders start to turn with the motion. I reach forward, my left hand meeting his neck as his body goes through a critical angle. He reacts, starts to mutter a noise, an inaudible grunt of a noise, as he throws his left arm around, in more of a defensive move than an offensive one. His hand is open so it would be a slap at best. It doesn't connect.

I grab his arm, and use it to pull him around, his momentum making him spin to his left as our eyes meet for the first time. I can see the fear this time, I can smell it. Then the surprise comes. Our bodies are entangled and my arms overlap his in a dominant position. I can see the fear in the whites of his eyes, the terror on his face. This is better. The proximity is making this so palpable I can taste it. My emotions continue to heighten as my senses overwhelm me.

Joe's body is now twisted completely, but he's exposed as he turns. My right hand reaches up. His neck is fully exposed now, with his old skin folding thickly like the nape of a puppy.

No more noise. He's contorted into a horrible position, rendering himself totally impotent. I hold him tightly with my left hand and pull him in towards me a fraction more, just enough. It opens up the right side of his neck further still.

The needle goes in.

CHAPTER 16

Rob had been looking forward to the weekend for a while. Even without the fresh case and the profile of a brutal murder, he hadn't been sat with his finger up his arse these past few months, and was very much looking forward to a weekend break, and to celebrate his sister Audra's wedding.

Spending quality time with family and friends seemed to be harder in 21st century Britain, a fact Rob had got used to personally, and something he was well used to seeing with the people he came across on a professional level, on the faces of the family members he'd come into contact with on a daily basis. Brothers who had got married and 'drifted away', sisters who weren't as close as they were in their inseparable teens, and friends who weren't as close as they thought when the secrets of their 'best mate' were laid bare post-mortem.

Rob had grown up in the north of England in the late seventies, him and his sister both having been born in Liverpool. An early move meant that neither had kept any kind of accent, something he'd been grateful for. He was proud of his roots, but there was still a stigma attached to accents, and he was happy that any twang he may have had as a young child had stayed on Merseyside.

Rob was the younger sibling. He had a good relationship with his sister, which had improved with age and on becoming an uncle to his nephew Ted, but other than at Christmas and the odd birthday, the relationship was unintentionally becoming one of weddings and funerals.

He'd spoken to Nicky first thing. She would take the lead with the interrogation of Alan Reynolds. Even if Rob was at work, he'd have asked Nicky to take the interview, and watch or listen to it online from his office. Nicky was a hard but compassionate interrogator, a quality operator. The fact that people like Alan Reynolds have tendencies of being anti-female, especially if the women has any kind of authority or power, would also be useful. Provocative. Rob had an inkling that he'd hate being interviewed by two women, and his criminal record merely supported that contempt.

Rob already had a strong suspicion that Alan Reynolds was not the man responsible for his father's death, but he wanted to be sure, wanted to find what knowledge was in that mind. Although he could acknowledge that Alan would no doubt need to grieve for his loss, he also wanted to make sure his time at Lodge House was as uncomfortable as possible.

The morning had been spent heading south down the M1 towards Bedford, with the Barns Hotel providing the venue for the day. Rob had booked a room; it looked nice online and a cooked breakfast was always an attractive proposition. This evening would no doubt go deep into the night, and although he had no plans to drink himself half to death, a few welcome lagers and a champagne toast were central to the day's plan. The journey had been good, and Rob had been surprised to see a sign for a Centre Parcs as he exited the junction near Woburn and headed along the A421 towards the town, increasing his glances at the sat nav as the venue drew nearer. Passing what looked and sounded like an attractive village, signposted as Marston Moretaine, Rob realised he'd never been to Woburn Safari Park, which was being advertised on the brown tourism road signs, and he made a mental note to go one day with his kids.

Rob had also shared a brief conversation with Jen whilst in the car. He knew she had the mettle to sit in the room with Alan Reynolds, but people like him could get to you. Get under your skin and into your head. People with nothing to lose and no respect for authority could say vile, hurtful things, and being exposed to it was almost a rite of passage, along with getting spat at, and getting thrown under the bus by your superiors. Life skills. Valuable experience.

Rob had every confidence in Jen, but she was still young. Feisty. These exchanges can affect you, and how you feel. Rob was more than conscious of it; mental health was becoming a key factor in any workplace, and the police force hardly reflected the average place of work. But he also cared for Jen and he wanted her to know he was there for her. He'd put in the call as a metaphorical 'arm around', something Jen had appreciated.

It was late morning when Rob arrived at the Barns Hotel, and he was delighted to see an authentic and very beautiful Tudor barn, where the ceremony would no doubt take place in a few short hours. The barn shared a large site with a more modern hotel and nicely kept gardens, a real contrast. There was an old versus new vibe that was working well and would offer the day an original scene for the wedding and some nice photographs post-nuptials. Plenty of character for the photographs. Quirky features and oak beams for the pictures, and a 21st century room with WiFi and a comfortable bed for later. A perfect contrast.

Rob found a chair inside and took it, sitting back and thinking about the contrast in the life of Alan Reynolds. An unprivileged existence on the doorstep of the gleaming city centre. Drinking his life away in the shadows while the young danced, partied and shopped, building towards their future. A very different type of contrast.

He picked up a glossy magazine from a coffee table, inhaling images of beautiful people advertising beautiful things. He reflected on how society continued to ram fashion, brands and high-end stores down the throats of the young, the fashionable and the obsessed. Alan Reynolds was none of those, and had probably never set foot in the Highcross, let alone parted with any cash there. The shiny billboards, magazine culture and social media would all be targeting the Instagram generation, with an overwhelming desire to conform, socialise and be accepted.

Alan Reynolds was an outcast. Did that just happen or did society do that to him? It didn't necessarily make him a murderer, but Rob wanted to know what was hiding in the depths of a conscience that may afford the investigation some progress.

He looked at his phone to see if there were any messages, which were usually short, even if just to update or guide on how the interview was going. Nothing yet, just a screen saver of Rob and his two sons smiling back at him. A photo of the three of them at the King Power Stadium for the Leicester versus Southampton game a couple of months ago.

He smiled. It was always a picture he liked looking at. His boys gave Rob an exceptional amount of pride. He loved being a father, and they provided motivation and resolve on the tough days. Days like last Thursday when William Reynolds was found strapped to a chair. He smiled again at the image. All three were smiling and wrapped up on a cold but sunny day. A great memory of a carefree weekend, one where nothing mattered.

He unlocked the screen with his thumb and hacked "Anything?" into his phone before sending it to Nicky.

Slipping the phone back into his pocket, he wandered into the reception to check in and offload his bags. There was plenty of time for a shower and a pint before his sister arrived.

CHAPTER 17

It was a bright Monday morning, and Nicky had messaged Jen and Jack to meet her in the office. She was expecting Rob to be in early for a full brief of the information that the team had been gathering. Nicky had arrived just before 6.30am, and was making sure that all of the current data and the findings of the recent days were either in place or on display, ready to be shared, picked apart and understood. Jen had messaged to say she was running late but only by ten minutes or so. She lived by the mantra that lateness was a relative concept. If she arrived before Rob she was either early or on time. Lateness only occurred when she arrived after the SIO, irrespective of the actual time.

Jack had messaged to say he was also about ten minutes out, but would be arriving with four Starbucks coffees of the standard order. He was picking them up from a drive-thru that had been opened in the car park of a trading estate, in the shadows of a closed down Toys R Us.

Nicky was just starting to crave her caramel latte when Jen arrived, lugging some hand-outs and prepared files that she had organised ready for the session, with Jack following shortly afterwards. Jen smiled broadly with her eyes bright, giving Jack a double finger gun salute to start the morning, with a loud "Hey!" to go with it.

It always looked good to be in the office, to be seen. The myth that attendance and commitment was a proportional relationship still existed. It was sometimes better to be in the office even if you were on eBay than not in the office at all.

All three were beavering away in growing company, with the chatter in the office starting to build nicely when Rob arrived, with the clock still shy of 7am. He was delighted to see the step change in what he could immediately see. The level of detail that had been gathered had expanded well, and the walls now looked more like an investigation building momentum than one still getting off the ground. Rob was already relishing the morning ahead, but desisted changing his facial expression to show as much. He managed a wry smile when he realised the flat white on one of the hot desks in the main office was his.

"One sugar, boss," said Jack, raising his own drink in a 'cheers' gesture.

"Thanks, Jack," replied Rob, raising his own cup with 'Rob' written on it in black pen. Classic Starbucks.

Jen still had an old Starbucks cup on her desk, from a time when the barista had misheard and inexplicably written 'Yen' on the side of her cup, a nickname that had stuck.

"Who wants to start then?" said Rob, eager to kick off, grabbing a chair from one of the desks and rolling it into the centre of the floor.

"I will, Gov," said Jack, the slight change in tone an acknowledgement that the small talk was over and it was game time.

Jack started to stand before Rob raised a hand. He apologised to Jack before asking Nicky to update first on the final output from the Alan Reynolds interview. Jack sat down with Rob still apologising, acknowledging Jack's willingness to kick things off.

Nicky swung her legs off the desk to stand and picked up a biro that she'd spin between her fingers as she spoke. A subconscious choice, a habit to occupy her hands when she was standing on the spot talking to a group. Partly a nervous tic. Partly just something to do with her hands when she stood in front of a group of people.

"So we got Alan on a good day. A day he didn't fancy a fight, and wasn't overly aggressive other than being a bit sweary. We got him talking, and more, he was prepared to talk. He didn't lawyer up, didn't "no comment" at any point and seemed happy to chat to us. I say happy…""He knew he was under arrest, knew it was on suspicion of murdering his dad, and if I'm honest, he was quite pathetic, to the point that I nearly felt sorry for him. I think we got him at the end of a bender. He looked like he was still coming down; the whites of his eyes were rolling but not enough to make me think he'd used in the few hours before we picked him up. He sat there looking blank and cried quite a lot when the realisation that his dad was dead landed. He seemed genuine, or as genuine as he ever is. He looked confused, tired and blank at times, but was as open as he's ever been and wasn't aggressive or defensive. We're all used to the aggressive wankers, the ones we all know have got something to hide, who think if they shout loudly or aggressively enough we might drop it."

Alan Reynolds was very much one of the wankers. He'd needed to be constrained by officers in the past even during a routine interview. Somebody who can kick off if the wind blows the wrong way. He was well known for it, and any experienced officer in the constabulary knew that he needed to be treated with caution at all times.

"He sat with his coffee, and asked for a smoke, and you could see him processing what he'd heard and was being told. I'm not sure there are many cogs left working in there, but the ones that are were whirring away to the point we could practically hear them. It seemed clear that what we were telling him or asking him was news to him."

"Alibi, Nicky?" Rob chipped in and was ready to hear what he had suspected for a few days.

"He remembered being in a pub on Church Gate at some point. The Sun. It's a pub that a few officers remember being nice around ten to fifteen years ago, but which has somewhat declined and now suits a lower social clientele."

Jen nodded in approval at Nicky's well phrased summary of what she had found to be a real shit-hole of a pub, and one she could easily picture Alan Reynolds looking at home in. At least with the bones of an alibi offered up, or where Alan Reynold's thought he might have been at the time of his father's death, it had allowed Jen to go digging.

A helpful element of the city centre was its plethora of cash points, mobile phone towers and endless CCTV cameras. Digital records, all offering the innocent man a cast iron alibi in the wrong set of circumstances, or solid evidence against the guilty. An Orwellian delight, but commonplace in any major city. Big Brother's uncompromising eyes and ears all around you. Something now oddly helpful to Alan Reynolds given his insobriety, and inability to accurately account for his own whereabouts.

Becky had only been able to give a broad window for the time of William's death, but it was something the team could work with, and something Jen had been able to check on. She'd spent some time with a number of city retailers on Church Gate and down towards the junction with St Peter's Lane. Junctions always increase your chances of a find, and with a large casino tucked in opposite a Debenhams and a host of fast food outlets, she could easily imagine picking Alan Reynolds up in the area. Buying a kebab. Buying an eight ball. Buying both.

There were some obvious candidates for decent CCTV coverage in the usual big chains, as well as a few independent coffee shops who had splashed out to avoid, or protect themselves against vandalism, and other petty crime that plagued the streets.

It had taken a while but she had picked up Alan Reynolds staggering down Churchgate at a credible enough time to the one he'd given.

He looked suitably inebriated, and was walking in a way that again seemed to help his cause. The team believed the killer was someone in control. Composed. Totally in conflict with the outline of the pathetic half-cut figure on the screen.

Jen had looked at the footage, which was undoubtedly of Alan Reynolds, recognisable both facially and by a distinctive grey Superdry coat with an orange band and logo to the back, which had made the identification easier. He was wearing the same coat when he was picked up by uniform.

Jen stood, coffee in hand, and addressed the team.

"Once we found him on one of the CCTV feeds we could corroborate it with several other cameras from local shops, as well as the main city feed of several other streets."

She pinned the best three images of Alan Reynolds on the board, each time stamped before continuing.

"We were able to follow him for a good mile on his route out, heading back towards the Haymarket. We lost him somewhere between there and the car park at Lee Circle, but he looks to be heading towards home. We'd hoped to pick him up on a bus somewhere. Jack has spoken to, and sat with the guys from both Arriva and Midland Fox, but we're certain he didn't get on a bus to get home; it would have offered more CCTV of his journey. They have some cracking cameras both on-board and on the outside of buses now, they even get decent images of pedestrians they pass. It's impressive stuff."

"The summary is, we're confident he was heading home, and his demeanor was of a man who'd been drinking heavily and was heading into the evening to carry on or sleep it off. The only missing piece is exact timings, so we're an hour shy of the critical time of death estimates, but he's pissed, he's heading the wrong way, and he's on foot. His dad's house is out at Markfield so it would be accessible, and it is possible he could have done the round trip, but in that state and without a car – it just isn't plausible.""Jack and I did it, wanted to gauge whether it could be done, and from where we last saw him we took the drive out there. Its eleven miles out of town, straight up the A50, but you've got to get out of the city first. He doesn't own a car, having had his licence revoked. Drink-driving. You can do it in the time but we're not buying it, not in his state. Would be far too off the cuff; there'd been no communication between them or reason for an argument to be brewing, and whoever did go into that house that night did so in a planned and prepared manner."Jen pointed at the image of a sad and drunk figure, tapping at it with her fingers."That is not a prepared man."

Nicky had made the decision to release Alan Reynolds that evening. He remained a suspect as the round trip was technically possible, but she was comfortable enough that he wasn't the man they were looking for. He still had some time left on his custody clock, but she hadn't wanted to waste their time on him. She had a hunch that somewhere in the back of his mind he may know something that could be critical in identifying the motive for the murders. There was a bigger picture and she wanted to play on it. They may need him, and there would be other times to antagonise him, no doubt. If there was something in that memory, it would be very deeply buried, eroded badly by years of alcohol and substance abuse, but Nicky wanted him 'on side'. He was the person who knew their victim the best.

Rob was happy with the content and comfortable with the interview. He was equally disappointed in having to rely on someone of Alan Reynold's ilk for quality information.

His stomach rumbled.

"Croissants next time, Jack," smiled Rob as he gestured to Jack, who smiled back, feeling slightly awkward as he had eaten one in the car on the way in, and worried that there may be a telling flake of pastry in his stubble, giving him away.

Rob downed the last of his coffee and threw the cup towards the bin in the corner of the room, scouring the desks to see if, or where, he'd thrown a Grenade bar or something else he could munch on.

"We need to get out to the prison. I think we need a steer on what happened inside, who got on, who didn't get on, and whether anything significant enough happened to make our gang fall out with one another."

"Jen and I are going over there now, Gov."

CHAPTER 18

HM Prison Gartree is a large Category B facility on the outskirts of Market Harborough, nestled in the affluent countryside about halfway between Leicester and Northampton. The drive out there is a pleasant one, straight up the London Road past the train station, then up the A6, clipping the top corner of Victoria Park, a majestic, rolling park framed with wrought-iron gates and the landscaped gardens of the De Montfort Hall.

Nicky regaled fond memories of Radio 1's Big Weekend to Jen as they headed up the hill in slow morning traffic. In the late nineties, maybe 2000. 100,000 people crammed onto the park with the likes of Dido and Faithless knocking out mighty sets. Heady days. The park had provided the same backdrop when Leicester City won the Premier League a couple of years back; the whole city seemingly decamped onto the park for a massive and impromptu Kasabian gig. How a simple park can hold memories of youth, joy and hedonism. Just a great time to be alive. She smiled.

The A6 flowed up and out of the city and into the leafy countryside of South Leicestershire on a long straight drag of ten miles or so, before finally landing at an island with a

McDonald's on it, a sure sign you were getting close to the prison. A fleeting glance was exchanged between the two women as the golden arches drew closer, with the question not needing to be spoken out loud. Nicky had already drifted into the lane for turning left and was indicating, ready to hit the drive-thru. A quick glance at the clock on the dash showed 10.12am, meaning there was still a full eighteen minutes before the breakfast menu stopped being served. Sausage and Egg McMuffins all round, with hash browns for chasers and a flat white apiece.

The food was accounted for in the car with talk around plans for the coming days, a quick catch-up on suspicions of an office affair and Jen's Tinder profile. There was always something juicy going on with somebody from the office, and the world of Tinder always brought amusement with the sheer scope of weirdo's on offer. Jen was surprised she hadn't met more in her professional capacity than her personal one.

With breakfast down and the brown paper bag dispatched into an oversized bin, the two made the final mile up the hill and off the main road. The barbed wire and high fence became visible. The prison sits on an old site, with original officers' housing outside the main gate, along with a scattering of small concrete buildings which have been converted into offices or storage. A large Samworth Brothers lorry had just arrived to deliver food supplies, sandwiches and ingredients, and was going through the full checks that a Class B facility demands. It would no doubt take him at least an hour to get through the gate.

Nicky and Jen left their car outside in a small staff and visitors' parking area, and, as pre-registered official visitors and serving police officers investigating a murder, used a pedestrian entrance. Full security procedures remained mandatory regardless of occupation or rank, so they'd still have to go through a stringent checking of shoes and handbags, including a full airport style X-ray machine. Nicky was a handbag fanatic, and was no doubt about to hand over one of her prized Mulberry's to some sour-faced bitch who would manhandle it like it was a sack of potatoes. Jen kept a keen eye on Nicky to enjoy the passionately disdainful look she'd give back, with absolutely no attempt to hide it.

It was twenty-five minutes before they cleared security, and started to chat about the main elements of the information gathering for today. They stood facing each other, strapping their watches back on after collecting them from a plain grey box.

A figure emerged from a side office and introduced himself as Gary Hunt, shaking hands weakly with both and stating his title as 'Senior Liaison Officer'. Jen thought it sounded like one of those awful job titles dreamt up by some overpaid bureaucrat, and told Nicky as much later on. She also noted the acronym as SLO, and imagined how shit it would look written on a business card or as an email signature.

Gary led Nicky and Jen into a room set aside for official business, and visits of a more formal nature. That it was a little used side room was their first impression, as it was fairly plain. It had a desk and three chairs in it, and clearly hadn't been anybody's functional office for a while.

Some files were set aside, which Gary would no doubt have had some skivvy dig out earlier on. He came across as a pleasant enough character, but his outfit, a short-sleeved light pink shirt and striped tie coupled with a navy tank top, was giving off more than an air of 'jobsworth' about him. It wasn't a good look. He hung around for a bit before Nicky told him they'd be fine and he could leave them be if he had work to do, something he seemed grateful for, and he scurried off along the corridor.

A number of boxes had been left to the side of the room. Dusty white and grey boxes with lids and various scrawls in black marker across them, visible under the dirt. There were some large black lever arch files alongside them and each one was crammed with paperwork.

"So what should be here, Nicky? What are we expecting to find?"

"Well, I'd like to think we can find something salient around the time William Reynolds and his likely lads spent in here. What they did, who they had fights with, and any other secrets that were documented, as well as who visited them, and how often. There may be a name we might not expect. A non-relative, a silent partner."

"And why isn't this all on the database? Why are we here?"

"Two reasons, Jen. One is people. I spoke to Gary yesterday. Sometimes there are people who know things, remember things. Things that aren't written down. Moods, feelings, emotions. Sadly for us, that doesn't appear to be the case here, and all the guys who worked B block at the time Bill and the boys were here all seem to be retired or dead. We'll need to follow on with the retirees but that's one for another day. Reason two is prison resources. The criminal records database is up to date, so we know when the guys were here, how long for and what for, and we have the court records and trial transcripts, but what we don't have is what happened once they got here, and while they were here. Everything's digitised now, so anybody currently residing will have a digital record, but the legacy records of the prisoners prior to about 1995 were on paper and have never fully been updated into the digital archives. They are being done, but the recession killed the progress, and it's been slow going since, so it's proper policing until they do. They're working chronologically backwards, and as our lot were here from the early eighties they're in the low priority pile."

Nicky and Jen spent a good amount of time setting the room up and separating the files out by each of the five names in focus. Starting with William Reynolds, they laid out a number of files, and various pieces of paper. The nuts and bolts became clear pretty quickly. William had been here between 1984 and the summer of 1989, something they already knew, along with the fact that William's sentence was the shortest of the five men.

His time here had been 'good', in that he'd stayed out of trouble, had a clean disciplinary record and had even taken a woodworking course to pass the time, something he'd become quickly accomplished and proficient at. No surprise, given his penchant for making things and the transferable skills he'd acquired on the factory floor.

It looked like he'd socialised well, and had even been trusted with putting the woodworking tools away, as well as taking delivery of some of the raw materials from a local timber company named in the file as 'Shires Timber'. Jen continued to skim-read the handwritten documents, and could easily relate the temperament she was reading about to what she already knew about William Reynolds. Not an inherently bad man. Not a troublemaker.

The files detailing the incarceration of Joe Davies and Charles 'Charlie' Worth were much thicker, and there were more of them. Nicky started to take out the key sections around discipline. A reports and incident section that was empty for William was anything but for both Joe and Charlie.

There were countless reports for both men, whose stays at HMP Gartree had been almost double the length of William Reynolds'. Both had served their sentences between 1984 and 1995, and were never at risk of being released early. Nicky flicked through page after page of A4, each seemingly detailing a fight, a 'minor disturbance', or suspicions around their involvement in several major brawls that happened during that period. Several were backed up with medical reports of stitches, head injuries and broken fingers, with most sustained whilst inflicting injury on other inmates. Jen slid her chair across and the two could see that fighting and violence seemed to be something both men enjoyed, relished, and certainly seemed to have sought out.

Violence is prevalent in most prisons, Category A's and B's especially, and is a 'Marmite' element in the prison fraternity. Some, like William Reynolds, steer clear of it, and some seek it out like pigs rooting for truffles. Joe and Charlie were pigs. Nicky shook her head as she spread the pages out, wondering out loud how many of the scuffles and fights wouldn't have happened without Joe and Charlie there to start, incite or fuel whatever was going on.Stirring the pot at every opportunity, cooking up the atmosphere in a place that simply didn't need the provocation.

The wardens must have hated the pair of them and dreaded going to work, especially for a late shift when the day's boredom had set in and Joe and Charlie had had all day to root out who was having a bad day, who owed who for phone cards, cigarettes, drugs, and to find a way to manipulate the situation until the outcome was inevitable, and fists were flying.

Jen had been digging and started to compile details for the fourth and fifth names from the list. Paul Harris and Daniel Mortimer. They were still relative unknowns from the group, and at first glance appeared to be nestled somewhere between William and the two clear 'bad eggs' on the prison behaviour spectrum. Paul Harris had spent some time in isolation, although it looked like the primary cause was for his own safety and his mental health issues, something which wasn't fully understood or catered for at the time, and in some parts of society, still isn't in 2019.

Jen felt more than a hint of sympathy for a man she imagined would have struggled to adjust to prison life, and who had passed away within a year of walking out of the gates that she and Nicky had passed through just a short while ago.

Jen was surprised at how a handful of files and documents in a boring and colourless room could paint such a colourful picture of the characters and temperaments of five men she had never met, or met alive, in William Reynolds' case. Simple sheets of paper that could articulate a group of men, their traits, and who would likely have held which roles within their group. Their micro-climate.

Daniel Mortimer was similar to William; a quiet character who avoided the limelight as much as possible and did his utmost to keep his prison life clean. He'd studied with the Open University, and had read to pass his sentence, and seemed to be the most academic of the five. He'd even studied at medical school as a younger man. Jen had found some background documents the day before where he'd used 'Dr' as a prefix to his name, but the team had been unable to locate whether that medical training was ever fully completed and to what extent Daniel Mortimer had practised medicine.

Jen sat back in her chair, looking up at Nicky, who was still digging through a folder.

"You can see it, can't you, Nic. You can imagine Joe and Charlie cooking this up, manipulating and twisting the other three. Chirping about how they should do it, why they should do it and getting in the ear of men who were either too vulnerable, too scared or too indebted to one of them to say no."

Gary offered to scan and send anything that Nicky and Jen deemed prudent back to the station while the two travelled so it was waiting for them when they got back, an offer which had pleasantly surprised them, and for which they offered genuine gratitude.

He'd be busy.

Jen needed another coffee, and was already thinking about dropping into Maccies for the second time on the way out of the prison. She was also feeling sorry for whichever Junior Liaison Officer Gary found to do his donkey work.

A phone vibrated on the desk and Nicky looked at it, It was a WhatsApp message from Jack. Nicky gave it a confused look, and spoke out loud to share that some residents on Brook Street in Syston had reported what they thought was a dead body inside their neighbours house.

Jen's face shared her perplexion. "Why does that sound familiar?"

Nicky sat, rustling away, flapping the papers in front of her. The frown on her face showed that she knew the address, had read it but was unable to place it. She found a page, pulled it out and read aloud what was in her hand.

"That's where Joe Davies lives."

CHAPTER 19

It was the wrong side of 6pm when Nicky and Jen arrived in Syston, after a prolonged departure from the prison, and a forgettable drive from Gartree. Brook Street had been cordoned off, uniform had set up a small roadblock and were already stopping cars on Barkby Road to take statements from drivers, hopeful that somebody had seen something out of the ordinary, remembered something useful, or, even better, that they would find a nosy local with a dashcam.

Jen spotted Becky Ryan, and jumped out of the car to cut her off before Nicky headed further up the street to park. It was dry, but the sky was threatening and the natural daylight was starting the early evening descent into darkness. It would be gone within an hour, two at most. Another night under artificial light.

Nicky found a spot on a side road and parked her car near a convenience store on a corner, a local Mace, which she didn't realise still existed. She thought they'd gone the same way as Safeway, Somerfield and Kwik Save. She'd started to walk back up the street when she heard Jen let out a loud, sharp laugh, the noise hard against a sombre background. She snapped her head up quickly to look, and could see Becky standing with a Starbucks coffee, having picked one up from a drive thru on the way in. A caffeine fix to fuel the body and mind for what was to come.

As Nicky got closer, Jen was pointing at it to get her to look, still laughing under her breath. In thick black marker the word 'Betty' was written down the side with a 'smiley face' drawn underneath it. Nicky sniggered and said hi to Becky before asking how she was. Becky replied with an affirmative nod and a characteristic smile.

The uniformed officers had arrived quickly, and Nicky recognised the collar reference numbers as belonging to Hamilton, a small station operating in the west of the county. Syston had had its own police station for years, barely 500 yards from where they now stood, but it had been closed a couple of years ago under political wranglings and cost reduction measures. Another community asset deemed unnecessary, no doubt by a group of people on the public sector payroll. Choosing to deprive the very people who pay their salary from a vital service. The police station, the library, the post office. Vital community services closed down in the name of bureaucracy.

Nicky had pointed the old station out when they'd driven past not ten minutes ago, now just a plain looking estate agents blending in opposite a modern doctor's surgery with a small Boots outside.

A number of recognisable faces had started to arrive, having made good time from Leicester. Bernie Copp and Emma Sharpe were both visible amongst the growing melee as the number at the scene continued to increase steadily.

Nicky, Becky and Jen started to walk towards the house along a street that had been fully closed, another cul-de-sac, as it was with William Reynolds. Always an easier location to isolate. Less contamination. No through traffic.

The three women had been getting to know one another as the investigation grew, and outstanding questions around the first murder were being tossed around as they walked. Becky strolled ahead, a tall woman with an enviable olive complexion and dark, sultry features. The sort of woman who would look good in a bin bag. Even now on a damp Tuesday evening, with her long dark hair tied back and up, just a hint of makeup and a white paper suit, Becky still managed to look effortlessly glamorous.

Nicky and Jen's relationship with Becky had blossomed both professionally and personally to the point where they could now pass playful and tongue-in-cheek comments, which were taken fully as intended, and met with a smile that would only enhance and highlight her features further. She even looked tall in the awful blue plastic mortuary Crocs she was wearing, but was walking as gracefully as if she was wearing a pair of sky-high Louboutins. Nicky wagered that she owned a pair, but would save that question for a different time.

The street appeared dark, but a patrol car parked across the road had its blue light flashing, and by sitting in the entrance to the street it was funnelling the light across the terraced houses like a strobe. Nicky gestured to an officer, and with a furrowed brow asked for it to be switched off. The neighbours had all got the gist of what was happening and she'd have a migraine within the hour if that kept going.

Her iPhone buzzed in her pocket. She pulled it out and looked at it. Rob. It simply said "Ten minutes".

Nicky shared the news with Jen and Becky, but gave the message, "We should get cracking."

Two other pathologists who reported into Becky were already on site and had secured and sealed the scene, ready to start their gruelling and unenviable evening's work. The three pathologists had a brief chat before Becky turned and asked Jen and Nicky if they could give her twenty minutes, explaining her reason about space in the property and concerns for preservation. She'd been told that space was tight in the mid-terrace and her priority was to collect samples, dust for prints, and run a number of initial tests for DNA while the scene was as fresh as it was. A small terrace always made for interesting logistics with photographers, forensics and detectives vying for space, to take a look and get an initial view of the scene. The first glimpse.

Becky had a casual way of asking, and both were happy to oblige. Having detectives hustling to do their job was natural, but in the wrong environment, or with the wrong mix of characters it could be invasive and cause friction. It could also contaminate any evidence if procedures were not followed, and cause the sort of doubt that a defence lawyer would welcome with open arms, would relish in court. Becky wanted the scene, wanted to find and capture what was there, before the other judicial personnel could theorise and fixate to their heart's content.

Jen put a call in to Jack. He'd been following a lead so was a good distance away. Jen told him to stay put, finish up at Lodge House and head home for some kip. He'd get his chance with the scene but it wouldn't be this evening. Too many cooks…

Rob arrived shortly after, Nicky went to cut him off and give him the initial brief and an overview of the crime scene and the surrounding area. She passed on that Becky's team were working the scene, as some timely flashes burst out of the front window of the terrace from a forensic camera. They started to suit up as they spoke, with Jen doing the same while sitting in the open side door of one of the pathology vans, a Peugeot Partner, parked in Brook Street.

Becky appeared from the alleyway to the side of the house, and gestured to the senior team to come down and enter the property from the rear, advising them to mind the cat that had appeared and was sitting meowing away in the kitchen.

Becky asked Nicky if she was able to feed him, having already called the RSPCA to come to collect him. Becky had mentioned to her new friends that she had a rescue cat at home; a tabby called Doris, and so she was more than sympathetic to the sad and hungry looking feline. She'd happily volunteer to adopt Doug too and take him home should the need arise.

The stench of death hung thickly in the air. Rob was already asking after the young couple next door. They had probably tried the letterbox to take a look inside, thinking something may be wrong, before being hit by the violent stench that would have emanated from the opening. Like a slap in the face, only much worse. Their statements were being taken but the early signs were that they'd heard nothing, just been unlucky enough to care.

Rob carried on walking with Nicky and Jen behind. The body came into view, a lifeless silhouette sitting strapped to a chair. They moved into the narrow kitchen, where two forensic officers studiously continued their duties, but were happy to share the workspace. Joe Davies was sitting in a wooden chair facing away from the kitchen, in the middle of the floor, where his killer would have had 360 degree access to his then live body. To inflict pain. To torment it.

Rob looked down at some smashed shards of wood that were littering the floor, and with tongue in cheek asked the forensic guys if they'd been clumsy on the way in. Becky peered around the wall into the lounge, smiled and replied to the negative.

"This is as it was when we came in. Looks like the twin brother of the one he's sitting in. We assume he put up more of a fight than Bill did, or that there was an initial struggle, and at some stage the second chair was broken. Joe was bigger than Bill was, and seems to have been in better shape, so it would have been harder for our guy to get started. But get started he did."

Nicky and Jen were walking around the body, taking in what had been done to it. Processing what they could see.

"We think within the last twelve to eighteen hours as a guesstimate for the time of death. Rigor's well set in so getting him off the chair will be fun. You can see the obvious damage, the similarities too. Most obvious variant is the fingers, though."

Becky watched each of the officers take a close look at the body, starting to form their own opinions on what was before them. The body was slumped forwards in the dark wooden chair, with cable ties strapped tightly to his wrists, and several others tied to his shins and ankles, which were most likely the only thing holding Joe Davies' body in the chair. Restrained, even in death.

"There was no gaffer tape to the hands or feet this time, just a double layer wrapped tightly around the head to cover the mouth. A bulge in the tape suggests there was something in his mouth with the tape covering it, no doubt to block the screams."

The absence or removal of any teeth wasn't obvious but would be determined back at the Royal, under Becky's hand. His feet were pointing inwards and were bare. His clothing was badly shredded where he'd been beaten, appearing as if he'd been thrashed as well as forcefully struck. There were clean cuts amongst it, and some that could have been made post-mortem. Blood had oozed from a number of cuts, grazes and wounds that were visible on the torso, soaking the torn areas of his shirt and laying thickly in his lap.

Joe had much shorter hair than William, and there was bruising clearly visible around his hairline. There was blood spatter everywhere. His face, head and neck had again been beaten, and the low light made the glow of the bruises appear more visible; iridescent yellows, bright blues and dark blacks as you moved around the body.

His left ear was missing, and the blood was heavy to the left side of his head as a result, soaking the skin below his jawline and down into his throat, as well as the fabric of the shirt across the collar and left shoulder. Dark blood was now dried onto the skin, but it still shimmered as bright scarlet on the smooth surface of the grey tape.

Becky looked at the team, all taking the time to inhale the scene. Looking at it. Processing it. Thinking.

"He took some punishment I'm afraid. We're in the same boat; cause may be difficult to identify, but there seem to be some subtle differences. There are less puncture type wounds but we have bruising to the neck that's new. Maybe an additional torture. Maybe the assailant wanted our new friend to share some information. But I'll leave those trains of thought with you guys."

Jen got down on her haunches to the left side of the body, being careful not to touch anything despite her gloved hands and body suit. Her mouth was firmly covered with a paper mask, which was offering little protection from the strength of the smell. She'd taken a good look at the injury caused by the mutilation and removal of the ear, but was more interested with the more obvious difference, one that Becky was surprised hadn't been the first point of conversation.

Jen was low, her eyes inches from the corpse as she explored the bloodied and restrained left hand of Joe Davies, which was missing not one but two fingers. The index and middle digits. Cleanly severed and no doubt cut from his hand while he was still alive. The blood had come out of the wound at force initially; a small projectile had sprayed away from the hand a good couple of feet across the floor in front of his body. Some thicker blood had followed, running down and setting on the leg of the timber chair, with some pooling at the base of the chair as he'd continued to bleed. Unable to move. All had noticed it immediately but had become transfixed on the myriad of injuries, recalling the sight that had greeted them at Bill Reynolds' house and comparing them like a macabre game of spot the difference.

Jen broke the silence with a subtle question.

"So why the fuck did he cut two fingers off this hand?"

CHAPTER 20

I expected to feel good after that. Better. Expected there to be a real satisfaction. But I'm not getting the feeling I thought Joe Davies would give me. I expected a real contentment. Happiness. Pleasure.

Yet the disappointment is rife, and a real void is eating away, consuming me. A hard numbness I simply didn't expect.

I'm sitting in a Costa Coffee in a large shopping centre just out of town. Beaumont Shopping Centre in Beaumont Leys. Sounds a lot nicer than it is. The estate surrounding it is a bit of a dump. It was only a couple of years ago that somebody threw a bomb into the front door of the police station here. An 'incendiary device', they called it. It exploded. It was a fucking bomb.

I'm drinking a flat white, but it doesn't taste like it should. There's nothing wrong with it, but my taste buds, like the rest of me, are feeling unsatisfied. Empty.

I thought last night would be euphoric. The itch that needed scratching so badly has been scratched, yet the itching is still there. William had felt good. Felt natural. He was satisfying and left me with a buzz that lasted for a good couple of days. A real energy that tingled through my body, made me walk straighter, chest out. I felt taller. Somebody at work even asked me what I was so chipper about. I even enjoyed the blatant lie I responded with.

Joe Davies should have been a money shot. I'd been building up to it, emotionally and physically. I'd learned a lot from William, which had gone so much better than expected, especially for the first time. It had gone to plan. Better, actually. I learned enough to make some changes for Joe. I'd used different, thicker cable ties, which were quicker, and less messy than tape, and the gag worked well. Only too well.

I needed him subdued, definitely couldn't afford any real outbursts or screams, but may have inadvertently gone overboard. His head had rocked, he was biting hard into that gag, his muffled pain was there for me to see. I enjoyed seeing it, that bit went well. I wanted to see him suffer, but he drifted in and out of consciousness, which pissed me off. I had to slap him about a lot more than William, who stayed with me throughout. The whole ordeal. I enjoyed that. Enjoyed him going through the full sentence.

Last night was *bitty*. Fragmented. I wasted effort when unconsciousness kicked in way too early. Too easily. That was my mistake.

Sure, he's dead. Dead as a dodo. So why isn't that enough? Why doesn't it feel enough? That's the one I'd thought about the most. I had planned it to take place second in the pecking order to make sure it went ahead. To make sure I'd had some practice on a weaker target.

I look up as a young mum shouting at her son commands my attention, breaking my train of thought. She tells him to stop dragging his feet and grabs him by his coat, pulling him along.

I look back down at the coffee but don't pick it up. Thinking about the moments when Joe Davies thrashed against the chair, unable to break free but coming close. What if he had? The chair was ineffective; I only just got away with that.

Maybe he's just more immune to pain than William, but Joe definitely didn't respond as much. That's it. He didn't respond. Gag or no gag, he took it better. Like a man. I wanted him to be pathetic and squeal. Wanted him to wizen up like a dying weed. Weak and pitiful. He didn't deserve to just slip away. So I'll reconsider how best to proceed. For next time.

My business is unfinished; it's the only thing that makes sense, the only reason my appetite doesn't feel fed. My desire to finish this remains strong, an insatiable desire that still burns brightly. I have to carry on. I will carry on. Only more death and more pain will free me of my chains. I look down at a stack of magazines lying on a table close to where I'm sitting. The top magazine is open at an article about Terry Goodkind, adorned with the words "I am dead; only vengeance can restore me".

They resonate strongly. I will go on.

CHAPTER 21

"Listen up, everybody!" Rob hollered across the room.

The team had assembled early and were well aware of the significance of last night's events in Syston. Some yawns were being stifled and bags under eyes were on show. Large mugs of coffee and the odd can of Red Bull were being cradled by officers. The pressure to catch a murderer until yesterday was big; now it would be palpable. Infinitely greater. The demands don't simply double along with the death toll, and Rob and the team would now be under enormous pressure to make an arrest. To deliver.

The room was full. Anybody who had been remotely involved in the case was in the room, and Rob now had more resources than he'd been used to. A physical reminder of the importance of the task. The hierarchy had given him what he needed, what he wanted, to increase the pace of the investigation and find their killer.

God forbid there was a break-in today, or some other mediocre offence. Petty crime. *Petty*. Like it doesn't matter, or is insignificant. Your problem, for today at least.

Rob scanned the room, standing front and centre, and addressing no one in particular demanded a focus. Demanded fresh impetus on the specific crimes of the men whose names were written on the board behind him. Five men, two of whom were now murder victims and whose pale and numbered cadaver photos were taped to the very same board.

"William Reynolds, murdered. We've all seen the images, we know what happened, and most of us crossed the line into that bungalow. Saw William in that chair.""Joe Davies. Postmortem results remain outstanding and Becky will be here within twenty-four hours, but there are more than sufficient similarities for us to be comfortable that we are dealing with the same man. A double killer, something not many of you will have come across, is now our target and the focus of this investigation."

Rob paused. The room held its breath. Silence."From this list, two men have been murdered, and Paul Harris died in October 1997. We've heard about the two heists, so we have an idea as to the characters of these men."Rob stabbed the names on the board firmly with his index finger, rocking its weak aluminium frame."Jen, prison update, please."

Rob asked abruptly and didn't make eye contact. The room looked at Jen, who was expecting to speak at some point but was taken aback by the lack of notice. She was standing already and was near to Nicky, who acknowledged her with a glance.

Jen moved into the centre of the room, in front of the board, still holding a coffee and with the benefit of youth to mask her tiredness.

"It was an interesting visit to Gartree. The reports give an insight into the mindset of the gang. The prison records paint a vivid picture of each of them as men, who they were. Their traits. There is still speculation surrounding some of the facts, in terms of the specific actions of the men in the jewellers, but the conviction documents from the eighties were very clear in identifying our gang and holding them responsible. They tie in well with the records of each and their time served, so it's easy to see how those conclusions came about, and were sold to a jury."

Jen cleared her throat, having warmed up with her opening. She took a couple of steps to the left so the photographs of the men on the board were visible. The gaze of the room followed her.

"Joe Davies and Charlie Worth were the out and out wrong'uns of this gang. They were bullies, they were violent. They *liked* violence, and they have wider criminal records, which by today's standards would class them as career criminals. Pub fights, burglaries, robberies, car theft, handling stolen goods. They did it all. Their time in prison seemed to be time they enjoyed, relished. Their company inside suited them, and they certainly don't look as if they would have been out of place. If anything, the opposite is true; these men were hardened criminals and would not have been intimidated in prison. It transpires from what Nicky and I found that they were the intimidators. They were unpleasant, nasty men."

She paused, drew breath and continued.

"We are working on the assumptions on roles, which were detailed in the convictions and which are totally supported by the characteristics we've seen from their time in prison. We believe Joe Davies and Charlie Worth led the gang. We believe they planned the robberies, but are working to establish this more accurately. They were aggressive men, they loved the violence and the aggravation, and they were the aggressors and stirrers in prison. We don't believe they would have had many issues in thinking up and carrying out hard, aggressive robberies.

"Paul Harris was quiet; certainly in prison he kept his head down. There is little around his life other than a history of mental illness, for which he wasn't treated well by the system. We failed him. He was vulnerable, he was quiet, he would have been easily led. Jack is still looking into when and where Paul was recruited by or met Joe, or Charlie, but he'd have done as he was asked. It's quite a tragic story of a young man who grew up in seventies' and eighties' Britain and was on the fringes of society. He was socially capable, he held several part-time jobs throughout his life, and married his wife, who later became his widow, but he had his demons. I'll share the full diagnosis from his file so you have it, but he would have been volatile at times, and would have been easy to manipulate. He died in October 1997, less than a year after being released, from breathing complications, which were attributed to natural causes."

Jen grabbed a can of Diet Coke from the desk and took a swig. She was in full flow now and wasn't stopping.

"Paul was labelled as one of the smashers and grabbers, along with Daniel Mortimer. Daniel Mortimer was reclusive, and studied during his incarceration. He's the most interesting of the gang, a real Jekyll and Hyde character. I'd be lying if I said I even remotely understand who the real Daniel Mortimer is at this point, so he remains a focus to this inquiry."

"He seems mysterious. He excelled at school, was highly intelligent, highly academic and pursued a medical career. He spent a number of years studying, and moved into work at the Queen's Medical in Nottingham after successfully completing his undergraduate degree. He continued his medical studies and worked at university hospitals, where as a student he seemed dedicated, popular and hardworking."

"Daniel was young at the time, a student, so we are looking at potential financial incentives for him. Student loans. Debt. The usual. We know Daniel failed to complete his doctorate and left under a cloud, so we're looking into that as a potential trigger, whether that was the point that forced his hand, left him short of cash. But he also went from being an employed, stable young man with a career and an education to raiding jewellers. He's younger than the others but is still in his late fifties now. The real issue with him is he's off the radar. He doesn't exist, at least not in his original guise, anyway. With William and Daniel we don't know at which point, or where, their paths crossed with Joe or Charlie, so that needs rooting out. Where did they meet? Both are unlikely to have been chance meetings, but at some point this gang formed and agreed to commit these crimes."

"William acted as the getaway driver and we don't believe he entered either of the premises on the days of the raids. He may have helped to recce the jewellers, but without CCTV we'll never know. Other than that, he did little except drive the car, but the law of the land made him an armed robber.""In prison, William kept himself to himself, was quiet and avoided any form of trouble. He served well and was trusted by the prison hierarchy, given responsibility."

Jen broke her presentation with an opinion."He was still treated to the same level of violence as Joe was though. There was no differentiation from the killers point of view, and he was treated and murdered as culpably as the others."

Rob wasn't a fan of opinions in briefings; they were rarely helpful and not always appreciated, although he couldn't help but see the point Jen had made. If the getaway driver had been subjected to the same level of violence as those who had planned the robberies, then anyone else in the crosshairs could be in for a rocky ride. Killers devolve. Their level of violence rarely eases.

Rob thanked Jen for her the contribution, and gave her a reassuring nod as the pencils and various scribes in the room continued to scratch at the paper. Thoughts, notes, more opinions. Things to do.

Rob stood, hands on hips, shirt sleeves rolled up and tie knot immaculate. Today was a tie day.

"So our immediate focus is on Charles Worth and Daniel Mortimer. We have a gang of five men, and three of them are dead. Two in the last week. Given the evidence we do have, the court has approved a search of Charles Worth's premises, as well as for his arrest."

Rob adjusted his stance and his stare, making eye contact with some of the junior officers and pausing to ensure they knew he was addressing them directly.

"To continue the groundwork, I want to know why they stopped at two raids. Why didn't they go on? It took a good period of time before they were all apprehended, so it wasn't their apprehension that stopped them specifically. How did the cuts work, and who got what? We know the original investigating team recovered £60,000 worth of jewellery stolen, but they lifted £400k in today's cash, so their payday was big, and this was well before the Proceeds of Crime Act existed and could relieve criminals of their cars and property. So where did the cash and the rest of the jewels go? Did they sell it? Who to? And what did they do with the cash? Did they launder it? Who decided the split? Was it an equal five-way split? What was William Reynolds cut? Did Paul Harris ever get his cut? Is the stash now the motive? Where is it and who knows about it?"

Rob was firing questions rapidly out into the room with vigour, almost shouting, demanding action. Demanding answers.

"Continue to look at early lives, marriages, who knew what. Leave no stone unturned."

Rob had a rhythm, and could see the positive impact it was having on the room. Jen's energy had set the mood up well. The room sat and listened, soaking up the information, desperate to go out and act on it. Chomping at the proverbial bit.

"There's nothing evidentially clear to isolate our attention between either of the two remaining names!" Rob stabbed at the board once more. "We know little about the recent lives of either of these men, but we know Charles is a bad egg and we know where he is."

Rob addressed Nicky and Jen directly. "Go out and pick up Charles Worth. Search his house and find out what he knows. See if he'll talk to us."

Turning back to the room, Rob concluded, "And go and find me Daniel Mortimer, or whoever the fuck he is now!"

The room started to move. Chairs were dragged across the floor and backsides were lifted from desks. Backs arched and fingers cracked. Plastic coffee cups and cans were tossed into the bin as the procession started to filter from the room, a bustling hum audible with numerous conversations having been started.

Rob wandered towards Nicky and asked her if she was clear, and if she was happy with the team she was taking to Loughborough, to carry out the warrant. Charles Worth could be their murderer, and today could be the first encounter with their double killer. The team were well aware that he could also be their next intended victim, or he may just hold the key, the information to lift the lid. All were clear, given Charlie's criminal record and the way he had treated his victims, that he would be treated with extreme caution. A guilty man until proven otherwise.

"Yeah, all good, Gov. You ok?"

"Yes, I'm fine. I need to see Becky. Joe Davies' post-mortem is due and she wanted to see me anyway. I'm going to head over now, see what she's found."

CHAPTER 22

Rob parked his car on Havelock Street, a short one-way street on a stretch behind the Royal Infirmary, and in the shadow of Welford Road Stadium. It was still early and Rob hated using the main car park, which always seemed to rinse him of significant amounts of time and money. He struggled to tolerate either.

The area surrounding the Royal is almost exclusively double yellow, or double red lines; the authorities like vultures, waiting to fine, clamp or remove those with enough gall to dare to breach the regulations. Rob had found a legal spot to park, due to the time of day, and had pounced into it. The early bird catching the worm.

He'd walked the short distance under dull street lighting, with his coat zipped up tight to his chin, and used a rear entrance of the Windsor building to find his way into a bright, sterile corridor. He'd sent a WhatsApp message to Becky after parking, and was delighted to see her appear along the corridor, the two of them well in the depths of the Royal Infirmary on yet another cold, wet Leicester morning.

Rob walked towards her, and could see that Becky had her dark black hair tied up in a bun, with a few stray strands escaping to the side. She stroked them back behind her ear with her right hand as she bid Rob a good morning with a bright, warm smile. Despite her efforts last night, her youth and energy made her glow as brightly as a woman who had slept solidly for eight or nine hours last night, something Rob knew to be untrue. Four or five at best. At most.

The two stood chatting. Small talk. Close enough for Rob to see an almost flawless complexion. Not a hint of a line, and not a mark of tiredness or a blemish on a face Rob was envious of for a number of reasons. Youthfulness. Energy. He'd clocked his own reflection on the way in, a large window pane against the pitch black early morning providing the mirror. Bags, crow's feet and lines worn onto the face of a man whose own sleep pattern had been varied in recent times. Family illness, work and all-hours phone calls were not conducive to the youthful appearance Rob himself had once worn, unaware of its finite nature until the day it passed. Gone forever. It was a phase of life Rob hadn't appreciated to the full extent that he now wished he had. Youth wasted on the young.

Rob sighed, aware he'd slipped into a daydream. A 4.45am alarm hadn't helped. He looked at Becky, who offered a slight smile and sympathetically gestured to an office.

"Shall we start with a coffee?"

Rob was grateful when the fresh and still steaming cup of coffee appeared. He took a sip from the drink he knew was still boiling, the sting on his lips providing an injection of life.

"What do you know then, Becky Ryan?"

Rob had a lot of questions. A lot of things had passed through his mind on the way home from last night's crime scene, in the car, in his kitchen and just before the moment he fell into a sleep that wouldn't be deep enough to repair his body, after another day at the metaphorical coalface. His initial question was short. He wanted to see what Becky was going to offer before filling in the gaps. Plus, he needed caffeine and was happy to be spoken to.

"So the post-mortem initially didn't tell us anything we didn't specifically know or suspect anyway. I'm more than happy to tell you you're only looking for one killer; this is the work of the same individual, so you have a double killer on your hands."

Rob nodded, accepting the comment and with no reason whatsoever to doubt the conclusion the team had reached quickly after arriving at the house in Syston yesterday evening.

"There looks to have been a struggle in terms of the scene; we saw the broken chair and shards of timber littering the rear room. Yet there are no defensive wounds on the hands of the victim, no DNA under his fingernails. Well, nothing useful at least, and no marks that would suggest a physical struggle. Joe Davies was a physically fit seventy-five year old man, with no illness or ailments that would have physically restricted him. Other than his advancing years, anyway. The theory we had before the PM was that they'd fallen over in the struggle and that Mr Davies may have struck his head on the floor, rendering himself unconscious, or injured enough to not be able to effectively defend himself further."

"You said that *was* your theory, Becky?"

"Yeah. So we got him open and carried out a range of X-rays and scans on his skull, hence it taking slightly longer than anticipated."Becky paused, her brain flicking onto another train of thought.

"I'll talk about tox tests in a minute as there are results we are expecting, which may come in while you're here, so this is something of a live feed."

She continued, clicking back onto her original track. "Anyway, so there are a range of head injuries, which we thought were going to be head on floor followed by the assault injuries, but they weren't." Becky looked at Rob. Half of the mug of coffee was warming him nicely and she could see the cogs had awoken. He'd need them. "Are you familiar with coup and contrecoup, Inspector?"

Rob frowned, the lines on his forehead creasing slightly. He was vaguely familiar with them and trotted a line out around skull deflection and the injury site showing how that injury was caused, and how the brain and internal bruising painted a fuller picture of what happened.

Becky continued, happy, and impressed that her audience had enough of a grasp for the explanation that was to come. "So we expected to find a serious contrecoup, and then a number of coup injuries, with the cerebral contusions supporting that. Only we didn't. The contrecoup would have shown that the moving head hit a stationary object to start with, i.e. the floor, or maybe a wall, first as he fell. The coup injuries would then show up as contusions that would identify that the stationary head was subsequently struck by a moving object, or objects i.e. he was assaulted with a moving object whilst his body wasn't moving."

"Ok" Rob muttered slowly, understanding the theory but unsure where Becky's implication was now heading. He finished his coffee and put the mug to the side, hoping that another one wasn't far behind it.

"His head didn't hit the floor. Well, not hard enough to leave a contusion on the brain, so if it did hit the floor it was minor, and he was still very much compos mentis afterwards. He should have been conscious. Conscious enough to carry on the fight."

Rob had already reached one of two conclusions in his mind, but was happy enough to let Becky continue an insightful explanation.

"It took a while because of the blood, and this relates to the tox tests I mentioned, but we don't now believe Joe Davies was conscious when he fell. It looks as if he was artificially inebriated before he hit the floor.""After we cleaned up the blood we found an amount of bruising to the right side of Joe's neck. It wouldn't have been visible before, but we found the entry point of a hypodermic needle. He wasn't diabetic, it wasn't medical as far as we can see, and due to the blood and the nature of the bruising we can conclude that the victim had something injected into him at an early point in the attack."

"So he was neutralised?"

"Looks that way. He was a big guy, and even at his age there was some strength and fight left in him. Given what the girls have said about him, he wasn't an angel and would have been happy to fight."

Rob knew that 'the girls' were Nicky and Jen, and that their friendship was blossoming. He knew the importance of good relationships in policing, but also knew he may need to have an occasional word to three lively personalities. To maintain professional standards and to keep all in his charge on the straight and narrow.

"There was no gaffer tape to the wrists this time, as you know, and the injuries have some differences from the first attack. There are still a number of stab wounds, from the same knife that was used to inflict stab wounds on William's body, but there are some other wounds. We've identified that a number of whip and slash type injuries are present, and we can see that a large broken piece of the chair has been used as a weapon, to stab, beat and cut Joe."

Rob's brain was now alive, his mind running at light speed. "Why the tape on the mouth, then? Why the gag?"

"I'm glad you asked, Inspector," Becky teased, enjoying spelling out the story her work had uncovered. "We won't know until we identify the drugs used, but it's highly likely that he was conscious for most of the attack. We know that courtesy of a screwed up piece of cloth that we pulled from his mouth; there were fibres from the cloth in his lungs, so he'd breathed them in hard while the gag was in place. If he'd have been unconscious, the fibres wouldn't have got to where they did."

Rob was now thinking out loud. "So we have a semi-conscious victim who our guy has drugged. Same MO in terms of the chair and the injuries, and a physical link with the same knife being used, but here our killer decided to nullify Joe Davies. Why?"

The question was rhetorical and Rob already had an idea in his head. Becky did too, but the question wasn't to her. She continued, having information she still wanted to share.

"We still have a vicious attack. We still have a huge range of injuries to his legs and feet, as well as stab marks and slashes to his torso, but to a lesser extent than last time. There is significant bruising, so again a blunt instrument was used to beat Joe, and again the blows are plentiful, without them individually having excessive force. The full injury summary will be emailed over to you later, along with a full image file."

Becky hadn't quite finished and continued. "So the key difference we have here is that the attack doesn't seem as prolonged as with William Reynolds. There are numerically less injuries than we saw in the first attack, and a number of them were inflicted post-mortem. The cause of death here is simple asphyxiation, which would have saved him further suffering at the hands of our perpetrator. Joe was asthmatic. We found his inhalers in the house and have corroborated it with his doctor's records; it was a lifelong condition. His age and medical condition, combined with the psychological pressure of being strapped to the chair with his mouth gaffer-taped shut, caused an involuntary reaction."

Rob interjected. "He was sick?"

"Yep. He was sick. Not a lot. But enough to trigger a reaction in his system that caused him to choke. He swallowed it. Had no choice. His death would have been an anti-climax, I think. He would have almost drifted off once the asphyxia reached critical mass, almost like going to sleep."

"Well, that would have really pissed him off," said Rob, abruptly. "Our killer."

"Indeed. We can evidence that as well, as the attack continued post-mortem. Joe was dead and our perp would have known it. Despite this, he continued to beat Joe violently, with a disproportionate number of injuries occurring after he died. It was angry, almost like he was trying to beat Joe back to life so he could continue to suffer. Joe got away with it compared to William. The killer would have wanted this to last longer, to have got more out of it. Yes, he suffered, but he died of asphyxia, he wasn't beaten and assaulted to the brink of death before his body finally gave out. If he hadn't, there would have been more injuries imparted pre-mortem."

"Including..." Rob led Becky neatly into the signature of the now multiple kills.

"The main commonality, Inspector Rhone, is a removal of not one but two fingers in this instance, and the right ear as previously. Same tool, probably; same person without a shadow of a doubt."

The mark that was now a signature had been clearly visible upon entering the small terrace on Brook Street, with the right ear missing, and two fingers from the right hand also removed, but not missing. Left on the dining table near to Joe's body for the police to find, as they were on William Reynolds' coffee table. There was less blood, although still a significant amount. Becky had her suspicions at the scene that these incisions were made after death, something she'd kept to herself. Becky was tactful, and knew when to share subjective opinions and when not to. She was a slick operator, and Rob had come to respect her greatly in the short time he'd known her.

Rob drew breath to speak, but Becky beat him to the punch.

"I've already ordered the re-testing of William Reynolds' body, before you ask," She added gleefully, her smile reappearing. "There was no evidence of drugs or any kind of intoxicant or anaesthetic found in the initial tox tests, nothing in his system to show foul play, but we're re-running the tests and widening them too, just in case something different was used. But I don't think there was. I've even checked his neck again this morning. Nothing was found on my post-mortem, but in the interests of thoroughness I wanted to double check."

Rob knew the answer but let Becky spell it out.

"There is no bruising, and no clear or obvious sign of an injection mark that would show William Reynolds was drugged prior to his assault."

"So, we have two kills from one person, and the MO seems to have been tailored slightly for each. The perp was happy to assault William Reynolds on a level playing field, but not Joe Davies." Rob stroked his chin, pondering. His head started to buzz, the early morning tiredness becoming a distant memory. "Call me as soon as you get anything on the tox tests, please."

Rob was already on his feet. He needed to speak to Nicky and share the information he'd just learned with his team. Becky acknowledged the request with a smile. Rob smiled back as he headed to the door. A Starbucks drive-thru would provide the next caffeine fix. The day was still young but there was already a lot to do.

CHAPTER 23

Nicky had already been on her early morning coffee run, and was on the phone to Jen as she headed north out of the city, up towards the A6 junction at Redhill Circle where a McDonald's sits next to an abandoned Blockbuster video, under the shadow of another of the city's concrete flyovers.

She had Jack riding shotgun, so there were two vanilla lattes in the central console. She looked at the curious expression on his face as they passed the now faded blue store with the old sign still hanging limply from the building. She sensed the question coming, so started to explain the concept of going out to rent videos from a shop to a member of the Netflix generation. Generation Z or Millennials, or whatever the media were labelling this crop as. Nicky knew she was Generation X without having the slightest fucking clue of what that meant. She also realised how stupid the concept of renting videos now sounded. Jack's face agreed.

Jack hadn't attended the murder scene last night. Hadn't minded either. It had been on the wrong side of town, and given the space restrictions in Joe Davies' house, the 'too many cooks' mantra had applied and he'd agreed to stay away. He was planning to go over later today now that all of the formalities had been wrapped up, and although the body was safely in the custody of the LRI, Jack wanted to see the scene and understand its intricacies. Visualise the crime being committed. There'd be plenty more occasions in his career where he'd be one of the first ones onto a murder scene, face to face with the victim in their raw state, after being left remorselessly only to be found by a friend, the postman or a neighbour.

Jack struggled to understand a killer who left a body openly to be found. Why wouldn't someone make a bit more *effort?* There were bodies found in shallow graves, or in remote locations where an attempt had been made to hide the crime, but to cross the line and kill someone and then just walk away, it felt a bit lazy. A bit half-arsed. Knowing that a poor somebody would unwittingly stumble upon the corpse, while just going about their day, walking the dog, playing golf. Maybe that was part of the thrill.

Nicky continued to brief Jack on what they'd found last night. Who they'd found and how they had found him.

Describing the scene in the house, Nicky set out the rear portion of the house and the simple chair on which the victim had been found. She winced at herself as she described how she felt that the scene wasn't as bad as the William Reynolds murder. *Not as bad*, as if there's a Likert scale for these types of attacks. 1 for mild, 10 for awful. As an experienced officer, she still felt a tinge of guilt for rating crimes. 'Not as bad.' Almost a good murder, one the victim's family wouldn't mind, could appreciate.

Nicky knew the absurdity of it all, but it was language that would be trotted out during the trial for all to hear, should that day ever arrive. The grisly details played out in open court in front of friends, spouses and children. Laid raw as a matter of public record for all to see. Who that person was, and what they were really like, what they were capable of.

Jack was naturally inquisitive and was appreciative of a brief from an experienced senior officer, before seeing the scene first-hand to form his own opinions. He was benefitting from working with both Nicky and Jen, and he was enjoying it. His focus on detail and his ability to ask prudent and searching questions was improving quickly. Accept nothing. Challenge everything. Trust no one.

The conversation had been broad and Nicky had been happy to toss thoughts around in the car as they drove up the hill into Birstall, an affluent village with a frontage of large period properties on an imposing route out of town. The conversation had quickly settled back onto Charles Worth. Another seventy year old who should be retiring gracefully, and not be the third pensioner to have appeared on a very undesirable police list in the last fortnight. At least he was still breathing.

Charles was seventy-two, another widow, although his wife looked to have been long suffering when she was alive. Nobody had yet had the pleasure of meeting Charles Worth, but his criminal record and the visit to Gartree outlined a man of bullish nature. A man of his generation. A baby boomer. But there was nothing remotely pleasant about how Charlie had carried himself throughout his life. A bully. A thug. Somebody who used his fists first and thought about it later. Or not.

Even for a man who had married for a second time and later in his life, there were two records of Charles being arrested for assault against his wife, Sarah, during a period of time when domestic abuse was largely ignored, acknowledged or even accepted as the norm. If it wasn't reported it wasn't happening,

But at some point there was enough for the police to make their way to the same door that Nicky, Jack and Jen were now converging on.

Nicky already hated him. She felt her shackles rise and she called him an 'out-of-touch old wanker' out loud. An aggressive outburst. Her tolerance and contempt for men who used violence towards women was visible, with a strip of her getting riled with the subject still being in the present tense. A heavily emotive subject. Something still happening that society still hadn't done enough to eradicate. Domestic violence, racism, gender discrimination, equal pay.

She'd called Jen to check on her progress. They'd arranged to meet on the edge of town, in an area near the crematorium and close to a large private school. A large layby on a dual carriageway near the crematorium was perfect. There was enough room for the small convoy of vehicles to gather before making the final mile. Nicky had called the senior team and uniform, and had agreed to raid the premises to execute both the arrest and search warrants for the house on Great Central Road. No knock on the door for Charlie. He may be a potential victim. Might be a target.

Nicky and Rob had reached the conclusion that Charles Worth was a suspect and would be treated as such. He may be a witness, might be a potential victim, but he could also be the man responsible for two savage murders of old colleagues. Nicky wouldn't have hesitated to take the cautious route under any circumstances, and she certainly didn't need any particular reason to go through Charlie's front door with the big red key. He was overdue, and Nicky wanted to go in. She really wanted to go in. Go in hard, aggressively, and worry about the consequences later. Just like Charlie.

Nicky would enjoy standing outside watching his front door getting stoved in. He was coming out in handcuffs regardless of whether he was a victim or not. *Victim*. So subjective.

Nicky pulled off the dual carriageway section of the A6 and drove past a well kept floral declaration welcoming you into the university town of Loughborough. Two of the marked vans had arrived with a designated number of officers to support the raid, enter the premises and make the arrest, as well as carry out the search warrant.

Jen was the last to arrive and Nicky had insisted the team wait for her. Jen needed to be there and Nicky wasn't going ahead without a full complement. Plus she wanted to show Jen how she thought people like Charles Worth should be treated by the law.

The sky was emerging into a blue hue as daylight broke over the town. A nice morning following a damp, dark evening at the scene of Joe Davies' murder. Nicky addressed the officers verbally one final time. All had been briefed and had received an obligatory pack outlining the suspect, his history, his background. Everybody was on high alert.

All were aware of the context of the warrant within the wider case, through being directly involved, or just through being in the station and not having their head up their arse.

Nicky articulated the importance of the next few hours, the importance of securing Charles Worth into custody quickly. She'd overemphasised his history, his lack of respect for the law and his nature as a violent bully, and suitably emphasised the need to search the property thoroughly and professionally. Emotions aside, this could be their man, but Nicky reiterated one final time what a piece of shit they were dealing with for good measure.

They arrived outside the house within five minutes of leaving the rendezvous point. The marked vans had been left quickly but precisely in the narrow road. Residents were still at home due to the hour, with cars still lining the street, making considerate parking impossible.

Nicky found a space for her Mondeo and took it, before joining Jack and Jen, who had ditched her car behind the vans on the road. The three were on foot, having walked up the street, and were positioning themselves opposite the house, waiting for the moment the team of uniforms stormed through the door.

Nicky calmly popped a chewing gum in her mouth, and held out the pack to Jen and Jack without diverting her stare. Three uniformed officers quickly made their way to the front door to lead the raid, with five additional officers ready to follow them in. They lined up with a short gloved countdown before smashing the large metal battering ram into the door, just above the lock and handle. Two more heavy swings and the door gave way. A number of officers marauded in in succession, over the remains of the uPVC unit, which lay in tatters on the floor.

Nicky chewed hard on the gum, channelling her energy and standing resolutely with her hands in her pockets. The three stood looking at the house through the gaping hole. Listening to the shouting. The resistance sounded minimal before a semi-dressed and bedraggled looking Charles Worth emerged from the front door, frog-marched out unceremoniously by two officers. He didn't look bad against the file photo they had of him. Clearly older, but very recognisable.

Nicky started to walk across the street directly towards Charlie. She didn't break eye contact as she got within range. He was still an intimidating man. Six feet tall or so, and no lightweight either. A solid man. His gaze met hers. He had a spitting, snarling face, angry at the intrusion. Angry at being *bothered*. He was raging, ranting under his breath but trying to hold it in, using every one of his seventy-two years trying to exercise restraint. He was already in handcuffs, his house already full of officers. Pick your battles.

She had no doubt that ten years ago he'd have head-butted her, or spat at her by now, or tried to do both. Plus at least one of the officers inside the house would have already shed blood.

She satisfyingly read him his rights, buzzing inside and eyeballing him as he was loaded into the waiting van, still swearing but to nobody in particular. She decided he could be the man. He had the temperament still; there was still a lot of anger in Charles Worth. Fire in the belly. She could imagine him as a fit and fiery forty year old, barking out orders. Snarling at people. Like he was just now but with a lot more menace. Venom. Intimidating anyone in his path into following his will. She imagined that if he had asked her to have done something as a young woman, she probably would have.

The van drove away slowly. Nicky was conscious that the street was now awake, and if the neighbours weren't aware of who one of their neighbours was, they soon would.She wandered across towards the house and shouted in to enter. She was the ranking officer but the team had secured the premises and it was in good order.

Nicky walked gently over the broken front door, which moved underfoot. Making her way into the front room to the right-hand side of the house, she was followed by Jen and Jack. All three had pulled on a pair of latex gloves, as common in a copper's pocket as a mobile phone, and were starting to take in the house. What it looked like. What it meant.

It looked *normal.* There didn't seem to be an obvious smoking gun, a bloody knife left on the side or pictures of the victims on the walls with crosses through their faces. Just a sideboard, a TV, and an armchair that looked old and comfy.

The senior officer who led the entry came downstairs as Nicky walked back through into a plain hall with an old carpet.

"Anything juicy?" Nicky asked, hoping for a weapons stash, an illegally held shotgun or some obscure cannabis farm in the loft.

"Afraid not," came the response. "It just looks like a lonely old man lives here."

"Keep me posted, please, and thank you for your efforts this morning. Good, clean job."

Nicky had already turned when the acknowledgement came. She had no desire to kill precious time loitering in a house full of trinkets and old shit when she could be back in Leicester antagonising Charles Worth.

CHAPTER 24

It was late in the day when Nicky walked back into the main office, exhaling loudly from puffed cheeks. She glanced across at the coffee pot on the side, which was disappointingly empty. She'd have taken old, slightly cold coffee at this point, the caffeine hit being all she needed to take the edge off another long day, one that had started around thirteen hours earlier.

Jen and Jack had also arrived back in the office, having picked up a line of inquiry following the early morning excitement. They had gone to follow a trail to see what else they could learn about the group of names still adorning the whiteboard at the side of the room.

WILLIAM REYNOLDS

JOE DAVIES

CHARLES WORTH

PAUL HARRIS

DANIEL MORTIMER

Jack couldn't help but notice how the order of the names had fortuitously been written. It was just the random order that

Nicky had written them in several days ago, but there was now a haunting quality to the order in which the names appeared.

William was top of the list having been the initial victim, and was the first name to have a line drawn through it, but the other four were written randomly, yet Joe Davies turned into victim two, Charles Worth was in a cell downstairs, and Paul Harris is dead.

Jack shut the train of thought down in his mind, satisfied enough of a pure coincidence, and that there wasn't a pattern that would help to save another home visit.

The impromptu and unplanned nature of all three being in the office was not lost on Rob, who was in his office with his door shut, and continued to work while his senior officers sat down together outside. He continued to ignore them, and them him, as they each continued the threads they were currently working on.

Rob's finished first and he wandered out of his door, loosening his tie and sitting down on a chair he'd wheeled from a hot desk near his office.

"How did Charles Worth treat you, Nicky?" asked Rob, before flipping the question. "And how did you treat Charles Worth?"

The hint of sarcasm was appreciated by the team, but all were genuinely intrigued as to the outcome of the raid and the subsequent interview, as all had been working other lines for the vast majority of the day.

"He's a piece of shit, Gov." The answer came from an ingrained hatred that had stemmed from the moment she'd learned who Charles Worth was. What he was about. A hatred that had only intensified when they had eyeballed one another just after dawn this morning. Tiredness, and a lack of food and caffeine were also contributing to an unusually snappy DS.

Nobody disagreed so Nicky chose to articulate herself more suitably.

"He lawyer'd up straight away, was very defensive. Started off chatty. I say chatty…he told me he'd either like to break my nose or kill me slowly if he ever saw me in Loughborough again. Even his brief winced at that. He was snarling for the early part; don't think the raid or the journey here in the meat wagon made him any better. Took about an hour to cool him down. He was seething."

"You ok?" Rob asked. He liked Nicky, cared for her. She was tough, really tough, but everyone has a limit and people are capable of saying disgusting things. Things that can slip off at the time, but repeat hours later. Days later. Late at night. At vulnerable times.

"Yeah, I'm fine, Gov. It's not every day you get to sit in a room with a man of that calibre. He despises us. The police. Although I think he despises anyone who doesn't do exactly as he tells them to. Plus all women. He hates all women."

"But does he hate old colleagues?" asked Rob, leading the conversation to where they all wanted.

"Well, yes, I think he does. I think he hates life. He's the angriest man I've ever met, even at seventy-two. I'm glad I didn't meet him twenty years ago. Anyway, he wanted to talk but very quickly went 'no comment'. I carried on at him. He wanted to bite, I could sense it. I asked him about William Reynolds; no comment. Asked him about Joe Davies; no comment. Asked him for alibis for both murders; no comment. All very routine. He sat with his cup of water, but it's when I showed him the pictures of the bodies, several angles and a couple of close ups, that his face changed, just slightly, and his manner altered with it too. He picked them up, studied them. His frown lines creased and he went silent."

"So what do you think, Nicky?" Jen asked. "Is he the man?"

"Well, if he is we haven't got enough to hold him for longer than twenty-four hours, let alone to charge him. His house was clean except for a couple of antique knives and an old bayonet. Neither are illegal but we've seized them and will test them for blood. But there was nothing that came out of that house this morning that tells me that he's definitely our man. He's capable of it. Frighteningly capable of murder. Just not sure he committed either of these. If he had though I think the beating would have been shorter, and much harsher. He has no control, there'd be nothing measured if he came for you."

"Did you change angles, Nicky? Try appealing to his better nature as a witness?"

It was a smart question from Jack. Flexibility is a mantra for new recruits and an ability to adapt your style to any given situation is key. Much more so than in the days when there were no cameras in those interview rooms and you could use other methods to crack a suspect. Charles wouldn't have been one to crack under physical pressure in the eighties and he wasn't about to roll over now either.

Nicky smiled. "It's quite hard to do good cop when you're on your own, especially straight after bad cop, but yes, Jack, I did!"

"And?"

"Well, it worked of course! I sensed from his facial expression that he was shocked by the photographs I showed him. He tried his best not to change his face, but it did change. Not surprised by the violence at all, but I sensed an apprehension in him, a realisation that two of his old cronies have been murdered. And if it wasn't him, which, going by the lack of evidence in his house and his body language, it might not have been, then it's a very short list that's left."

She sat back in her chair, finishing up the unplanned debrief of the interview.

"He actually opened up a bit towards the end of the interview. He stopped no commenting, which was when I started asking him if he'd seen or heard from William or Joe in recent years, or weeks. He did no comment initially, but then said very calmly that he hadn't. The same for Daniel, and he said he didn't see Paul after his release and before he died. He was calm and I believed him."

"You haven't released him, have you?" Rob asked, looking almost appalled, as if Nicky's soft side had got too soft, and she'd tossed their second suspect back out onto Leicester's streets inside of the twenty-four window.

"Have I bollocks. He's in his cell downstairs enjoying a night on us. Plus I think he knows something, if not about the reason for the murders then about Daniel, or one of the victims, which may have triggered or led to the kills. If he thinks he might be on that list he might feel a bit more compelled to chat to us in the morning. We've got until 8am so will give him a coffee and a bacon sandwich, ask him again and cut him loose."

"And what did you pair learn for the rest of your day?" Rob asked casually and with a smile. He had switched his attention to Jen, knowing her and Jack had peeled away following the raid.

"So we had a win, Gov." Jen smiled, pleased at what her and Jack had found, and excited to be able to share it in such an intimate environment. Hot off the press. "We'd heard a sniff that there might have been a link at Parker Plant. It's a big engineering place on Canon Street, the Viaduct Works. It backs onto the London mainline."

"Yeah, I know it," Rob said. "They make big heavy rock-crushing stuff, right?"

"Right! They do! Big heavy stuff for quarries. It's a real hard-core manufacturing site! It has a working foundry and everything! We met with one of their site managers, a nice guy called Alan Carter, and he spent some time with us and took us through some records. He dragged a couple of guys in who he thought might help, a couple of old boys called Max and Joe, and we've pieced together a credible link."

Jack chipped in. "I'd found from the background I did on William that he'd spent fifteen months working at Parkers as a fabricator in the early eighties. He actually left there to take the job at Corah & Sons. It was a short period, unremarkable, and he left of his own choosing to go to a better paid job nearer to home."

Jen took the conversation back onto the crux of the day's find. "It was unremarkable to William, and to us, until we found that Joe Davies worked there for two years as a welder while he was on the straight and narrow, so he'd have been on the same production line at the same time."

"Good, so we have a link," said Rob, feeling energised despite the length of the day and its toil. He leapt to his feet to write PARKER PLANT on the board, and drew big arrows between William's and Joe's names.

"It gets better, Gov," Jen teased, having saved the best until last. "We have a record showing that William and Joe were employed there at the same time, we have contracts of employment, payment histories etc, so it proves the link between those guys. But we took all of the mug-shot photos and one of the real old timers in the foundry, also called Joe, remembers Charlie Worth, or claims he does. They couldn't find a record for him while we were there but they're going to have another dig. He could have been short-term, could have been a subcontractor, or it was the eighties so he could just have been cash in hand, but we have a witness on record saying he remembers Charles Worth working at the plant."

"Did he seem credible, Jen?" asked Nicky.

"He said if it was him he remembers him being an abrasive character, not getting on very well with other people, and he seems to remember him being let go for causing fights in the yard."

"So very fucking credible then!" Nicky's thought out loud caused a smile from the team. "That'll be the first thing I ask him in the morning."

Jen wrapped up neatly. "And just for the record, we have absolutely no sight that either Paul Harris or Daniel Mortimer ever set foot in Parker Plant, let alone worked there or met the crew there."

"Progress and great work, team." Rob always liked to thank whoever was left in the office at the end of the day for their efforts. He felt it made a difference to those who had gone above and beyond to be going home with simple affirmation. "Go home and get some rest. Then come back and we'll do it all again tomorrow."

Jen was wearing a big dirty grin by this point, and smiling at Nicky as she energetically told her to get some sleep tonight, as she'd need to be in a fit state for tomorrow night.

"Why?" asked Nicky, trying to recall what day it was and what the hell was happening tomorrow.

"It's quiz night!"

CHAPTER 25

The team had a good social relationship on all levels, and regularly enjoyed a drink together. There were several WhatsApp groups kicking around; The Pig Pen and The Dumpling Clan were two of many. They had another one for their lottery syndicate too, Mo Money Mo Problems, for when the Euros jackpot hit £170m and they all fancied a bit of it. Like many, they didn't bother with the 'regular' Euros when the jackpot was a miserly £20m. Split five ways it was barely worth the £2.50 buy-in, although even Bernie raided his pockets when the jackpot climbed north of about £50m. Pity the poor bastard in any workplace who didn't go in on any syndicate that went on to win big. The lone soul left holding the fort.

The current haunt was a big old pub on the corner of Wilberforce Road; down off the Narborough Road and situated on the banks of the River Soar, with Bede Park to the other side and a huge new futuristic building emerging on the bank, casting a huge shadow over the modest and traditional looking inn.

"Welcome to the Western!"

Jen was vibrant and energetic, and smiled with her eyes. She loved quiz night, and loved a Tuesday night in the Western. Any night really. A good old-fashioned pub with decent, reasonably priced drinks, down-to-earth, working-class clientele and a nice laid-back vibe.

Some pubs just feel like home, and Jen shared her love of this one. There was a warm vibe, the music was good and there enough in for the vibe to be building nicely. A good place to go, especially in the summer. It was equally good for meeting friends, or family, on your own, or as a meeting point for an evening destined for casual sex, following a successful exchange on Bumble or Tinder. Generation Y didn't want to wait for it, and why should they? Wait four, five, six dates or longer. For *it*. Commit time and effort getting to know somebody, only to have the crappest sex of your life, and realise you've wasted three months of each other's time.

Date one; get in there, get off, and if it works or was a good distance north of awful then it's time for date two. The shackles are off and you can open up and move onto the really enjoyable stuff while still getting to know each other. Great fun and no time wasted.

Rob loved listening to Jen socially. Fresh, vibrant and brutally but beautifully honest. It was why he'd liked her when they first met, why he knew she'd be perfect. The team liked her. Liked her humour for its darkness and inappropriate quirks, and loved her for her honesty and 'what-you-see-is-what-you-get' persona. Warm, intelligent and popular. She'd been a quality addition.

Jack arrived for his first quiz with the team, walking in sheepishly, convinced he'd got the wrong place or been tricked, with the rest of them a couple of miles away in a different pub.

"This is the right one, then?" Jack asked, taking his coat off and sitting down on a stool around the team's table.

"It is, Jack. Let me buy you a drink," offered Rob. "Anybody else?"

Jen was never backwards in going forwards, so asked for another pint of Stella, to park next to the half-full glass still sitting on the table in front of her.

As Rob headed to the bar, Jen shouted; "Nicky's only ten away, Gov. Large Sauvignon, please, New Zealand if they've got it."

Rob gestured to keep the noise down, and to stop calling him Gov whilst in a pub. It was expected at work, it had been earned and it was healthy, but he wasn't a stickler, and to the passer-by this was a group of friends who could work in an office or factory. He hated the term when any of them were in a pub, and people were kicking back, relaxing.

Nicky arrived, saw Rob at the bar and headed over to him to say hi first, offering to help carry the drinks, or any crisps, but Rob waved her away.She trotted over to the gang, arms out for hugs all round, greeting her friends warmly. Nicky's personable nature shined outwardly, warm and bubbly with a strong and hearty personality. She was also a fucking diva at pub quizzes. 'Nicky-pedia', she'd been dubbed in the office. She had general knowledge to an endless degree. Films, actors, music, celebrities, who was married to who, who was divorced from who. Some of the shit she knew was so obscure it was brilliant.

Nicky looked up just as Becky Ryan walked in, looking equally as lost as Jack had just a few minutes ago.

"Hey!" Nicky ran over to Becky, hugging her and beckoning her over to the table. Jen and Jack knew Becky was coming and were delighted to see her. Nicky had forgotten to let Rob know, it wasn't exactly mission-critical in the office yesterday, but Rob was equally delighted to see the well-heeled pathologist, and added another drink to the round, an elderflower G&T in a glass that looked like a small fishbowl. It had huge ice cubes and what looked like some petals floating on the top of it. Rob was surprised the Western served drinks like that; he felt it was more of an Everard's Bitter and Walkers crisps type pub. Only the good flavours though. No prawn cocktail or Worcestershire sauce.

Rob divvied the drinks up while standing over the small wooden table. He sat down, picked up his pint and chinked glasses with Nicky, causing the team to follow suit.

Rob sat back, pleased with where his evening was going. Less so the investigation. He was enjoying the company. Colleagues, yes, but friends too. Good friends. He looked at the diversity around the table. Age, experience and background. Geography. Rob had been born in Liverpool, Jack Northampton. Nicky had been born in Winchester in Hampshire, and Jen in Peterborough. From recent conversations, Rob knew Becky had been born in St. Albans, in the posh bit, where she'd grown up with her sister Katie. He had joked about the north/south divide with her and commented on how he'd wondered where the posh-ness in her accent came from. Five separate counties, hundreds of miles, yet all five people had found their way to each other, in a way that only life can weave, and were now sitting around the same small table in the Western.

Rob thought about the gang, the pub noise fading away as he zoned out and into a murkier world. A world where five other people had met in very different circumstances, and with very different norms and social values.

They now knew that William Reynolds had met Joe Davies on the production line at Parker Plant across the city. Parker Plant had provided the scene for a married man, talented with his hands and something of an artisan, to meet and acquaint himself with a violent, narcissistic bully. He thought about what they'd have spoken about, what brought them and kept them together. Their ideals. Their circle. Football. Women. Music. Two very different men, poles apart and seemingly with little in common. But within two years both had planned, discussed and carried out the raids. Raids that now seemed central to the ongoing downfall of the gang.

He could easily imagine Joe and Charlie meeting. Both were criminals. Rob had a suspicion that his team wouldn't be able to pin down the exact moment that these two met, but knew it wouldn't have been with good intentions.

The quiz had started, something Rob had been unaware of, until he was nudged by Becky, who realised that Rob had phased out. She checked he was ok before asking him if he knew what the capital of Madagascar was.

"Antananarivo," replied Rob, before grabbing some crisps from a bag that had been split in the middle of the table.

"Something on your mind, Rob?"

"Always, Becky."

Rob picked the lime from the top of the bottle of Kronenbourg, and took a large and satisfying gulp. He heard the next question, the first one he'd been 'in the room' for. Something about a film or an actress. He had nothing, but saw Nicky lean in and whisper "Jada Pinkett Smith", before sitting back, pleased with herself. Jack scrawled it on the team sheet.

Why would Charlie Worth have killed William Reynolds or Joe Davies? He wasn't a man who would wait for revenge, and if either of them owed him money or had been on the take he'd have beaten them to death years ago. Unless they had something, knew something. But then the time element comes back in. The Why.

If Charles Worth wasn't their man, was he a potential victim? Or was he somehow not involved? Rob told himself not to be stupid. Charles Worth was involved with this, perhaps more so than even he knew; they'd be seeing him again.

Rob's mind flicked to the perpetrator. Maybe Charlie, maybe somebody else. And if it was somebody else, he almost pitied them going toe to toe with him. With Charlie. A man prepared and willing to fight.

He'd been offered support and protection, had been told the police were prepared to monitor his house. That went down as well as expected, and had unsurprisingly been declined. Charlie Worth looked after himself, and was the last person the police would ever expect to be looking out for. He'd take his chances, and if somebody did come for him, they'd very much be taking theirs.

And what of Daniel Mortimer? A mysterious character. Educated, a man of medicine to some degree. But a ghost. A National Insurance number that had only been used fraudulently in the last five years. Rob had been picking the scab that was Daniel Mortimer. Effectively missing in action. He was using his years of contacts to try to locate a man who seemingly didn't want to be found, or had good reason to be hiding. The name nothing but a shell corporation for a man out in the world, with secrets to hide or information to give. He could be one of the geeky turds on the table next to them for all they knew. A team aptly calling themselves the Cunning Stunts.

Rob heard a question he knew the answer to as his mind continued to flicker, and said "The Verve" out loud. He was shushed by Jen.

"Tell everybody, Rob," came the put down.

Rob had escalated Daniel Mortimer to his senior officers. The top brass. He'd felt there was a reason Daniel Mortimer didn't exist, in the usual channels anyway. A reason he was in the shadows. Maybe he'd changed his own name, morphed into somebody else or just plain stolen or created an identity.

Becky and Jen high-fived across the table, snapping Rob out of his daydream.

Nicky had been and brought more drinks. She hadn't asked Rob, who she knew was thinking shop if not talking it, but had bought him another Kronenbourg anyway.

A picture round had been delivered to the table, and everybody huddled round. Whispers of 'George Michael' and 'Michelle Obama' were being thrown into the middle for Jack to write down. Rob recognised Gaz Coombes from Supergrass, and consciously whispered it to Jack, who hadn't a clue who he was or what Supergrass were.

Nicky took her phone out of her pocket, realising she had several missed calls from the station and one from an unknown number. Rob looked at Nicky's face, realising somebody was trying to get hold of her urgently, and it wasn't likely to be a PPI cold call.

Rob's phone vibrated on the table. The station. He picked it up and answered it. The on-duty desk sergeant introduced himself as Martyn Duffy. Rob knew him, he was a good bloke. The quizmaster looked upset that his rules on mobile phones were being flaunted, but Rob's face made him carry on reading his questions, holding back any admonishment.

"Alan Reynolds has been arrested for trespassing and breaking and entering, Sir. Bernie Copp has just brought him into custody to be processed."

"Why is this relevant to me?" asked Rob, almost annoyed at the intrusion into his evening for a simple misdemeanor.

"Well, according to Bernie it's the allotment that used to belong to his dad, back in the day. The actual day. It isn't his now, though. They've had a number of recent break-ins at the allotment, petty theft and an arson attack on some sheds, so a couple of the local green-fingered boys had some cheap sensors and cameras installed on their sheds. One picked him up and triggered on a mobile so they called us."

Rob's annoyance hadn't subsided. "And the point, Sergeant?"

"It's insignificant, other than why he there in the middle of the night? He was arrested with a shovel on him, and a metal detector he 'bought in a pub', apparently. That old chestnut. Wish I'd got a quid every time I'd heard that."

Rob had got the picture. He told Martyn that he wouldn't be showing his face this evening, and to lock Alan Reynolds up for the night. Nothing he wasn't used to. Plus, he was probably drunk or high, and a night in the cells would benefit all parties.

Rob thanked Martyn for the update and hung up. He delivered the news to the team a lot more subtly than his last contribution to the quiz.

"So what was he looking for?" asked Jen.

"Very good question, Jennifer," replied Rob, aware of his use of Jen's full name. "I don't know, but I am sure it's what you'll be asking him first thing tomorrow morning."

CHAPTER 26

"Listen up, guys," shouted Rob to an enthused office, especially to the senior team at the front, buoyed following their respectable second place showing at the Western last night. Jen had enthusiastically claimed their £25 team winnings, which would no doubt be spent on today's lunch. Anything but Martin's Meats had been Rob's only stipulation.

"Big day today! Jen and Jack will be unpicking Alan Reynolds, finding out why he was midnight gardening last night. For those of you who haven't heard, Alan Reynolds was arrested on the council allotments on the outskirts of Groby village last night, shovel and metal detector in hand. We want to know why!"

"The rest of you, I need whatever we've got going over again with a fine-tooth comb. I want witness statements checking, alibis going over, the old documents reviewing for anything we've missed or wasn't relevant a week ago. I need to see some energy from you, so wind it up please!"

Rob felt as if some air had come out of the balloon in the last forty-eight hours. Investigations ride on waves, on momentum, and the last few days had been at the lower end of the scale.

Rob knew it wouldn't take much to reinvigorate the team, just something new, something that linked person A with piece of evidence B. They were like dogs, and as soon as there was something fresh to pursue and they were let off the leash, they went for it. His job was to keep the team motivated when the mood was low, marshal the troops on to the next high.

The team anticipated a breakthrough. Needed one. In fairness, everybody had expected a bit more from the raid in Loughborough, maybe even the big result, but it was all based on hope rather than gradually building towards a result, creating the luck yourself. The arrest had been satisfying, but there was an anticipation that something would have come out of it. Crucial evidence, information, leads, names.

As it turned out, all they'd achieved was taking a narky, dangerous old man off the streets for twenty-four hours. Rob had always been pessimistic, so had very easily kept his emotions in check, but even he was expecting a bit more than nothing. 'Jack shit' was the phrase used following the raid in Loughborough, along with 'very little material of interest'.

It's not as if Rob was expecting to find a bloody knife on the kitchen worktop, soaked in Joe Davies' blood, but *something* would have been useful. Something to nudge the investigation, allow it to focus or confirm a suspicion. Allow simple progress.

A man like Charlie Worth was a leopard whose spots would never change, so even the real 'half empties' thought they'd find something incriminating. A bag of tools for a burglary, a couple of nicked car radios, a few lifted wallets. Whatever criminal enterprise he was currently engaged in.

Rob was beginning to not enjoy investigating the elderly. The only piece of hardware they'd found in the house was an outdated Motorola flip phone, not even a smartphone. He thought about the number of times a cocky twenty-something had sat opposite him no commenting, only for him to be able to produce an abundance of digital data: WhatsApp messages, deleted text messages, Google searches, drug deals agreed over email, knives and guns sold on Gumtree and various other channels of the dark web. Even location data proving where someone had been. Or hadn't been.Not needing someone to speak. They're the best cases. There is nothing more compelling to a jury than a rake of digital evidence, and DNA to top it off. The cocky little shits can sit there and say nothing all day long and they're still going down.

Charlie Worth was old school. In every way. Nothing was written down, nothing existed in the cloud, and there was nothing to incriminate anyone in that house. No leverage. They needed him to speak, talk to them. Co-operate. The issue with people of Charlie Worth's ilk is an ingrained hatred of authority, and a defensive mechanism that simply does not allow them to talk to the police.

Rob knew he'd react to Nicky, just knew that putting the two together in the same room would create the sort of friction that could provide some fruit. He might have sat in silence with Jen, Jack, or even himself, Rob had reflected, but Charlie needed provocation, would react to it. And he did, but the result was still one of little relevance, and not even the suggestion to him that his life may be in danger did anything to stir a shred of worry.

If anything, he seemed grateful that there might be some excitement in his life, something to focus on. It seemed like the gauntlet had been thrown down. The thought that somebody from his past was now coming for him and his cronies seemed to light his animal instinct. His chest was puffed out, and he had retorted along the lines that if somebody was coming for him, they'd need to come well prepared or bring an army.

Rob headed into his office and sat back in his chair, with the video of Charles Worth paused on his laptop. Sometimes you miss something in the heat of the moment and later pick up a word, a piece of body language that was insignificant at the time. Like an old film you watch over and over, each time picking up something new, something you've never noticed before. Rob sat, unmoved. Thinking. Subconsciously squeezing a small rubber stress ball and tossing it back and forth. A green Leicester Tigers ball he'd picked up from somewhere. An evening do or a conference.

What did Charles Worth actually know? And what was the best way to relieve him of that information? Rob needed a reason to get him to cough it up and it wasn't on the horizon.

He was still sitting thinking when Jen walked into the office late in the morning to find a bustling hive of activity. A lot of officers, heads down. Phones going, mobiles tucked behind ears, as sandwiches were being ripped out of their packaging and bananas peeled. Those who started their lunch early or just grazed throughout the day were out of the gate.

Jen was impressed with the level of activity happening around her. Definitely a notch up on yesterday. She was hungry, but headed in to see Rob before settling down for food. She'd spent the morning sitting next to Jack and opposite Alan Reynolds and his brief, and knew Rob would expect an update. Jack had headed out to pick up lunch, so Jen needed Rob's order first and foremost, and would update him on the morning's graft whilst she was in his office.

"So did he say anything, Jen?" asked Rob, exhaling loudly and continuing to squeeze the life from his stress ball.

"In real terms, no Gov, he didn't. He sat with his arms folded. His solicitor had told him to go 'no comment', so he did. Barely said a word throughout." She paused. "Nobody is talking to us."

The interview itself had continued the theme of the last forty-eight hours and had been fruitless. It had started late due to Alan Reynolds' physical condition, which was a hangover-induced sickness; plus his solicitor had turned up late so the whole thing had taken a while to get going.

The frustration was clear on Jen's face. Two people had died, at least two more were alive but knew a lot more than they were sharing, and the status quo was not yet sufficiently in their favour. For the time being there was more reason for Alan Reynolds and Charles Worth to stay quiet, and contain their secrets than there was to spill the beans.

It was tragically likely to take another murder or a direct threat to life for one of them to cough, and even under pain of death, somebody like Charlie would despise coming cap in hand to the boys in blue.

"What have we done with Alan for now?" asked Rob.

"I've locked him back up. I wanted to confirm with you but I want to charge him with trespassing and breaking and entering. I think we can get a charge to stick on both."

"Agreed, get him booked. We might be able to use it as leverage, especially if we can dig something else up to use against him." Rob smiled at his unplanned reference to digging, and pointed his stress ball at Jen. "And while we're talking about digging stuff up, what do we think Reynolds was looking for last night?"

"Well, he wouldn't say, Gov, but it has to be some kind of loot, right? I'm just not sure what though. It could be completely unrelated to the murders and just be something dodgy he's buried, but then why hide it at an allotment that isn't his? And if it is related to his dad, why has he gone digging there now? It's nearly thirty years on, so finding anything would be a task in itself. It would be hard enough for a normal person, let alone him. And if there is something down there, the chances of it being in any kind of condition just seem very unlikely. It all seems random and a bit bizarre, but the timing makes it relevant. It has to be."

"I agree, Jen, I agree. Keep poking the bear, keep digging, metaphorically at least, and get him charged!"

"Will do, Gov. We're contacting the allotment association later. We'll get some guys over there with metal detectors too, to do it properly. There's something there, or he thinks there is. It would be nice to find something tangible that ties the crimes to Alan or William Reynolds."

CHAPTER 27

Two down. Everything is going to plan so far, or enough to plan anyway. I've got the disappointment of Joe Davies out of my system. It took a few days of moping about, and it still bites me when I think about it, but he's dead and he knew why it was happening as it was happening to him. I made sure of it. I'd have liked to have spent more time with him, would have liked to have been in the house for longer and got more out of it, but I extinguished his life, and he died miserably, horribly, and that makes me feel better.

With hindsight, it helped getting away a little bit earlier too. It was late but the dead of night it wasn't. The pub goers had gone home and it was quiet. Any longer and a hint of a noise would have stood out, and even without the young couple there must have been several dozen people within fifty yards of where Joe had sat. Had died.

There will have been a lot of knocking on a lot of doors since they found him. The neighbours, the other houses in the street, on the adjacent road. Anybody who may have seen something. Nobody has come knocking at my door, or is even looking in my direction, it would seem. It's been long enough to think that nobody has clocked anything suspicious from the local CCTV, so I'm clear on that one for now. That may change when they look back. They may see it then. See me. But for now they haven't, and I can move things forwards.

Onwards and upwards.

It feels good. It means I've avoided all the obvious mistakes, both inside and outside the house. I've kept those wolves from my door thus far, so I can crack on with my plan. I will continue to hide in plain sight. I can stop worrying about getting the tap on the shoulder, for now at least, and go back into operational mode. I have work to do, plans that have been a long time in the making. These people aren't going to kill themselves, so I'll just have to continue to do it for them.

I will definitely have to re-assess the next one, though. That's going to be a lot harder than I was hoping for. A lot harder. For somebody like *me* to be taking on somebody like *him*.

I just need some thinking time, time to revise the plan, but it's full steam ahead and it's going to happen, it just might have to be a bit different now he's half expecting a visitor.

I've crossed the line and there's no going back.

CHAPTER 28

It was a good phone call, as far as they go. Nicky had winced when she saw the number, one she'd added to her contacts after her and Jen's visit the previous week, just in case she ever needed him. She had considered letting the call go to voicemail so she could at least filter it, ring him back if she deemed it necessary. Sort the wheat from the chaff.

As it turned out, he'd kept the card she and Jen had left. Nicky could imagine it had been neatly filed somewhere, probably in alphabetical order on a well organised and slightly OCD desk. She'd answered the call expecting to lose five minutes of her life for good.

"Is that DS Nicky Green?" he'd asked very formally, and despite having called her number. She'd rolled her eyes, already regretting taking the call. "I know you said to call you if we thought of anything, or found anything, and we have."

Nicky waited. Silence. She realised Gary Hunt was expecting a response.

"And what have you remembered, Gary?"

"Well, not me exactly. We have an old guy who's been off sick, Ben. Ben Miller. Not the actor, he gets that all the time..."

"And what has Ben remembered, Gary?" Nicky was trying to mask the impatience in her tone, but wasn't convinced she was doing a very good job of doing so.

"Well, he's been here for a very long time. He was here when your gang were incarcerated here, and he's remembered an occasion during a visit where Joe Davies attacked Alan Reynolds, or tried to attack him anyway. He's having a good think why but he recalls several incidents of disputes between the men. I just thought it would be worth you speaking with him."

Nicky's mood tempered quickly. A glimmer of hope had shone and Gary Hunt now firmly had her attention.

"I'll come over now, Gary, if that's ok?" It wasn't really a question. "Is Ben working for the next few hours? Could I borrow him for a bit?"

Gary agreed and Nicky felt a twinge in her spine. She actually felt something tangible could come from speaking with Ben, and she was eager to find out what it was.

She was already walking towards Rob's office at pace, with her mobile phone still in her right hand, slipping her coat onto her left arm mid-stride. Rob looked up as she got nearer to the door.

"I've had a call from Gary Hunt at Gartree, he said he'd like to see me. There's a guy who's been off on long-term sick. He's just got back to work and he might know something of interest. Alright if I head off now, Gov?"

"Yeah, course it is, go!" Rob wafted Nicky away with his hands. "We need momentum and an injection of pace; anything new will feed the masses and keep the wheels turning, so go and find something!!"

Nicky enjoyed the drive out to Gartree. It was drier than last time and with a hint of blue sky overhead, with the sun trying hard to put in an appearance. It was a quicker drive out too, with the time of day making conditions more favourable, although Nicky was missing the banter with Jen. She smiled to herself as she got closer to McDonald's, but resisted turning left, impressing herself with her own show of willpower as she bore down on the prison. She decided Gary could make her a coffee rather than parting with £3.60 for one in the golden arches.

She felt a glimmer of regret as she parked up, realising it could be another three quarters of an hour before she was shaking hands with Gary Hunt, despite him being no more than 100 yards from her. The security procedures, bag checking and searches would rob her of her time. A flat white was looking cheap all of a sudden, and would have got her through, the caffeine fix taking the edge away. Plus she'd brought one of her finer bags today, an oak brown Mulberry Bayswater, which she considered leaving in the car rather than having it tossed around by the warden on duty.

As it turned out, it was a pleasant enough twenty-five minutes before Nicky was in, the searches completed with relative ease. She'd had a different officer from last time, who seemed to possess something approaching compassion for both people and personal belongings. Nicky assumed she was new, or still serving her probationary period, ironically.

Strapping her watch back on, she walked through into the same office and corridor area as before, assuming Gary would meet her as he had previously. He didn't appear so she was escorted through to the same grey room, where she left her bag and her keys and, assuming they'd be safe, she headed through to another room where she'd spied a water cooler.

She was sipping at it when Gary appeared, looking pleased with himself and over enthusiastically offering an outstretched hand.He tried to make small talk with Nicky, but she didn't make eye contact and continued to scan the posters on the walls, reading the various signage that looked as if it had been stuck to the walls for years.

She dialled back in as Gary was explaining that Ben would be along shortly, and said how he'd been here for over thirty-five years, having started as a young twenty-something. He was Gartree's longest serving officer. He then started to nervously make excuses for why he hadn't mentioned Ben when they'd first met. 'Slipped my mind' and 'hadn't seemed likely or appropriate' were muttered, as if he needed to justify his omission.

Nicky swatted it away, reassuring Gary in the process and scarcely blaming him for not thinking that an officer who'd been on the sick for over nine months would suddenly reappear and recall something decent, something worthy. The fact that that's exactly what had happened was pure fortune.

It was another ten minutes before Ben walked through the door, looking nervous and as if he was about to give evidence at a trial. She was unaware of the reason for his absence from work for the past nine months. Stress and anxiety had both crossed her mind, and looking at a figure weak in complexion and with a slow shuffle, she was sticking with that theory. For a police officer, Nicky had seldom been inside a prison, so twice in two weeks was new territory. She knew from various reports that littered her inbox that sickness rates were high and rising in Britain's prisons. She couldn't imagine Gary was the type to call in sick, although he was barely at the coalface of the place.

She shook Ben's hand as he introduced himself, and could see every last impact that three decades in a category B prison could have on a human being. In his face. In his walk. In his manner. He seemed pleasant enough. He was overweight and carried himself badly. Didn't wear the navy blue uniform well. She imagined he didn't dish out much to the prisoners anymore, and if he ever had, it would have been in the days when she was still in uniform herself.

"So you remember some people I'm interested in, Mr Miller."

Nicky started jovially, wanting to warm Ben up, make him feel at ease. People have a knack of recalling and sharing more when they're at ease than they do when they're under pressure, or feeling it. For some reason, Ben looked like he was feeling it.

"Yeah," he said, scratching his head. "There was an occasion when Joe Davies, he was a nasty piece of work, and William Reynolds were having a visitation at the same time. It was in the same room, they still are, but there were a load of small tables for each of the inmates. Alan Reynolds was here to visit his dad, and Joe Davies had a lady here. She came a few times. I can't remember her name so she may have been a girlfriend at the time. They sat a few tables away. It just went off, and really quickly. I was at the inmate end by the door, so Joe had his back to me, but it just kicked off."

Ben was using his hands to articulate the fight, his arms moving around his own head subconsciously. He continued to not make eye contact with Nicky, his head bowed.

"Can you remember why? Or do you know what triggered it, Ben?"

"Not really, or not officially, anyway. A report wouldn't have been filed. You have to understand that fracas and worse were commonplace in the late eighties. We didn't record stuff like that; if we broke it up and nobody got badly hurt, that was enough."

Nicky reassured Ben that she completely understood the times were very different, but said that anything he could remember would be helpful.

"There were a few of us in the room and we got Joe off Alan, got Alan out and William too. From the shouting we thought it was to do with some of their stash that had gone missing."

Nicky was nodding, encouraging but trying not to lead Ben Miller. She wanted to see what he could recall under his own steam.

"They'd nicked some jewels and some watches and some cash, and we don't think it all ended up where it was meant to. We got the impression that William may have had his fingers in the till, so to speak. Taken more than his twenty percent's worth."

Nicky felt happy to interject. "And you think that if William did take a bit extra, he used Alan to move it or stash it while he was in here with the gang? And you think Joe knew or suspected what was going on?"

"That was the theory. It was harder to track things back then. Serial numbers on bank notes and records on products weren't as they are now, plus there was no Proceeds of Crime Act. I doubt they knew what they'd got so it was even harder for you lot. The police, I mean. It must have been hard for them to know how to divvy it up."

Fair point, Nicky thought. It was the same thought that had been shared by the team. Cash is easy. Count it. Split it. Goods are harder, unless you know exactly what they're worth, and this lot didn't.

Nicky couldn't help but think that if William had been on the take it was very brave, very stupid or very out of character.

Crossing Joe Davies or Charlie Worth was not a decision that would have been taken lightly, but with a shorter sentence, knowledge of where the stash was would have played in his favour. Plus he had Alan, who, if he was involved in moving anything, wouldn't have batted an eyelid at being asked to do so.

Nicky was pondering. There was only one of the three protagonists still alive from the fracas Ben Miller was recalling, and given his arrest for midnight gardening, the link was now exceptionally timely. She'd worked out in her head that his custody clock would have expired, and was sure he'd have been charged and released by now. She'd give him a couple of hours and then have him picked up again.

"Was there anything else you remember from any of the men Gary has asked you about, please?"

"Nothing really. Well, nothing you don't know. There were a lot of fights but it tended to be Joe and Charlie. They were horrible men, DS Green, I can't tell you how bad they were. They were difficult people to… manage."

He chose his words carefully. Nicky was in the process of thanking him, and had got a contact card out to give to him, just in case something else came back to him from days he didn't seem that fond of.

She was almost standing, thinking the meeting had concluded, when he nonchalantly carried on.

"The only other thing I remember, and thought was odd at the time, is Daniel Mortimer. He was a smooth bugger, something of a ladies' man. He wasn't married but I remember a lady coming to visit him. Think she only came a couple of times but she was the most attractive woman that's ever set foot in here. Caused a real stir, it did. Amongst these animals anyway. That wasn't odd per se, but he wasn't married and she was a good-looking woman."

Nicky thought that was useful but not in the wider context of being able to do much with it. But Ben Miller wasn't finished.

"The bit that was odd was that it was Paul Harris' wife."

The perplexion on Nicky's face manifested itself, her poker face slipping slightly.

"I can't remember her name but she obviously visited Paul on a regular basis, but there were several times when she visited Daniel Mortimer too. As in separately, when Paul wasn't there. I'd hate to cast aspersions but it seemed… odd, and I don't think Paul knew she was visiting him. Or would have been very pleased about it."

"And you're absolutely certain that Paul Harris's wife visited Daniel Mortimer while he was here, Ben?"

"Yes, no doubt at all. It's not the sort of thing you forget. We all just thought they must have been carrying on."

"Well, thank you, Mr Miller, you've been more than helpful."

Nicky was already excited about calling Rob, and letting Jen and Jack know what she'd just learned. She also realised that she still hadn't had a coffee, and Maccies for a flat white was now inevitable.

CHAPTER 29

It was an impromptu session amongst the team, a level of spontaneity that happened occasionally and was usually for a good reason, a development or two.

After a slowish week, the last forty-eight hours had seen Alan Reynolds arrested for trespass and effectively breaking into an allotment, combined with Nicky's discovery and meeting with Ben Miller. Two pieces of good fortune that could well prove to be linked, but in different circumstances could both have gone undetected. Ben Miller's memories could ultimately lead the team down a path and uncover a killer, but had Ben taken early retirement or had another month off sick, the truth may never have been known. Gary Hunt may never have made that call.

A double killer could have got away with murder, or killed again, because an old man was ill. Fine margins.

Rob was sitting on one of the desks in the middle of the office, chewing on a peanut Eat Natural bar and trying to speak between bites.

"Alan Reynolds. We've followed this line of inquiry, but could he have been involved in his dad's killing? Either directly or indirectly? It seems unlikely based on the distance, travel and timings but I think we need to keep an open mind at this stage. He's definitely involved somehow, he definitely knows more than he's told any of us, so we need to find out to what extent."

Rob looked at Nicky, who hadn't long arrived back at Lodge House, for confirmation that she'd made the call on Alan Reynolds. He didn't ask the question so Nicky replied to the look.

"Yes, Gov, all done. Uniform are out to pick him up. Hopefully he's at home or in his local. I haven't heard anything but he'll be back here before we know it."

"Thank you, Nicky. Right, we need to keep digging while this is fresh. I want Alan Reynolds dragging over hot coals. He knows something critical to this and I want to know what it is. He also needs reminding that he's running out of chances, so he can either take one with us or if not, he could be the next one getting strapped to a chair."

Rob turned abruptly, addressing Jack directly. "Jack, Paul Harris."

"What about him, Gov?" Jack looked perplexed.

"I want to know whether he's dead or not."

The statement wasn't one the room was expecting. Nobody responded.

"We've ignored his name because we think he's dead, which would clearly rule him out. Joe was a good suspect, Charlie Worth is still a clear focus, but we know where he is for now and can keep half an eye on him. I'm just pointing out that the status quo has changed sufficiently for us to not rule anything out, and for us to go back over what we think we know in case we've got it wrong. I'm getting nowhere through the hierarchy with Daniel Mortimer in terms of identity and location, but given what Nicky was told this morning, we've got a potentially philandering wife, missing goods and a very good motive if finances in the here and now have become stretched, and as of yet we haven't fully 'crossed the i's and dotted the t's' on him."

Jack nodded, his instructions clear and his task in front of him. Rob continued for clarity.

"I want to see a death certificate pinned to this board. I want the doctor who issued it and pronounced him dead speaking to, if he's still alive. Was it his own GP, was it a doctor who certified his death? Could it be fraudulent? Could he have faked it? Was he cremated? Was he buried?"

Jack was mentally noting the questions, the pace too quick for writing anything down.

"And while you're at it, find out where Mrs Harris is now. Is she still alive? Did she remarry? Who too? Are her and Daniel Mortimer in contact and are they now unpicking the past together? There's an angle here and we need to work it. Find the people. Find the answers."

All realised the magnitude of the task Rob had blurted out. Jen was already leaning forward, effectively volunteering herself, which Rob both noticed and accepted.

"Do you want her bringing in, Gov, assuming we can find her?" Jen asked, placing herself in that role alongside Jack.

"Not unless you think she has something to hide. Check her finances, find out what she's been doing, where she works, if she's in debt. All the usual stuff. Make no bones about making her aware of what's happening. What has happened. She could be our best link to Daniel Mortimer at the minute, however unlikely that may seem. He could be in a house with her right now, or she may not have seen him in a decade. We don't know because we haven't taken a step back and looked at it from a different viewpoint."

The team nodded, agreeing how the focus had been reactive following the double murder. The investigation was diverging, and it was happening in real time. A narrow focus hadn't provided a result, so a different approach was needed. Rob was steering it and his charges knew the team was going in the right direction.

"So in other news, Gov," asked Jen. "Daniel Mortimer. Who the fuck is this guy?"

A few of the team had thought about it, but the focus hadn't squarely been on him, given the links to Joe Davies, Charles Worth and Alan Reynolds, all of whom had afforded the mystery man some breathing space, until now.

"It's a fair question, Jen."

Rob had been frustrated at the lack of progress on Daniel Mortimer. He'd left Gartree prison in 1991 and at some point very quickly thereafter had dropped off the grid. He didn't own a house, didn't have a credit card. Had a driving licence that had expired and was never renewed.

His National Insurance number hadn't appeared or been used legally, and his tax code was dormant and hadn't been used post release. At the time it would have been very easy for him to pick up a pay as you go mobile and disappear. His bank accounts had little in them pre-conviction and hadn't been touched. He wasn't a fraudster, officially anyway, but Rob was learning that Daniel Mortimer was smooth. A talker. Well educated, good looking and confident. The sort who can convince, blend in, morph, and nobody would be any the wiser.

The key issue was the identity. There was no evidence to suggest Daniel Mortimer had changed his name by deed poll, or any other legal means. It had taken time to establish, but Rob had requested information from his superiors on whether his identity was being withheld at the request of the state. Whether he'd been involved in something much bigger and had been poacher turned gamekeeper, and was now being afforded protection by the very same people paying Rob's wages.

He didn't have a specific answer, he rarely did when politics was involved, but he had more than an inkling that Daniel Mortimer hadn't been given a new identity by the Government, and wasn't being looked after as an informant. Time would tell, but Rob was convinced he'd stolen an identity and was living under an assumed name that he'd found or stolen shortly after release. In the years before the turn of the millennium, a decent forged driving licence could get you a current account opened at any High Street bank; that in turn could get you credit for mobile phone contracts, and within three months of renting a flat and paying a few utility bills in a false name, you could acquire a fully legal UK passport under your new and assumed name. The world was your oyster, it just didn't know who you were.

Death of course was an option, but Rob was now working to the theory, like with Paul Harris, that death was something that needed proving beyond all reasonable doubt.

Daniel Mortimer was out there. Rob was convinced of it. He hadn't shared his thoughts with his team, not even Nicky, but he'd considered whether Daniel Mortimer might have inserted himself into professional life within the city. One of the three city hospitals, a GP surgery, or in another professional capacity, but one with privilege or access. Maybe even one where he had access to the police. Rob had shared his concerns with Chief Constable David Parker, who had a natural diplomacy for things of a certain nature, as well as Assistant Chief Constable

Laura Mathers, who was more visible to Rob. He had a better relationship with her too. They were both doing all they could to quietly dig into the backgrounds of senior and medical professionals of a specific age group and appearance, without rocking too many boats.

The concern was real. If a convicted armed robber had fraudulently blended into city life, obtained a job and was currently working at a professional level whilst murdering his way through his old colleagues, the shit-storm would be immense. The sort of headlines that would cost jobs, perhaps even Rob's. The scandal, the controversy. Rob had been in these situations before, not of this extremity, but the type where you can imagine the headlines being written nationwide, none of which flattering, all of which demanding resignations. Dismissals. Rolling heads. The chief constable would have to go as a minimum, no doubt about it. No wonder he was being so accommodating.

The complexity was dawning on those involved. The answer was nowhere near to presenting itself, so all the team could do was keep moving forwards. Keep asking questions. With the initial suspect pool now either dead, shown to be incompetent, on the police radar or still in the wind, the future was uncertain. Nobody was screaming guilty, and the lack of physical evidence wasn't affording the team any breaks to run with.

Rob wanted proof that Paul Harris was dead, and if he is, he wanted to find his widow. Wanted to find Elizabeth Harris, even if just to buy a few more days that may provide a result on Daniel Mortimer. Something. Anything.

Rob had a thought on Daniel Mortimer, something worth checking. He picked up his mobile and dialled the chief constable, and prepared himself to leave a voicemail before the first ring.

CHAPTER 30

Now is risky. It isn't the best time at all, but I'm not sure if I leave it any longer that there will ever be a best time. The truth in life is that there's never a perfect time. To marry, have kids, divorce. They all happen at inconvenient times, and we all still bitch about it. Dying, losing your job, falling in love. Like they're choices you can just make. 'It wasn't the right time, but when you know, you know.' All that bollocks.

If there's never a good time, there definitely isn't a right time. So I need to force the issue. Make it happen. It'll be difficult for a number of reasons, some practical, some just down to access and time. There are more reasons to abort than to proceed. Like that's an option. I'm neck-deep already and there's no backing out when you've taken two lives. You're in.

Stopping now isn't an option, and besides, I'm enjoying myself.

This will be very different to William Reynolds. Different from Joe Davies too. It has to be. I could have changed the order, but it feels better like this. The behaviour of those in line has been as expected, and even the behaviour of the police has been relatively predictable. Nothing that will prevent a third murder anyway. I'm not deterred, and there's insufficient protection to prevent it from happening.

The MO will change. It has to. That's a good thing. I've been toying with the details of this one for a while. Another break-in attack is possible, but difficult. Too much risk for me. Too much caution from him. Any whisper in that house at the minute and he'll kick off, plus he hasn't got a cat to cause a distraction; any noise and he'll be swinging or stabbing before I get close.

Regrettably this needs to be different, but I can live with that. This is about preservation as much as execution. Getting in, getting the job done and getting out. That's what success looks like today. No mistakes, no injuries, avoiding being caught. By anybody.

Then it'll be time to re-assess and take stock. Continue to plan, and continue to fly under the radar. But tonight belongs to me once more, and I'm buzzing for it.

CHAPTER 31

It's a nice day for it. Cool but dry. The best weather so far. I'm bang in the mood today but the excitement is more suppressed. Maybe two murders can do that to your emotions. I can feel the energy levels, can feel the adrenalin in my blood, but I'm sitting chugging on a Diet Coke calm as you like, breathing in deeply and sucking it all in. It's not every day you become a triple murderer.

Loughborough is weird. An eclectic mix. It has the usual mix of modern shops for the young, countless bars, restaurants and an obligatory Wetherspoons for the heavy student population, as well as some dated cafes and an eighties cinema for the retro crowd. It's trying hard to be all things to all men. I can't decide if I like it or not. It seems to vary street by street. The park is nice; Queen's park, just past a pottery shop where dads are sat painting teapots and giraffes with their kids. It's a large wide open space that is well kept and with the carillon in the middle. A large red brick bell tower with a beautifully weathered green copper roof in the middle of the park, which is visible from miles around. It's the sort of thing you might see in Boston, but it sits proudly in north Leicestershire. A war memorial. A big one.

I've definitely been in worse places, and there's a nice focus of what is to come. I almost feel normal. Calm.

I'm only three miles or so from the house, but it's still light so I'll wait. I enjoy the build-up, and hate feeling rushed. I'd hate to drive there feeling stressed, park badly and go straight into it, full of negative energy and all pent up. I get none of that this way. It's like a regular day out, only with a slight twist at the end of the day.

No rushing, no mistakes.

Charles Worth won't be a person to make a mistake on. He's on high alert. He's had the police barge into his house and work him up, and he's an old school fuck-up full of anger and hatred. Full of animosity. He's anti-establishment and anti-police and does not take fools gladly. Almost classic punk era but more old school than that. A touch of Ronnie Kray about him. Seriously fucking psycho.

I'll head over later, avoid rush hour and keep my head down. CCTV is less of an issue; there's none on the A6, and there are countless back roads out through Quorn, Rothley, Woodhouse Eaves, Barrow upon Soar and several other villages that could all afford an easy route out. A number of options to get out of the town and back to the city undetected. It's perfect. Highly accessible and with multiple options to remain in the shadows. Maybe I do like it.

He's not being monitored, so that doesn't need to be taken into account. He may know it, he may suspect it, but they're not babysitting him. He didn't want it anyway and they haven't got the resources. Charles Worth looks after himself and doesn't need the police to do it for him. He'll go toe to toe with anyone stupid or brave enough to come looking for him. At least his house has been swept, so if there were any firearms lying about or other offensive weapons they'll have either been confiscated or moved to a safer location for when the police don't have a microscope on him.

Game on.

It's getting quieter in the park and the shadows start to lengthen. The young and old alike have started to go home for tea or warmth, and a smattering of dog walkers and couples remain. A few wander back to a pay and display car park, and a few more into the Coffee Pot across the road. A retro cafe offering great value food. A cash-only business and no CCTV. Another good choice. Sandwiches are good, too.

I walk back to my car, which is parked on a residential street adjacent to Queen's Park, close to the town centre but it's pretty innocuous. I'm only ten minutes from where I need to be. No need for the sat-nav to be employed, even with the one-way system which will take me the wrong way out of town, and around a large B&Q.

I've recce'd this scene countless times, as I have with all of them. Something I'm proud of. At different times of day, weekends, almost as if I was buying the place. It's on their turf so it needs to be done. Meticulous planning has got me here, and it's not about to be dialled down for Charlie Worth. Quite the opposite. It's an evolution, and scales up from here on in.

I follow the Leicester Road in steady traffic before turning up onto New King Street, which is significantly quieter. Barely a car. Another side road leads me up towards the spot where I've planned to park. It's a few hundred yards away from the house but is ideal. Up passed all of the houses and by an old, abandoned and derelict scrapyard with a cricket club next to it. There's nobody here at this time of year. The close season. The scrapyard too. Not a soul. Almost eerie.

I park my car where I planned to, on some hard-standing to avoid leaving any tyre marks. The walk back towards the house is quiet too. Nobody about. I take care not to step in any areas of mud by the scrapyard; leaving a footprint here or on Charlie's carpet would be amateur. I've taken precautions. My shoes are two sizes larger than my feet, just in case. Three pairs of socks on and all strapped up. Just in case a print is detected. It could help to cast some doubt on a jury. OJ's glove is in my mind as I walk towards the first houses at the top end of the street; several semi-detached houses with simple bay fronts. The street is dead, and it's unlikely there'll be any police visits this evening.

If it don't fit, you must acquit.

My heart rate starts to climb as I get within about 150 yards of his house. I've been thinking about this for months, and the last few weeks have made it all so real. Palpable.

The plan has changed. Is changing. The anger from Joe Davies mellowed into peaceful reflection, and allowed me to think differently. Adapt. Tonight will be very different. Has to be different.I'm not sure how much time I'll get with Charlie Worth so it needs to be well spent and it needs to get the job done.

I'm aware of the danger here. Not just because of who Charlie Worth is. Was. What he represents. William Reynolds was a soft target, frankly speaking, and I knew I could get into Joe Davies' house comfortably and take it to him.

As I continue to walk down the street, I start to question my decision making. What I'm about to do. Breaking into Charlie's house would be dangerous. His neighbours are on high alert thanks to recent days and any noises, let alone screams, would mean an immediate 999 call. I need to accept that the media is now in play too. The murders are big on social media locally, and the story is national, although I'm disappointed I haven't got a moniker yet. Boston Strangler. Yorkshire Ripper. Maybe this one will do it.

I can see his house down on the right-hand side. The curtains are closed but there are lights on, the glow emanating through the curtains and making it clear that Charlie boy is at home.

There's a dog walker at the other end of the street, but I can't tell whether they're a man or a woman at this distance. It puts me at ease as they head out of view. They can't have seen me either, not in any detail anyway. Its bin night as well, so I need to be careful of any late evening bin runs or last-minute recycling. Potential witnesses.

It's time to front up. Time to take a risk. A big one. I don't know if this will work. Only one way to find out. Nerves have started to appear so I'm having to breathe slowly. Breathe hard. I inhale one final long breathe, walk up the short pathway and, sucking in the cool air of the night, reach up and knock on the brand new front door.

There's no immediate response. I consider knocking again but don't want to over-egg it. I drop my hood as I don't want to completely give him the wrong impression when he answers. I don't knock again. Choose not to. I can hear movement inside, and after what feels like several minutes, I can sense him moving towards the front door. He takes the chain off. It's a new door but inexplicably there's no spy hole. I breathe a sigh of relief. He's opening the door without me having to do anything. Still time to abort. The initial relief merges into fear. Some doubt kicks in. This really could go wrong. And if it goes wrong it'll happen quickly. The intensity is crippling me. The danger. The fear.

He says something behind the glass. I don't make it out. The doubt grows. How will he react? Will he have a knife in his hand? A bat behind the door? It's too late to change my mind now. I'm committed to this big time and a long way over wherever the line was.

There's a clunk of a lock before I see his hand through the narrow opaque glass moving towards the top Yale lock. He's wearing something blue.

The door opens. Whatever he was expecting, I can see he wasn't expecting me. His face softens a little. Perplexed. His hand remains behind the door. Guarded. Defensive.

I say good evening and tell him my name. Not an alias. My actual name. He looks confused. More so, he looks curious. I'm sweating but controlling my breathing. Still not convinced this is the best way, I talk to him, ask him how he is. Ask him if I can have ten minutes of his time if he wouldn't mind. Real charm offensive.

He sighs heavily but doesn't look immediately threatened. It's perfect. I look up and down the street casually just to check we're still alone. His posture softens a little, his hand drops from the door. It's empty. He looks me square in the eye, nods and mouths a curious 'alright, then'.

I've got him on the hook.

This is the bit I pondered while I was walking around the park this afternoon. The details of this bit. How it would play out. How it would start. Would he slide in next to the door and let me walk past him, or in front of him? And if so, at what point could I play my hand?

I've hedged my bets. I muster up the best smile I can with the sincerest 'thanks' I can manage.

He turns his back. He turns his back on me. I nearly smile. A brief moment of surprise and excitement. I'm rushing now. I dreamt of this but was playing to the worst-case scenario.

A second or so passes as I slide the needle out of my jacket pocket.

He walks forward a pace or two into the hall with the stairs to the left and the kitchen ahead of him. I step inside behind him. He starts to turn and say something but he's too late. My moment has presented itself and I grab at it.

I reach up and stab him hard in the side of the neck.

He reacts immediately and swings hard but I sway. He catches me towards the top of my head and I fall against the front door, pushing it shut.

He swears. He's thrashing hard but his arms are wild. I manoeuvre myself out of the corner as he continues to swing wildly. He catches me in the chest and lunges forward, sensing me. I push him away and step back into the door frame. Give myself some room. He's slurring now. He gets close again so I push him hard and step back.

He starts to sway. The syringe isn't in his neck anymore but that doesn't matter. *Bide your time.*

The groaning gets slower. I pick my moment. Walk to his side and grab one of his arms. He's so out of it now he's almost grateful I'm there to hold him up.

I guide him forwards into the lounge and drop him into a chair. It's hard. He's a big guy and he's collapsing as we reach the chair, his own bodyweight too much to bear. For both of us.

He's down. He's unconscious.

I close the curtains and find the empty syringe in the hall. That couldn't have gone much better.

It's playtime.

CHAPTER 32

It had been a tough few days on the team; the workload had been heavy and with the results light, it was always going to take its toll on morale. Nicky and Jen were both feeling the squeeze, but knew they had to keep pressing ahead. Had to keep battling. There is no other option in a murder case. Lives depend on it. Neither took any pride in knowing that the killer was probably only a few miles away and mocking the police while still at large.

Mocking the public, too. The Leicester Mercury had gone big online and the local news crews were starting to get stuck in. Kicking them when they were down. 'Serial Killer at Large in City' was splashed across one homepage, with all the usual shit about staying in after dark, locking your doors and not walking home alone.

Nicky was experienced with the media, and knew and understood its powers. She had used it to her advantage on many occasions and was well connected in certain circles, but there was never a moral high ground. Their job is to sell newspapers and drum up readers, and they'd have no issue sensationalising a double murder to do so.

It was also the reason Nicky and Jen were spending the night in the pub. A midweek blow out. Not always the sensible option on a school night, but rolling with the punches can sometimes lead you down that path. The spur of the moment.

Both were fatigued. It had started innocently enough, but after three large glasses of wine both knew they were in for a session. They saw it coming but let the evening wash over them as the wine became vodka and they became louder without knowing it.

The early talk was shop. Nicky voiced how she felt that they'd already met the murderer, spoken to them face to face, maybe even shook their hand. The suspect pool wasn't that wide, and Nicky and Jen had spoken to everybody associated with the gang to this point, with one notable absence.

Jen was in the camp of that notable absence; Daniel Mortimer, convinced it was the only remaining theory of any viability. They both felt the Paul Harris move was a clutch at straws, but were totally respectful of Rob's need to fully eliminate it. It wasn't the first time he would have made such a bold statement only for it to be the shining light in an investigation, and Nicky was well aware of that fact and of Rob's record. She still felt Paul Harris wasn't their man but was happy to let Jack do the legwork and satisfy that line of inquiry.

The back end of the night devolved rapidly into the juicy stuff, and who was shagging who; the really sophisticated conversations. Jen described her recent love life as 'up and down', which had made Nicky snort vodka up through her nose. The night continued to take its toll. They messaged Becky, hoping she was in town, but she'd headed south to see her sister, who was starting a new job. Jack very sensibly ignored their messages and stayed clear.

The last recollection Nicky had was of walking out of the pub, the fresh air hitting her like a slap in the face. The need for grease high. Anything beige and filthy from a local vendor would do the trick. She remembered hugging Jen, who had sorted herself with an Uber, and Nicky had decided to walk the mile home to sober up, hoping her husband was sound asleep and their dachshunds wouldn't go too crazy when she put the key in the door.

She'd try to be quiet, which is never easy when you're this drunk. She needed to sleep.

CHAPTER 33

Nicky woke up on the sofa. One of the dachshunds was pulling on the sock she still had on and was demanding breakfast. Her glasses and a notebook were on the coffee table in front of her. She felt like shit. Head banging. Throat dry. She slid her glasses on and picked up the notepad, reading the message written on it. 'Hope you feel ok, your coffee's still in the kitchen. Love you xxxx'

She smiled and headed into the kitchen to boil the kettle when her phone beeped in her jeans. Assuming it was Jen she ignored it for a second, the need for caffeine much greater.

She couldn't decide if toast was a good idea. Nicky wasn't a cereal person, but couldn't find any croissants or fresh bread in the kitchen either. Maybe later.

She looked at her phone, expecting a picture or a gif of someone vomiting from Jen. She got neither.

A message from Jack: 'Loughborough, you know where. Quick as you can.'

Nicky mustered a 'shit' and hit dial. Jack knew they were out last night. They'd told him, he'd seen their messages, and on another night he may have been there with them. He was grateful he'd declined. His phone only rang once.

"They've found a body, Gov. Charles Worth, in his house. Postman asked a neighbour if they'd seen him; the curtains were closed and he didn't like what he could see through the letterbox. The neighbours hadn't seen him so it was the postie who called us."

"I'll be as quick as I can, Jack. Are you on the way?"

"I'm ten minutes away, I'll sort the early scene, and Rob isn't far behind me. He's spoken to Becky and sorted cover for her this morning. We'll be here a good while, I reckon, so see you later?"

Nicky thanked Jack for the message. She knew he'd have made an excuse or two to cover for them. Tried to.

Nicky was sobering up more quickly with the news of another body. She dialled Rob within seconds of Jack's call ending. She knew the call would be brief, knew Rob would know she'd been drinking immediately. She wouldn't deny it and he'd rip her a new one at some point when she thought he'd forgotten. Only he wouldn't forget.

He acknowledged her and told her to get over as soon as she could, then cut her off. The abruptness she expected.

Jen was the last call before a shower. Another Uber was in order. Last night already seemed like a very long time ago.

It was 10am before Jen's Toyota Prius parked at the bottom of the street near to another cab, which had just dropped Nicky off. The street was all taped off, with patrol cars parked sideways to block any determined Amazon driver from thinking twice.

Nicky walked towards Jen with a bottle of water in hand. There was a nod between the two for a greeting before they walked towards a house, as they had done only last week. The swagger of seven days ago had vanished. The cockiness of standing in the street while Charles Worth's home was raided now seemed so trivial, so worthless.

Nicky could picture the press reporting on another old man being failed. Let down by the system. She decided it was the hangover talking, but she knew that whoever picked the story up would forget the decades of brutality that Charles Worth had imparted on the city.

Jack had got wind of their arrival and headed out of the house, fully suited up in his white paper overalls and blue slip-on shoes. Rob did the same and nodded at Nicky, an acknowledgment was as good as it was going to get today.

"How are you feeling, Gov?" Jack asked.

"Better than Charles Worth is, Jack. What's in there?"

"It's not pretty, Nicky. Really not pretty."

"Same killer?" asked Jen, her eyes straining at the daylight.

"No doubt about it. It's different again but yeah, it's the same guy." Jack looked at Nicky and Jen. Both were happy for him to guide on what was happening inside the house. "He's in a chair, cable ties again. Hands and feet are well strapped. He's been beaten badly. Something blunt like a club or cosh. His left ear is missing, there is a lot of blood to his head and face, so it is the same killer. There's more blood though, a lot more."

"More? How can there be more than there was at Joe Davies' house? He had the living shit kicked out of him." Jen's question was blunt but Jack took the point.

"He's been cut. Like, a lot. His trousers are shredded and his legs and parts of his torso are completely gashed to bits. His legs are in tatters. I don't think I've ever seen this much blood. It's hard to tell if he fought back but it looks like he let his attacker in, which is the interesting bit. No sign of any break-in or forced entry, so it looks like he either knew or trusted the person who did this to him enough to open his front door to them and let them in.

"The gaffer isn't happy but you may have clocked that. He's pissed off. Seems pissed off with me and I haven't done anything. He snapped at one of the pathologists too, but I guess he was feeling it enough before we got this call."

"Obvious question, Jack..." Nicky didn't need to ask it.

"Three fingers. All cleanly cut off and left on the table in a neat little row."

CHAPTER 34

It was late in the afternoon by the time the body of Charles Worth had been transported the eleven miles back down the A6 to the Leicester Royal Infirmary, in a very different van to his last trip.

The day had been long and the crime scene was still being processed in minute detail, something which would continue further now the removal of the body was complete.

The house was one the team knew well, having gone through a police raid in the last week, albeit in a search capacity. It was rare for a police team to be going into familiar territory. Most crime scenes are new and fresh ground. You have to start from scratch. Not today. The house and the body were very much on their radar. The layout, the decor, the smells.

Rob had already spoken to the assistant chief constable. The politics of how Charles Worth's death could have been avoided were already underway; how he could have been protected, especially with him being a potential target. Those games had started. The murder took centre stage, but the internal dealings were off and running too.

The early morning start had afforded the police some daylight to work with, unlike the previous murders, and Nicky and Jen had benefited from the fresh air as they coordinated the forensic work and early response. A Subway had also helped, and by mid-afternoon Nicky was firing on all cylinders, and was starting to make arrangements for what was to come in the next twenty-four hours. There was no legitimate next of kin, and the team would need clear direction as the investigation continued to unfold.

If the team felt the heat turn up after Joe Davies' death, the gas rings were about to be cranked up another notch or two. Gas mark seven at least.

Nicky had put in a call to Bernie Copp, his gravitas and persona perfect for motivating and preparing the troops for the storm that would come as soon as Rob and the team got back into Lodge House, when the next wave of information processing, door-knocking and covering of old ground would kick off.

Rob would be demanding of the team. More demanding. Nicky knew it was coming. She also knew that her and Rob would deal with their differences at another point. The timing was poor, so any conflict would need parking while the criticality of the investigation continued to climb.

Jen was on the phone to Becky, having got through to her, and was arranging the timing of the post-mortem. Becky would carry it out as soon as she arrived back from Leighton Buzzard in the coming hours. Jen would meet her at the hospital and stay for the duration. Nicky would work remotely whilst Rob and Jack got stuck back in with the team, a situation that was mutual whilst tempers were frayed. It also allowed Rob to stay clear and get his head into the key elements that had just nudged up on the priority scale.

The missing links. Paul Harris. The whereabouts of Daniel Mortimer.

CHAPTER 35

It was early evening by the time Becky Ryan had scrubbed up and was kitted out for the impending autopsy. Both Becky and Jen were wearing their hair up, following what had been two long days for very different reasons, although Jen's hangover had drifted from her memory and into the history bin several hours ago. The sobering sights of a Loughborough crime scene and a mortuary were both very capable of forcing sobriety through the hardest of systems.

Jen knew where her focus for the next forty-eight hours was headed, but had a more pressing few hours ahead of her. Several hours of sleep would be afforded before another mammoth day tomorrow. Two or three days would pass in the blink of an eye and they needed to bear fruit.

Becky started with the support of one of her colleagues. Jen's nervous energy and over-tiredness was causing her to walk the corridors, in and out of the viewing gallery, and over-indulge on vending machine coffee. The nasty stuff in beige plastic cups that burns your hands as you hold it.

The procedure was well underway when Jen found herself staring in at Becky, wondering how she did the job she did.

Jen's job wasn't a picnic; dead bodies, house calls, car crash victims. But there were positive sides too; reunited families, victim recoveries, convictions to provide closure to those left behind. The survivors.

Becky was voice-recording her findings when she lowered her head to take a closer look at something that had caught her attention. Something that saw her head come within inches of the pale chest of Charles Worth. The blood had largely been washed away, the cold steel tray showing slivers of scarlet rinsed from a body that was bearing the physical signs of a brutal assault.

Even from behind the glass screen, Jen felt a retch in her stomach. Not a vodka retch, although that wouldn't be helping, just a realisation of the death that was being served up for them to deal with. A production line that was keeping Becky and her in a job, and one she would be happy to stop.

This was the third corpse in a little over two weeks, and this was going to end with either an arrest or the perpetrator's shopping list being exhausted. The risk of a triple murderer remaining at large was more viable than anybody wanted to acknowledge.

Jen looked up to see Becky was looking at her, she stifled a yawn and continuing to tip what was meant to be a cappuccino down her neck.

"Why don't you go and get some rest, Jen? There's a family room down the hall you can use. There's a loo and a sofa in there. We'll be at this for a while and I'll wake you when we find something."

Jen wasn't going to look a gift horse in the mouth and she knew she needed sleep. She was happy to get some shut-eye while the post-mortem went on, and knew Becky would be true to her word.

She was, and three hours later Jen was stirred by Becky, who dropped a bottle of Evian on the table and told Jen she had news to share.

Jen thumbed a message to Nicky to tell her the post-mortem was done and she was about to be briefed, knowing the news would get to Rob. She asked Becky for ten minutes. A loo break and a splash of water to the face was needed.

Jen met Becky in the mortuary, with screens showing several close-up images of the body, and she wanted to start from a slightly different angle. "So how is this different to what we've already had, Becky?"

"The key difference is an attack to the legs, which you'll have seen from him being on the slab. There are multiple deep gashes to the soft tissue areas of both legs, which would have been inflicted with a razor blade or a Stanley knife. Deep and clean, several long incisions. Could have been a scalpel. Designed to cause maximum pain, and the blood loss is heavy as a result. The blood loss is heavy overall. So much blood. You'll have seen it heavy on the clothes and body in Loughborough, and inside the house in general. The area under and around the chair was bloodier than we've seen at either of the previous crime scenes too. Exsanguination is the clear cause of death as a result. He took a pounding again, but he bled out sitting in that chair."

"So slightly different to what we've seen again? Third murder and third variation of the theme?" asked Jen.

"Yes, definitely. Same guy, no doubt about it. This isn't a new perpetrator. I won't roll Mr Worth over, but the thighs have been slashed at badly, you can see on the lower part here." Becky ran her little finger down the region of Charles Worth's left leg. Jen didn't need the graphic version but there wasn't a softer equivalent. "The hamstrings would have been agony, and this area of the thighs wouldn't have been a great deal more pleasant. This is savage, looks less measured and perhaps even rushed, but is just a bloody assault on another restrained victim. He was well restrained again, as the bruising on the wrists shows you. He was trussed up tight and going nowhere. He was a big strong guy and you wouldn't have wanted him free, although the beating and the blood loss would have rendered him stricken quite quickly."

Jen continued to look the body up and down, the blood now cleaned away, but the deep wounds and bruises were shining brightly against pale white skin.

"This looks like it would have been agonising, Becky?"

Becky nodded to the affirmative.

"And if somebody did this to you, you'd scream?"

"Like a baby. The pain would have been excruciating."

"And the area is built up and he has neighbours, people who walk by?"

"Yep." Becky knew exactly where Jen's line of questioning was taking her. It had occurred to her too but she already had an outline of the answer, or a hypothesis at least.

"So was the perp less careful this time or just didn't they care if they were overheard? Those noises would have been hideous. You'd have called our lot immediately if you heard them."

"Well, he was silenced to a degree, Jen, but better than Joe Davies was. I say *better*, I mean more efficient. Less fatal, at least. He was gagged, only he didn't have the good fortune of choking to death. The gag was tight but there wasn't anything stuffed in his mouth, so the noise would have been heavily muffled, probably only audible to our killer."

Becky pointed out the harsh marks to Charlie Worth's mouth. Deep purple bruises emerging from the corners of the mouth, the bruising easing into a deep red across the cheeks. Evidence of how tight the gag was. Nobody could hear. The pain could be maximised. Enjoyed.

"The other element that is new is a number of needle marks. There are several of note. We don't think Charlie was a perpetual drug user; there certainly wasn't any paraphernalia around his house on either of our visits."

Jen looked curious as a frown appeared. Becky continued.

"We need to run the full tox tests but I think the killer has used drugs to keep him conscious, or allow him to regain consciousness throughout the assault. To endure it more. I may be wrong but it looks from the bruising like the piercings to the skin were made at a similar time to the rest of the more obvious injuries you can see."

"That's savage if that's what happened. Maybe more cruel than savage. Both."

Jen had an appreciation for the darker things in life and was borderline impressed at the length that had been gone to in order to make Charles Worth suffer. Not just once, but over and over until his body had finally given up on him.

Jen took a look at the left-hand side of Charles Worth's corpse. If the varied nature of the killings caused any doubt as to whether this was a fresh killer, some other traits very clearly let the team know that the same man had just dispatched his third victim.

She bent down to look at the clean removal of three fingers from Charles Worth's left hand; the little to middle finger, all gone and in a bag somewhere in Becky's care, to be stitched back on before the funeral.

Jen switched her attention to the now-familiar missing left ear. The cut again was clean. Becky had done a very proficient job of stitching and closing the wound, but the left ear, like the fingers to the left hand, had been competently removed.

Jen stood upright and pondered. She looked at Becky and said, "This fucker's getting worse. We really need to stop him."

CHAPTER 36

It was a bright and early start for a Wednesday morning. The third murder had lit the blue touch paper locally, and the press was now having a field day running the story. Rob had spent more time than he'd have liked on phone calls or in offices with senior officers, explaining their lines of inquiry. His lines of inquiry. Justifying.

The chief constable had been very clear that he expected a full and co-ordinated response from the investigating team, wanted the investigation moving up a notch, and wanted a result. He also didn't want the BBC or ITN parking their trucks outside and "turning this into a fucking carnival". Rob recalled the words being spat angrily out of his mouth. He always resented the discussion. *That* discussion. The naughty schoolboy chat that suggested he wasn't doing enough, wasn't good enough, and that he was somehow sat on his arse deliberately not catching a murderer. It always made him feel shit, and even if he was critical of his own performance, it was right up there in the helpful stakes with chocolate teapots and glass hammers.

The farce of bureaucracy.

Rob had left the meeting and gone for a walk to catch some air before going back to the office and getting on with it. The job. Up and over Tigers Way, turning left onto New Walk and continuing up its wide and magnificent boulevard, stopping at one of the green spaces; De Montfort Square. Rob walked towards the central statue of the square's namesake and pondered. In the shadow of St Stephen's Church, Rob looked around at the beautiful Edwardian terraces and palisaded villas standing proudly before him.

He looked around at some of the men, women and children going about their daily business. He always felt a responsibility to them. All of them. Nobody knew who he was, but if they did know he was leading the investigation into Leicester's triple murderer, he knew some would wish him luck, some would shrug their shoulders, and some would tell him to pull his finger out and catch the killer. Or worse. Law of averages. But he still felt responsible. Duty-bound.

Leicester was his city, a place he called home, and every last taxpayer paying his wages deserved the streets to be safe. Or as safe as the streets can be nowadays. He saw yesterday's Daily Mirror in the top of a bin by the path, detailing yet another stabbing in the capital. Words such as 'epidemic', 'disease' and 'cancer of a generation' were splashed across the pages. He wondered how the mayor had the bottle to pledge 'safe streets' and a 'serious response' when the statistics showed there'd be another dead teenager on his hands by teatime.

He wasn't the only one not doing enough.

CHAPTER 37

It took Rob half an hour to get back to the office, including a stop at Tesco Metro on the London Road for a Diet Coke that he wished he'd had in the square. The office was busy and Nicky had marshalled the investigating team well. Jen had done an equally good job with the wider support function staff, who were now going over every piece of evidence collected so far to find anything they'd missed. Could have missed.

Rob slipped his jacket off and rolled his shirt sleeves up. He stood in the middle of the room and addressed the team. "The goal posts haven't moved. The death toll doesn't change our focus, which is to catch whoever is responsible for these crimes."

The room was listening.

"Your determination and resolve *will* make a difference. It will stop this man, because he isn't done yet. Our task is to find him and bring him to justice before he completes his mission, whatever that mission is. He is hell-bent on revenge, and only we can stop him."

The room had stopped. The team knew what needed doing. There was no lack of effort. No lack of vigour. Rob knew it and his tone told the team he knew it too. He chose to impart his words more wisely and more empathetically than his superiors had chosen to do with him. He wanted his team to feel valued, to keep spirits and energy levels as high as they could be at a time like this. Making them feel inferior and inadequate now would kill their work. Their critical work.

Rob carried on. "Our focus remains on finding Daniel Mortimer, and at a senior level that will continue to be the case. We need to go over everything we have, the full background, again and again. When he went off radar. Why he went off the radar."

The team nodded; it was a task already being vigorously worked on.

"In addition, we have been granted access to sophisticated software that will allow us to review and recognise facial similarities. A number of you won't have come across it during an active investigation before, but we've been investigating the possibility that Daniel Mortimer is engaged at a professional level in the city and is hiding in plain sight. This has been sanctioned at the highest level of the police force, by local government and GCHQ. They have our back, so stay focused and we'll crack this. This team will solve these crimes."

Rob himself was spitting out the words by the end. He felt the raw emotion in his own delivery. The passion and care in his voice was deafening. The room was stone dead. Nicky was surprised Rob had chosen now to disclose the information at such a sensitive point of the investigation, and was certain it hadn't already been sanctioned by Rob's superiors. She also knew the power of inclusion, and that if the team knew they were being trusted with key information at such a critical time, as well as what measures were going on behind the scenes, it would spur them on. Motivate them.

They needed it today.

CHAPTER 38

Becky had promised Jen she'd call the team as soon as she knew anything on the tox screening that was ongoing across town. The office had settled back down following Rob's impassioned team talk and was bristling nicely when Jen's phone vibrated on her desk. Becky Ryan's smiling face filled the screen of her iPhone; Jen answered the call with her headphones in, whilst still reading a document on her laptop.

A short Tinder update ensued, with debate about the weirdos, the definite 'no's and the potentials for a casual encounter. Jen regaled a short story about one guy she'd met recently in a pub whose profile picture must have been taken about a decade ago. About three stones ago, too. She'd passed a comment on it. He'd got upset, asked her for a blowjob and then left, disappointed.

Becky loved a Tinder update. The extended version and juicy details would follow at the next social meet, but in the meantime, Becky had an update for Jen.

"So we've completed the full toxicology tests and had some initial results. They're saying a lot, Jen. It may be worth hooking up Google Hangouts in Rob's office and getting Nicky and Jack on it too."

"Ok, cool, give me five minutes and we'll dial you in. See you shortly."

It took Jen less than five minutes to get Nicky and Rob together and into Rob's office, and just a couple more to summon three coffees from Jack, who then wandered in. Jen was dialling in on the TV screen Rob had on his wall for such occasions. The team tended to use conference calls, but had started to use Google Hangouts as a free and easy way to host a meeting where they could see each other, as opposed to just a bland, impersonal voice call.

Jack was doling the coffees out as Becky appeared on the screen to a cheer from Jen. Becky was alone and Rob and the team adjusted their chairs to ensure they were all in Becky's view. In the picture.

"Good to go, Becky," Jen shared with a thumbs-up and a 'whoop whoop'.

Becky shared her outline of the developments for the benefit of the wider room, repeating the fact that more in-depth tests remained ongoing, before sharing the bones of what she had.

"There were a number of needle marks on the body, which were inflicted during the fatal assault on Charles Worth. In addition, we found traces of Propofol in the bloodstream."

Becky could see the blank looks on the faces of her audience on her laptop. The benefit of being able to see faces and gauge reactions.

"It's a barbiturate, and is also a very common anaesthetic. It's also identical to the substance found in Joe Davies' body, so we're dealing with the same MO. He was incapacitated before the assault started, so he was a sitting duck, the same as Joe Davies was."

Becky looked at the room once more. She had their full attention and with no questions forthcoming she carried on.

"The bit where it gets interesting, and different from Joe Davies' murder, is that there were additional needle marks, and we identified traces of Provigil in his system too. Now this is different in that this likely would have revived him, reinvigorated his system and made him stay conscious for longer. He'd have been able to feel for longer, his nervous system unable to shut down."

Becky checked in with the room again, taking in the faces and reactions of the four officers in front of her. On screen at least. She could see them processing what she'd just shared.

"So the second drug revived our victim so he could suffer more?" Rob asked, knowing the answer already but saying it out loud to clarify for the room.

"Exactly that. It's a sadistic use of a drug. It also caused a patchy rash on his skin, which is why we thought it was there and were able to test for and identify it so quickly. It wasn't an abrasion, just a reaction to the drug. It's used to treat narcolepsy in the mainstream, but it's been widely abused by people who want to stay awake against the will of their bodies. Students, festival goers, ravers. Lorry drivers, at one stage."

Rob wanted to summarise. "This is the second killing where drugs have been used to inebriate the victim, with William the only exception. What we now have is another drug used that made Charles Worth recover consciousness, allowing the attack to continue."

Rob checked the screen to see Becky nodding in full agreement. She responded.

"It's another evolution. We saw the subtle changes made for the Joe Davies killing, but we saw an earlier departure from the pain than the killer would have wanted. It would have annoyed him, aggravated him. Joe Davies escaped the pain that Charles Worth was made to sit through. And then sit through some more. There was no early death for Charles Worth, and even unconsciousness didn't save him. The killer prepared measures that meant this murder was endured to its full extent."

The surprise was etched on Jen's face. Jack's too. Neither had experienced this level of human perversion before, not first-hand anyway. It's different when you're exposed to the details. When you've seen the bodies. Society knows what the Wests did, but only a small group of people got to see the house, smell the fear in the walls and sense the horror in that basement.

Becky added her final view of the drugs used during the attack.

"Usually, once unconsciousness has set in, the pain threshold falls, and only if you cease and desist, or even treat the patient, will the body recover enough to regain consciousness. Our man wasn't that patient so wanted to inflict enough pain to cause unconsciousness, but then medically stimulate consciousness so the assault could go on in the knowledge that pain would still be felt."

What had happened to Charles Worth was slowly sinking in, and the level at which the killer was devolving and tailoring his method of killing was about to become a serious concern to the team, if it hadn't hit home already.

Becky could see by the expressions on their faces that the officers were struggling to fully understand the depravity and extent of what had happened in Loughborough, in Charles Worth's front room less than forty-eight hours ago. With no one chipping in, she added an afterthought.

"It's not uncommon in the tortures of some drug informants or those who haven't been loyal to a cartel. I've seen cases of it in Columbia, Mexico and South Africa, where the drug gangs rule with pure fear, and victims have been tortured and revived like this for days. Either until they give up the information they have or just so they can suffer for longer."

Rob took the point but added, "Yes, but this isn't Columbia, Becky. It's Leicester city."

CHAPTER 39

Rob started the day by sharing the news that the search for Daniel Mortimer hadn't so far detected any visual similarities at the locations in the city where there was hope of a result, and that he'd had the authority to widen the search area.

The day had started in a more positive fashion for Nicky and Jen. With Daniel Mortimer still in the wind, they'd been working away on a theory that Elizabeth Harris had less reason to hide and was therefore eminently more findable.

Nicky knew it was something of a needle in a haystack, but had developed a list of potential candidates. Rob had asked her to keep it quiet, so she'd enlisted Jen and Jack to work on it. Several hundred names had been whittled down to a few credibles. Jack had then been able to use bank records, as well as trace official records which had got them down to a single suspect; Elizabeth Warren. The name had belonged to a seventy-nine-year-old woman who had died in April 1992, less than twelve months after Daniel Mortimer had been released and only two after Paul's death, but at that time had been miraculously resurrected. Nobody, seemingly, had noticed. Jack had started to data mine into the digital side of the now

Elizabeth Warren's life, and was satisfied enough to have gone and sat outside her house in Enderby with Jen for a couple of hours. The woman they saw was easily identifiable as an aged version of the Elizabeth Harris they had a photograph of, and they'd left her untouched for further surveillance as instructed, while Rob and the team held out for the bigger prize.

With the past forty-eight hours proving fruitless, Jen and Nicky were on their way to execute a search warrant and an arrest. The initial charge of identity theft and fraud was bolted on. Jack had more than enough evidence to make that stick. He'd even managed to acquire dental records from the late eighties in order to prove who she is. Who she was.

The bigger plan involving an otherwise law-abiding citizen, with no criminal record under either pseudonym, was to leverage the charge against what she knew. The levels of expectation were mixed amongst those who knew the plan, but Nicky and Jack would take the interview, and Jen would oversee the search warrant in Enderby. Nice and tight.

The arrest was clean and went well. It was a knock on the door with the warrant presented to her. No broken door, no home invasion. She'd almost looked relieved, and came across as a quiet and pleasant woman. Normal. She'd be a different character to interview than those who had been on the list of people of interest so far in the case. Jen had started the search at the house with a small team. It was a very ordinary house in suburbia. Average in every way. Jen wasn't sure what she'd find, if anything. A long shot, but the investigation was at long-shot stage.

It was 9am before the interview got underway. Elizabeth Harris, who she'd been arrested as, had accepted the offer of a duty solicitor, and after a short private discussion with him was ready to talk. Rob watched intently from his office, the interview hooked up to his flat screen.

Nicky cut to the chase and laid out the bare facts on the table. Irrefutable facts. A decent lawyer might struggle with this, let alone the half-wit who was sat cross-legged and silently opposite Jack.

Jack spelled out very clearly the detail and data they had, including the dental records. He then made it very clear that their core investigation was into the murders of the three men her late husband had once called friends.

"Have you seen, spoken to or heard from Daniel Mortimer within the last six months?" Jack asked very clearly and very articulately. Then he sat staring at Elizabeth Harris. Inviting a response. Waiting for it.

Rob was impressed. He sat watching. Waiting.

Elizabeth Harris sighed deeply. She looked at the solicitor who didn't respond.

"I haven't *seen* him for years," came the start of the reply.

Jack and Nicky continued their gaze. An awkward silence. They sensed there was more.

"He contacted me by email." It followed heavily, a response she really hadn't wanted to give. Knowing her phone and laptop would have been removed from her house shortly after she was, what she was now sharing seemed more of a pragmatic decision than a voluntary one.

Rob was already on the phone to the director of forensics; Justin Lennox, a tall Richard Osman lookalike from Leeds. Whatever their workload, it was about to be dropped like a stone.

Jack continued, "Could you describe your relationship with Daniel Mortimer, both in 1992 and now, please?"

"Now?" she asked, seemingly in shock at the suggestion of a current relationship. Elizabeth came across as a woman who wasn't comfortable in this environment, any more so than she would have been as the wife of a convicted thief. "I don't have a relationship with him now. I haven't seen him for years."

"And in '92?" Jack continued to dig. He wanted to hear the answer. Needed to.

The pause hung heavily in the air. The words were hard to release; she didn't want to say them. They crept out reluctantly.

"We had an affair." A hint of embarrassment came with them.

"He came to the house a few times when it turned out they were preparing for a job. He was charming and educated and he complimented me. It was flattering and I fell for him. He was that sort of man."

Rob had half tuned out. He had the first confirmation of Daniel Mortimer being alive, and better still, there was an email. A digital footprint.

Nicky and Jack continued the interview. Elizabeth went on to reveal details of a short affair that she believed was love. Daniel had helped her to get a new identity and had gifted her a large cash sum that she thought was to start their new life together. Away from it all. In reality, it ended not long after it had started, and Daniel disappeared as easily as he'd slipped into Elizabeth's life. Like a tornado; short and destructive. She recalled feeling foolish. They were looking for a sociopath.

She'd spoken with less emotion about what she knew about the rest of the men. She hated Charlie and Joe, that was easy to believe, and she'd only met William on a few occasions, but recalled a pleasant enough character who she always felt seemed out of place.

She explained how, at a low point in her life and as a widow with little to her name, she'd used the money to buy her house in Enderby under her assumed name, one that Daniel had helped her to get, as well as cut all ties with the very few people she had known. No family, no children and a widow. It had been easy to cut ties from friends who had turned their backs when her husband's occupation had got out and into the mainstream. She had the opportunity for a clean break. A fresh start. Far too good an opportunity to miss. She took it.

She spoke more fluidly as she became less apprehensive about her surroundings. Her solicitor was happy enough to let her talk, and with the evidence of her identity irrefutable, she was now just helping the police with their enquiries. She had admitted an affair with an armed robber, as well as having been married to one. Rock bottom had happened a long time ago, and admitting it was just raking up the memories that had long since been buried in a dark corner of Elizabeth Warren's mind.

She'd gone on and had been employed for the rest of her working life, something she spoke about with more comfort. More pride. She'd settled down well after what must have been a traumatic experience of a marriage and an affair, then a court case, incarceration, prison visits and widowhood. The slight woman in front of them simply didn't fit the bill. She was decent. She denied ever seeing any of the spoils, other than some cash from Daniel, and Jack believed her. The Proceeds of Crime Act didn't exist then, and neither did money laundering diligence on property deposits. With the mortgage fully settled and paid up, that sleeping dog would lie.

"I got nothing from Paul, not that I wanted it. Maybe Daniel had more than he should have. I simply didn't ask."

It made sense. She had learned quickly that Paul was in bed with some bad people, but while the bills were being paid and Paul was either stable or happy she turned a blind eye.

Nicky and Jack let her talk as she continued to tell her story. They listened intently as she talked more of her limited exposure to what she came to learn was a criminal gang, and not just her husband's 'friends'. She volunteered that Paul knew William from a local cricket club. Both had played briefly and they'd lived nearer to one another at that point, with the two men sharing a beer from time to time.

Jack asked her casually how Paul had met Charlie and Joe. He dropped it into the conversation seamlessly and left it hanging in the room. Elizabeth pondered, thought about it, then with a furrowed brow said she didn't know, but thought that it was something to do with William.

"Paul had never met them and got involved through William. I'm sure that's how they got Paul involved. I trusted William, quite liked him, but he got in with the wrong crowd, and then got Paul mixed up in it too. He owed them for something, I'm not sure what, and they used it to get William involved with what they were doing. Paul knew William and was probably just in the wrong place at the wrong time."

Elizabeth smiled, knowing she probably just looked like a weak-minded housewife making excuses for what her husband did. Irrespective of his mental state and his illness, he knew what he was doing. Knew it was wrong. So did she.

Nicky looked happy. She felt that she'd just learned some of the links that until now were only tenuous or suspected, or not known at all. That digging would carry on outside of these four walls.

"Do you know what he owed, Elizabeth? Or who he owed it to?"

"No I don't, sorry. I think it was to Joe but I'm not sure. The way Paul described it was that Joe pulled William's strings and Charlie did most of the overall planning for the jobs."

With the interview at a stable point and with Elizabeth Warren unlikely to flee the country, Jack looked at Nicky, who nodded, ready for the tape to be paused.

"The one I really didn't like was Alan Reynolds."

Elizabeth dropped it in like an afterthought. An FYI. She wasn't aware of the bomb she'd just laid on the table. Nicky struggled to keep her usual poker face straight.

"Sorry, how do you mean?"

"Well, William brought him round to the house a couple of times, no more than that, but he was a little shit." Elizabeth was a well-spoken woman of ageing years, but she spoke the words with an edge and more than a hint of malice. "He was a teenager but he was a horrible child. Vile. He went bad long before his dad; he was just horrible and fitted in with the worst of them more than his dad ever did. William either brought him as he was lumbered with him, or he felt that Alan wasn't out of place amongst them."

Nicky was still struggling, the incredulity written large across her face.

"So he was in on it? The plan? The robberies?"

"I don't know as I tended to disappear out of the way quickly, especially if Joe or Charlie were about, but he was there so I guess he was involved, or certainly had knowledge of what they were planning. I recall asking Paul once as I thought it was odd. He said Joe didn't want Alan to have anything to do with it; he was young and far too petulant, but William was indebted to him so he just hung around. Paul said that William was always apprehensive and didn't say much, he just listened and did as he was told largely, and there were times when they had to physically remove Alan, who had more to say than a young man of his age should have, especially in that company. Crazy, really, to think that Alan wanted in and William wanted out."

CHAPTER 40

"So William Reynolds and Paul Harris were cricket buddies."

Rob sounded surprised. It was sometimes difficult to envisage somebody you only knew after death or as a younger man, let alone an athlete or a sportsman. It was always difficult to picture an ageing criminal in poor health running about, carefree. Especially with the time lapse.

The same was true of Paul Harris. Jen still held sympathy for a man only brought to life from prison and court documents, and a few old photographs. A man whose life had been challenging from a number of perspectives. His psychological demons and mental illness during a period of low social tolerance; of low understanding, and during periods of recession and high unemployment. Not to mention that the people who would become his friends ultimately led him down a path of no return.

Jen found contentment with a picture of a young Paul Harris running around a cricket field on a Saturday afternoon. Part of a team. A proper one. Running around in the sun. Enjoying himself. Free.

Rob got the marker pen out. He loved adding their

learnings to the board, lines to show the progress with the links displayed visually.

"I don't think there's any value in pursuing the initial links between Charlie and Joe. They were criminals. They were in each other's circle and would have been robbing and pillaging in the same places and at the same time. Could have been a natural meet between two like-minded men."

Nicky, Jen and Jack all nodded their approval. A thick black line was etched between Charlie's and Joe's names and their mugshots. Rob then added a similar line between Paul Harris and William Reynolds, along with the word 'cricket' above it. He then added a third line, albeit a dotted one, between William Reynolds and Joe Davies. On that line he added the word 'DEBT?' in capital letters.

"So the bits we don't know are what William Reynolds 'owed' Joe Davies for to get himself involved in the underworld, and at what point this man joined the fray." Rob stabbed at Daniel Mortimer's name, adding several large black blobs to the board in the process. "He was another outsider, and if he was a criminal he wasn't of the same ilk as Charlie or Joe, so how did he get roped in? Did he owe one of them too? Or was he a more willing accomplice?"

The phone on Rob's desk started to ring. Rob looked at Jack, who picked up the phone on the hot desk and intercepted the call.

Nicky and Jen were already getting up. Getting ready. They had been looking forward to this moment.

"Alan Reynolds is downstairs, Gov. Just been booked for obstruction."

Rob and Jack would continue their lines of inquiry while Nicky and Jen had another dig with Alan Reynolds.

He'd already requested the duty solicitor and with his abrupt arrest half an hour ago, he knew he wasn't back here for a friendly chat. Rob had the live link on and Jack would hover near enough to enjoy the stream of questions and the 'sport' of what was about to ensue downstairs in a sterile interview room.

Jack was sifting through documents pertaining to Daniel Mortimer's time in Gartree. The degree, the training. Useful skills. Skills he wouldn't be able to use or claim under a different name. Jack continued to ponder how he could live a life under an assumed name, but with a range of qualifications and training under his birth name.

Downstairs, Nicky opened up pleasantly enough, asking Alan if he'd ever donned his whites and joined his dad at the local cricket club. Alan looked surprised at the line of questioning, and after looking at his brief, who shrugged at him, decided to play along. Entertain them.

"Once or twice," came the irreverent reply, followed with, "wasn't really my thing, though."

"What was your thing then, Alan?" asked Jen.

"You know. This and that,"

The small-talk tennis continued before Nicky's boredom quickly set in.

"Does that include robbery planning with your dad and his mates, Alan?"

Alan's facial expression quickly changed and he opted to ignore the question.

"We know you were present when your dad met with the rest of the gang to plan the heists. Only Joe Davies wasn't too happy about it, because you weren't his cup of tea, were you?"

Alan swallowed hard and looked guilty.

"Your dad and Paul were cricket mates. That's nice. But we're not sure why your dad felt compelled to join the gang." It wasn't really a question, more of an invitation. Nicky and Jen weren't sure if he'd take it.

Silence.

"Your dad owed Joe Davies. Enough to agree to carry out two robberies with him. For him. Now he's dead, and I think you know why."

Silence.

"Who are you protecting, Alan? Yourself? It isn't your dad. Way too late for him. The men most likely to have wanted him dead have also been brutally murdered. Slowly, and painfully murdered. Somebody doesn't like what they did, Alan. What you did, and I think you know who it might be."

Alan Reynolds squirmed in the chair. Nicky and Jen relished the moment as a bead of sweat formed on his forehead.

"And worse for you, Alan, we think the killer knows who you are."

He continued to look heavily uncomfortable. He wanted to talk. His brief raised a hand but Alan had started to spill out the words, "I don't know who it is. I really don't."

"Do you feel safe at night, Alan?" Jen asked quickly, enjoying the look of fear on his face. "Do you feel responsible?"

He looked shell-shocked. Like a boxer who was taking a pounding but was still on his feet.

"What were you digging for on the allotment?" The question followed quickly and was like a punch to the head.

Alan held a hand up, temporarily stopping the fight. He took a swig of his coffee and pondered his response, palpably considering whether to share what he knew, or some of what he knew, with the two women in front of him, or take his chances with whatever the bigger picture was. Whoever it was.

His solicitor leant in to offer some advice, but Alan Reynolds wasn't listening.

"I was looking for a stash of watches."

Nicky took a sip of her coffee. Waited patiently.

"I knew what was happening, and I know how the robberies were planned. Joe and Charlie planned them well, really well, and they went down well too. It was afterwards that got messy. The spoils weren't split cleanly and Joe realised he'd stitched himself up, but by that point Daniel had a load of cash, and Dad had a shitload of watches that turned out to be more valuable than anyone knew."

It was the first admission of discontent amongst the gang. The valuables hadn't been a straight cut, and the inequality caused a rift.

"So what did you do with them, Alan?"

"Dad was scared. He was in deep and it wasn't his thing. I suggested he hide them at the allotment in case Joe came knocking, which he did. We managed to sell a few, but then Dad buried a stash of them at some point to hide them further, and all was forgotten. Until you came knocking, anyway, and raked all this up. Then I remembered where I thought they were and realised if they were in good nick they could still be worth a few quid. They were nice watches."

Nicky and Jen were satisfied enough with the response, without showing it. Nicky reminded Alan that he was a teenager at the time and wasn't directly involved, and that any accusation against him on the robberies had long since been beaten by the statute of limitations. They were on his side. The mood had softened. Alan was talking.

"How did your dad get involved, Alan? *Why* did your dad get involved?"

Alan swallowed hard again. But he'd started talking and almost looked relieved to finally be sharing a secret his father had taken to his grave.

"I got involved with the wrong crowd at a young age. I was dealing by the time I got to secondary school. Small time stuff at first, just some skunk, bit of weed. Y'know, the normal. But it escalated and I was dealing LSD and ecstasy within a year or two."

There were no surprises in the revelation, and the caution on Alan's criminal record for selling drugs as a thirteen year old was already in the domain of the team.

"I sold drugs to one lad who reacted badly. He ended up in hospital. His name was Chris Davies. He was in my class and he started fitting and blacked out."

"Chris Davies?" Nicky said loudly and clearly.

She'd met Chris Davies after his dad had been murdered. Only briefly, to notify him as the next of kin. Now married, living fifty miles away and with a crystal-clear alibi for the night that his own father had been murdered, as well as the other victims. A man who was well clear of his father's murky shadow; married and decent. Honest. Employed and working nights. He'd been on CCTV at his workplace, a warehouse in Nottingham at the time, and with no apparent motive or means had been excluded almost immediately as a suspect or a potential victim. He had no reason to be involved in his fathers death, and from the conversation Nicky had had with him, he'd got as far away as possible at a young age to build his own life. The apple had fallen a long way from the tree.

Alan continued to talk. "I took a kicking for it. Not sure

who from but I could hazard a pretty good guess. But then they wanted to know who I was getting the gear from. I thought at first they wanted me to deal for them too. Joe was looking at scaling down the violence of the robberies; they were getting too much attention. It was the late punk era heading into the nineties; everybody wanted new drugs and I had them. It was an easier way to make cash than to keep holding up jewellers, and we could have all scaled up."

Jen wasn't sure if Alan Reynolds had been this honest in decades, even to himself.

"I agreed, but Dad had got involved. He threatened me, but I think even then he knew it was fruitless. I was arrested for supplying the drugs to Chris, but his name was withheld and Dad gave me an alibi, so it was dropped. He really didn't want to, but he was trying to keep me on the straight and narrow. He hadn't given up by that point. Joe held it over my dad and said he'd either make our family pay or make sure that we suffered for what I'd done to Chris."

Nicky was pleased with where this was going. The duty brief had been shit again, which had helped, plus they'd got Alan on the right day. She offered him another coffee and even asked if he wanted to take a break. He accepted the coffee.

"It seemed ok at first. I ran some errands for Joe, but then they started planning the robberies and they told dad he needed to do it to clean his slate with them. Dad really didn't want to do it. He shouldn't have done it. I wanted to be in the gang and wanted to keep dad out, but he fitted the bill. Joe was the sort of character who enjoyed punishing people and loved having people who owed him so he could manipulate them. Dad resisted and tried everything to not do it, but they needed a driver. The compromise was that he didn't have to enter any of the buildings. There was no CCTV at the time so he thought that if he did it and kept his head down he'd be ok."

The interview reached a natural lull. Nicky and Jen let it sit, allowed Alan to catch his breath. He didn't look done and Nicky and Jen weren't either. Then, as Elizabeth Warren had done twenty-four hours earlier, he spilled the last of his secrets.

"There was a third robbery. A plan for a fourth, too, but that never happened. Another jewellers in the city went down after the second one but before they all got nicked. The third robbery was lower key, and they were starting to split by that point. The police could never prove it was them. It was different, smaller. Only three of them went to that raid and your lot didn't know who to charge for it, or link it well enough to get anything to stick. The deal in the end was for them to plead guilty to the two robberies and the charges would be dropped for the third."

"Was your dad involved in the third robbery, Alan?"

"He said he wasn't, and I believed him. I think him and Paul were shut out by that point, but I couldn't say for definite."

"Alan, do you know where the third robbery took place?"

"No, I don't know." He looked genuine.

"Ok, do you know *when* the third robbery took place?"

The look on his face told Nicky and Jen that he might do. He decided to chance his arm.

"So could we drop the obstruction charges now, then?"

CHAPTER 41

Rob couldn't hide a tinge of disappointment from the team. He'd become convinced that Daniel Mortimer was heavily involved in the case, perhaps entirely, but as a bare minimum he had a plethora of questions to answer.

After a positive twenty-four hours, which had seen Elizabeth Warren questioned and acknowledge the existence of Daniel Mortimer, and Alan Reynolds being re-questioned and sharing new information, Rob had hoped for something *quicker*. He was under pressure. Nicky was happier with their position, and knew the leads could be picked at. She knew progress was happening in real time and was keeping an upbeat front to Jen, Jack and the wider team.

Alan Reynolds had given as detailed a description of Daniel Mortimer as he could remember, along with several character traits that seemed to align with Elizabeth Warren's recollection of him. He'd stated categorically that he didn't know who he was, didn't know how he'd got involved and hadn't heard from him since one night at Paul Harris' house several decades ago. The team's initial reaction was to believe his version of events. He'd been honest on everything else, and given that Daniel

Mortimer was currently the person most likely to be trying to hunt down the gang and their associates, Alan had a powerful motivator to share information if he had it; to save his own skin.

Rob was continuing to harass the team, who were currently digging into the online life of Elizabeth Warren. His impatience failed to appreciate the level of skill and effort required to isolate the required metadata, to separate the bits that may be useful from the Amazon orders for cutlery. To clear the wood from the trees, and then dig into the specifics of the interesting bits.

Rob had asked Jack to investigate the unsolved third heist from the archives, and pull all and any detail relating to it. The robbery that never was. Until now. More new information, a new crime, albeit one never attributed to the gang of men whose names still stood out, written large and bold in the middle of the board.

WILLIAM REYNOLDS

JOE DAVIES

CHARLES WORTH

PAUL HARRIS

DANIEL MORTIMER

"Well, it's either Mortimer or we're fucking missing something."

Rob's outburst wasn't surprising, and was nothing that hadn't been discussed in corridors and toilets and on lunch breaks amongst the wider members of the team. Jumping to the endgame, maybe, but with Mortimer being the only member of the gang still alive, it was an obvious conclusion, given Paul Harris' death from natural causes, and with the other three accounted for.

"While we're waiting for the techies, I want us to keep digging. I still think we've missed something."

Rob's propensity to keep battering away was a strong trait. He had clear views on who he wanted in custody, but he was far from ruling out that Daniel Mortimer was just the last in a growing line of suspects. He hated being presumptuous.

Jack had been assigned the third robbery and was about to go digging, something he was becoming very proficient at. An eye for detail and the default position of not trusting anybody was developing, and Rob was confident he'd find something.

The links were starting to fall out. Shaking Elizabeth Warren's tree provided the link between Paul and William, as well as the tenuous outline of the debt William owed to Joe, something Alan had finally coughed up. Rob wondered how much of this simply wouldn't be happening if Alan Reynolds hadn't sold pills to Chris Davies all those years ago. Twenty quid here and there that to date has cost three lives. Expensive quick bucks.

The missing link in every which way was still Daniel Mortimer. They had limited past case history, just a handful of details about the time he served at Gartree, and still nothing close to evidential as to how he met and became involved with any of the other four men. Even the physical description was patchy and most likely dated. Paul Harris seemed to be the strongest credible candidate for a link, but that was nothing more than a deduction, and in truth the team still didn't have a clue. Even Elizabeth Warren seemed to know little about the man she'd fallen for and taken a significant sum of money from.

A ghost doing a very good job of hiding.

Rob was working on some new theories. In his mind, at least. The relatives list the team had found for the old crimes had been completely fruitless; there was no clear or obvious candidate from the assorted victims, no clear motivators for revenge. Nobody, other than Alan Reynolds knew anything about the possibility of some goods of value still being out in the world.

Rob pondered, thinking that a few buried Rolexes wouldn't have caused this. It was much more personal to whoever was committing these crimes. It meant something.

Jack was already straining at the leash. The prospect of new leads starting to appear and a third heist that the team were never charged with was juicy, and right in his wheelhouse. The fact that the link hadn't been found could be a cause for concern, but in truth a number of internal factors could account for that. No charges were ever brought, and Alan Reynolds' recollection of this robbery was one of a three-man effort.

CHAPTER 42

I feel tired today. Lethargic. I am not a morning person, never have been. My Fitbit didn't register me being awake before 10am yesterday, despite the fact I started work at eight. It's sometimes problematic in my line of work, but people don't always notice what's right in front of them. Only caffeine and food will stir the senses and get me going today. A croissant will do it. A chocolate one.

Things are going well. I can still go about my daily business like a regular civilian, blending in. Carrying on. People in coffee shops and supermarkets are nice to me, smile at me. Unaware of my elevated status. Unaware of who I really am. I like that.

I'm still showing horror when conversation of the murders comes up. Feigning how appalled I am by the senseless killings. It's been quiet these last few days. The press are continuing to hound the police, and with Brexit gaining pace, some cabinet resignations and some other local politics taking some column inches, I'm barely on the brink of being unmasked. Of being found out. I'm trying not to be arrogant about it, but I am now the City Slayer. I'm not sure it's my favourite but it's a phrase that's being used abundantly. How we love a nickname. I've always thought it sounds like an old word. *Slayed. Slayer.* I'm not fucking Buffy. There hasn't been a murder in a good few days, and after a brisk spell for me, it's not like I can stop now; I still have unfinished business. The plan gets sketchier from here on in, but only I know that.

I feel satisfied enough. The empire could have crumbled by now, it could have gone wrong, I always knew that. Only it hasn't. I'm 'still at large', as the Mercury worded it yesterday, and I still have my plan. Incomplete vengeance is no result, so the show will go on. Joe and Charlie were fun, they helped with the healing, but I set out to wipe them out. All of them. Although I'm struggling to find this one, he's doing a good job of hiding. I was hoping that with his mates going down like rats on a ship he'd slip up, stick his head above the parapet and reveal himself. Only he hasn't. Yet.

I'm on the fly now so this could be more testing. I'll need to adapt. Be more versatile than I have been so far. There'll be no recon next time, no sitting outside a house for weeks planning my 'in', planning the attack, no learning the territory and honing the best way to kill.

A blitz attack will be different. Maybe it'll be fun. I'll test myself. I have got one new focus anyway, that's a real bonus. That one will be staked out, watched and planned for. It'll either throw the police right off the scent or help them out, so I just need to decide on the order and see what falls out over the coming days. My itch to kill isn't fever pitch like it was after Joe Davies. I'm almost content.

I haven't planned much for the aftermath in terms of my life. I'm no suicide killer and won't be bailing out. I'm either getting away with this scot-free, I'm going down for it, or I need to find door number three and bail. Brazil is the front runner, and my go bag and fake passports are stashed already. Just some loose ends stand between me and an early retirement to Rio.

Three down, two to go.

CHAPTER 43

"Good morning, all," Rob shouted. He repeated his welcome for the benefit of those who hadn't heard him. "Settle down and listen up everybody!" Rob bellowed to get the attention of all those who had gathered to hear the breaking news.

There was an energy in the room and a real buzz. Word had spread across the station like wildfire, without the full details being known, but those whose recent weeks had been spent dedicated to this investigation knew this morning was important. There was going to be a revelation that might change the course of the team's focus over the coming days. The proverbial crossroads.

Nicky hadn't seen this many officers in the room since the second murder, when proceedings were stepped up and the response needed to be measured in people and resource. When it needed to be seen.

Jen was scanning the room too. She met the eyes of Emma Sharpe and Bernie Copp, who were standing together towards the back of the room. Emma nodded at Jen, who smiled back. Everybody of note was in the room.

"The tech guys have been working hard; trying to track our missing man. There was some complexity with it, but Elizabeth Harris' laptop has given up its secrets. The team have been picking at a couple of scabs, and they've been able to reverse engineer the metadata." Rob spoke clearly and loudly, looking at a number of people as he explained the findings. "There were several emails of note from an encrypted email address, which had been rerouted, so they were harder to trace than regular communication. This guy is good, but our guys are better."

Rob nodded. The masses in the room were stretching and leaning to get a better view, like a rake of middle-aged men standing on the terrace of an old-fashioned football ground. Vying for position.

"It has taken a while but they have a hit. *We* have a hit. They've traced the emails back to an IP address, and more importantly, a specific location."

The room rippled with anticipation. A few conversations started and palpable excitement broke out. Rob's raised left hand seemed to stop a full outburst, a combination of celebration and relief.

"This is a major step but it isn't fully cut and dry, so listen up!"

The room died back down. Seldom was a piece of information black and white, clean. Just another piece of information leading to more work leading to more information. A crawl towards the finish line. Baby steps.

Rob continued his explanation, consciously not wanting to take any edge off the positive news he'd just shared. He'd been speaking to his contact, Justin at the tech facility overnight. The explanation and discussion had focused mainly on location. The IP address used had been consistent for all of the emails, which was generally good news, but the address had been isolated to an internet cafe just outside of Liverpool Lime Street station, and had needed more work.

The last twenty-four hours had been a furious high-level effort to affirm the identity of Daniel Mortimer, using the highest powers the state had at its disposal. Rob's cards were close to his chest. The variables too great to risk.

The cafe itself had no CCTV, one of the likely reasons for its selection, and Rob had been working to establish whether Liverpool was a dot on a journey or a place Daniel Mortimer now called home.

Rob's relationship with his Merseyside counterpart had helped the efforts, as had his scouse heritage, but the work of DCI James Crofts' team had plotted the IP address and times against CCTV in the locale, and they'd got a hit. One that matched closely enough the facial features of an aged graphic of the man being hunted, found on two CCTV feeds within fifteen minutes of the emails being sent to Elizabeth Warren, walking north, away from Lime Street. Away from the heart of the city and Liverpool ONE, but crucially past a tight and popular area around the Liverpool Empire, where the same face had been found twice on a security feed. The right description, the right place and at the right time. No coincidence.

From those crumbs, his mobile phone had been accessed and triangulated, and located at what the Merseyside Constabulary now believed was Daniel Mortimer's home address.

Twelve Field Street was a regular looking house on a regular looking street. Normal. Jen pulled its image from Google Street view up on the screen behind Rob, as he continued to share the direction of the investigation that was now jointly happening over a hundred miles away.

Rob pointed at the red brick terrace on the screen behind him. "We believe this is Daniel Mortimer's house. We believe he lives alone. He isn't married and, as you'll see from the map shortly, he'll have walked from his house to the internet cafe. His house, ironically, is less than 500 yards from St Anne Street Police Station, and only a quarter of a mile from the Royal University Hospital, where we believe he's employed as a radiologist."

A raised hand from the masses broke the flow. Rob looked up and gestured to the individual with his hand raised to share his mind.

"So is he in custody, Sir? Has he been arrested on suspicion of the murders?"

The question was fair. The nods and murmurs from around the room always showed when the thought shared was a common one.

Rob responded with what could be construed as a negative response in a clear manner. "Daniel Mortimer is *not* in custody as we speak." He enunciated 'not' to avoid any confusion. To ensure those who might have misheard didn't have an excuse to put their feet or up disappear to the pub to celebrate the win. Rob continued.

"There are still many unanswered questions about this man."

Rob started to half point at the screen again, then realised there wasn't an image of Mortimer on it for him to address. Even he hadn't seen an image yet, but he knew pictures of Daniel Mortimer were now in the domain of the authorities. DCI Croft had promised to have an image over by 9am, a deadline that had not yet passed, and Rob was itching to see the face of the man who had been so elusive thus far. He was desperate to share it with the team whose efforts had also failed to track him down.

"Daniel Mortimer is currently under full surveillance by Merseyside Constabulary. They have eyes on him, they have his phone tapped and they can trace his whereabouts through his laptop and through his iPhone, as well as through the hospital CCTV when he's at work. For the first time, we're on the front foot!"

Rob had felt some relief when he'd hung up from the phone conversation late last night. Relief that a positive identification had been made, and relief that, although the still faceless suspect was working for the NHS, that it wasn't at one of Leicester's hospitals or healthcare facilities. It wasn't on his watch.

He'd smiled later that night at home, when he realised that until that point he had been getting desperate. He'd organised a sample of Daniel Mortimer's DNA from evidence, which Nicky and Jen had arranged with the help of Gary Hunt at Gartree. He'd even considered some form of localised DNA testing in the same way one of his predecessors, Detective David Baker, had done so three decades previously when trying to apprehend Colin Pitchfork. Alec Jeffreys' DNA breakthrough and methods of testing had become a viable option to Rob. Desperate times.

"The news is great, but for us as a team there are still a significant number of unanswered questions. If Mortimer is the man, has he been travelling up and down the motorway to kill and then return? And if so, has he been doing that while working around his shifts? All of this is still breaking. We're continuing to work on his phone to see where else that's been, but until then the 'fit' isn't perfect, so we're keeping him under watch to see what he's up to. If he isn't our man then we are merely protecting him, and if he is our perp we'll be standing on his coat-tails waiting for him to show us his true colours."

There was a pregnant pause. With no immediate questions aired, Rob confirmed that the operation was ongoing and had the full backing and authority of the chief constables from both forces. All resources were going into this, and there would be no respite for the Leicestershire team in the coming twenty-four hours.

Rob nodded and looked at Nicky. Nicky stood up, ignored the several hands which had now raised and started to speak, stating that a team of officers was required to travel to Liverpool to support the Merseyside force, and carry out the arrest. To continue the operation, just in a different county and in different surroundings. The hands dropped as Nicky confirmed the requirements, as those with their hands raised started to realise what was required of them, and it became crystal clear what the next steps looked like.

One hand remained in the air. Nicky stretched to see that it was PC Emma Sharpe with her hand up. She josticulated, inviting the question.

"Yes, Emma."

"Are we able to volunteer please, or will this be assigned? And secondly, if it isn't Daniel Mortimer, are we continuing to work on other lines of inquiry?"

It was a fair question. Leaving all of your eggs in a solitary basket is seldom a good idea, especially with such uncertainty still in play.

"A contingent will need to remain in Leicester and look after the consolidated efforts here and the ongoing investigation into a possible third robbery carried out by the gang, as well as all and any key outstanding leads."

Emma's hand went up again.

"What do we know about the third robbery at this stage, please?"

"At this stage, not a lot, which is why we're treating it as a priority. It may have nothing to do with the murders; it may mean everything."

Rob stood up and addressed the room. "This is major progress so you should all be pleased that your work has got us to this point. There are still a lot of unknowns, so stay focused and we'll get over the line. Nicky and Jen will assign the resource over the coming days for the operation. There are shift requirements here and a need to be in Liverpool for a short period of time. We'll be flexible if we need to be, but the expectation of you is high."

The murmurs started around the room. Like any team of people, there were those straining at the leash to be involved, some who'd be doing all they could to keep their heads down and stay in Leicester, and a few inbetweeners. The non-committals.

Nicky and Jen had had a chat offline around who were the right people to go to Liverpool. Those with the right skill set, or the right traits. Jack had been involved too to ensure there was a credible team to continue the Leicester end of the work.

Bernie voiced a question to the front of the room. "What's his assumed name then, Gov? Who are we going to get?"

The room murmured again. An appreciation for the question.

Rob had no issue in sharing the name. The Merseyside force already had it in their domain and there was now nothing classified that prevented the name going out. With some of the links that existed online and between different forces and personnel, it was already possible, if not highly likely, that there were more in the room than Rob, Nicky, Jen and Jack who already knew the pseudonym of the man they'd been trying to find.

"Briefing packs will be issued out to you all, but our man is now trading as Johnathan Christopher Alexander. We've already established his employment records and property are registered under this name, so we now need to keep unpicking his alias and the last two decades of his life.

Daniel Mortimer had made a mistake, and for the first time Rob knew where he was. And to make it even better, he had eyes on him.

CHAPTER 44

It was mid-afternoon before information packs had been fully issued and digested, along with a combination of Burger King and Subway take-outs. Wrappers and Coke cans littered the office, but they would be cleared more easily than the pungent smell of meaty baguettes and quarter pounders filling the room.

The positive buzz remained, and Rob was happy to ignore the smell for the energy and the vibe it had created. The officers who had been assigned or had volunteered to travel had been afforded the time to collect belongings and prepare for the forthcoming phase of the investigation. The chance to apprehend an individual in a separate county with the co-operation of another force was something few of the team had any experience of, and Rob knew that for Jack especially this was big. To continue the search for a man who had proved more than elusive, had kept his head down and stayed strong despite the national coverage and the clear knowledge that he was being hunted. A wanted man. But the net was now closing, and fast.

Bernie Copp had been assigned, having played a key support role throughout the investigation, but to Rob's and

Nicky's surprise he'd been vocal and defensive, making excuses about not being able to travel, feeling unwell and not being prepared or able to be a part of the effort in Liverpool.

Rob's face had shown his utter disdain, but after a short and contemptuous exchange he'd batted him away without so much as a fight, which had surprised Nicky. She'd questioned Rob afterwards, not wanting to question his authority in open forum, but he'd argued the point that the days of strong-arming people were largely in the past. Energy is finite. Pick your battles. He also made the point that he didn't want somebody who didn't want to be there in his ranks at such a critical time. He needed a team who was engaged and on board with what was happening, and he was happier to leave behind a straggler than take a passenger.

Fair call, Nicky had thought.

Emma Sharpe was scheduled on leave, and was unable to attend. Rob was disappointed. He'd been keen to have her in his ranks, as she'd been highly involved and shown willing throughout the investigation. There was a dogged determination in her work that Rob liked, but she'd taken some time and he was respectful of it. Some junior officers had also taken some time following the earlier crime scenes. The force needed to be seen to support its officers, and the HR team had had a busy few weeks.

Rob was happy with the core team that had been chosen and had assembled, and he'd advised those travelling that the chief constable had been speaking to his counterpart, and therefore some local support would be available and numbers would be good. Covert surveillance was in operation already, although on an arm's-length basis to avoid suspicion, but any mistake would be pounced on from this point onwards.

"We need to get on the road, team, let's move!"

Rob was getting restless and didn't want to be kicking around Leicester. He'd already geared himself up for a shit journey, one he'd done countless times between his adopted home city and his place of birth. M69, M6. Sounded simple. Never was. Even the assumption that you could get past Fosse Park without stacking up was complacent, and with evening rush hour approaching, the team needed to move.

"Jen, grab your stuff and let's go! Jack, you too!"

Nicky was also getting restless. She had an energy that was making her edgy, and she wanted to be on the road. Heading north.

The team had agreed to rendezvous at one of Merseyside Police's key stations, opposite the Royal Albert Dock and at the heart of the waterfront and the Cavern Quarter. Jack was looking forward to it, having never been on Merseyside, although there'd be no beers and good times on Mathew Street tonight. Not for him, anyway. Another time.

Jack and Jen were travelling with Nicky, the Mondeo proving the preferred option as Jen had already thrown all of her belongings in Nicky's boot, although there was still plenty of space leftover. PC Keith Wainwright had volunteered and was travelling with two other uniformed officers who were in plain clothes for the trip, and Rob was travelling alone. Partly so he could make a number of calls, some of which would no doubt be for his ears only, but mostly because anybody who'd travelled with him in the past wasn't queuing up for round two.

Bottles of water, Diet Coke and chewing gum were already being passed around Nicky's car, with food hitting the discussion almost immediately.

"I'm not stopping at Corley, so don't even ask!"

Nicky liked to get some miles under her belt before stopping on any long journey, and she didn't feel inclined to stop at the first services barely twenty miles up the M6. Jen was hoping to manipulate a visit to a butcher's and bakery place she knew, an artisan cafe offering top-notch food that was broadly en route, but she'd drop that in later when stomachs were growling, but before hangry had set in.

Tinder also came up quickly. Nicky brought it up, usually for entertainment. For a woman of her experience and wisdom, she seemed to find interviewing rapists easier than the concept of dating in the 21st century. She was glad to be married and, although a career woman, she'd be glad to be back at home in a few days with her husband and the dogs.

Jack had inexplicably owned up to dating a girl, something he'd kept to himself for a few weeks, but being in a confined space with two vivacious women for several hours was akin to having lights shined in your eyes. The interrogation started immediately.

He confessed to having had a number of dates and already having the girlfriend discussion. Nicky and Jen clambered over one another to get the questions in. What was she like? Did he have pictures? How old? They came thick and fast. Jen was half turned around in the seat and Jack could feel Nicky's eyes piercing him in the rear-view mirror. He picked up one of the bottles of water rolling around the foot-well and took a swig, realising he was warm. He still had about an hour and a half of the interrogation left.

He took another large swig and realised he should've asked Rob for a lift.

CHAPTER 45

It was late in the evening before the team arrived on Merseyside, parked up and made their way into central HQ. It was dark but not cold, and yawns were being stifled across the team. Rucksacks were slung on shoulders and the last to arrive were still arching backs and cracking knees whilst being ushered inside, the remnants of car cramp well settled into joints.

The station was visually similar to Lodge House, only without the obvious disrepair; it was of a similar age, a brick and concrete mix, and was sitting in the shadows of the contemporary and cultural parts of the city. The Royal Albert Dock, Liverpool ONE and John Lewis shone brightly next door, making the police station look decidedly out of place, the contrast stark.

The team were greeted and ushered into a large brightly lit room, which provided a shock to the eyes after three hours of darkness in the backs of cars. Handshakes and introductions created a murmur as counterparts met for the first time, and although Rob had acknowledged Nicky on arrival, he'd disappeared into an office with a figure who Nicky had assumed was DCI James Croft. Nicky had started her own introductions; the welcome was hospitable, considering both the hour and the nature of the meeting.

DS Alison Smith was a larger than life character. Nicky liked her as soon as she said 'hello' in a broad Liverpudlian accent. She'd offered a flat white as if she knew Nicky was partial to one, and in a way an old friend would ask. At this time of day Nicky was usually caffeine free, but following the drive and the fact they'd stopped at what seemed to be the only services without a Starbucks or a Costa, a flat white sounded irresistible. The food had been very good, the drinks selection less so. Score draw on Jen's recommendation.

The energy in the room was interesting. The hour was not an uncommon one for a police officer of a certain rank, but caffeine and nicotine were both contributing to the hum, and officers who had been strangers only a few days ago, and had become email acquaintances, were now meeting face to face. Nicky had many such acquaintances; some she'd known for years, had horse-traded favours and information with, but in many cases she had still never met them. A friend without a face. A digital relationship.

Nicky scoured the room, looking at the officers, thinking it must feel strange to them. To read about an ongoing murder investigation and see the headlines, and then become embroiled in it with the missing link living on their patch. Tabloid newspapers, TV news and social media were all loud with the coverage, but being a story over a hundred miles away, it would warrant a quick scan before heading off to the gym. Forgotten in an instant. *That serial killer in Leicester.*

The room had become fluid, almost like the evening part of a wedding, or a speed-dating night. There were lots of introductions, small talk and 'nice to meet you's, before moving onto the next person and seeing what their interest in the case was, who they were and whether you'd emailed them in the last week. Nicky had already heard the phrase 'nice to put a face to the name' several times over and had decided she wouldn't be using it. She hated small talk and wanted to crack on. Plus she wanted some sleep, knowing tomorrow would be busy. Demanding.

Alison ushered Nicky into her office. She left the door open but the noise became more distant, even through a thin partition wall. The coffee was on the desk steaming away, and Nicky mouthed a very genuine 'thank you'.

"Operation update?" It was a question of sorts from DS Smith, but was also rhetorical in nature. Nicky sipped on her coffee as Alison continued. "The teams will be briefed this evening before close. My DC; Edward Butterfield-Berridge will take the brief, but our man is tucked up at home as far as we can see."

Nicky was still swallowing that name. She'd seen it on several emails but to hear it out loud was interesting. She wasn't a fan of double-barrelling names on the whole, and this one wasn't going to do much to change that view.

"Johnathan Alexander – we're using his assumed name, but your man Daniel Mortimer – has worked a shift until early this evening, picked up a takeaway and a bottle of Malbec from a Tesco Metro and headed home. He walked in his front door just before 8pm and hasn't emerged since. We've got a visual on his front door, albeit from a soft distance, but he's in there. His calls and messages are being intercepted and other than some chatter on a hospital WhatsApp group he seems to be having a quiet night in, alone."

Nicky shrugged. "Well, it is Wednesday."

Alison laughed and gave Nicky a knowing look that said she'd rather be at home too. Nicky had clocked a lack of a wedding ring. Maybe a divorcee, maybe she'd never married. Maybe she'd been happy in a relationship for years and was one of the growing number who just didn't feel inclined to tie the knot. Either way, she'd rather be at home, but Nicky knew there were some loose ends to tie up tonight. The intricacies of roles and jurisdiction for the morning. Make sure everybody was crystal clear and there'd be no mistakes. The powers that be had decided enough was enough and had issued an arrest and search warrant. Everybody needed to go to sleep knowing exactly what was expected of them at 6am tomorrow morning.

Nicky stood up to lead the charge. "Are you ready?" Her question was equally rhetorical.

Alison nodded all the same. "Let's get this done, then we can all go and get some kip."

CHAPTER 46

It barely felt like a couple of hours had passed since they'd last been in the room, since they'd wrapped up the brief for the operation that they were now here to execute. Arms were being stretched, backs cracked. The yawns were wide and the early morning coffee was strong.

The tension in the room was palpable. A real nervous vibe, which was a contrast from the previous evening, when the energy level was one of tired anticipation. There was a mix of experience in the room, with a group of people who didn't know each other from Adam. They didn't know how they'd each react in the environment they were about to enter. Training is always consistent. People are not.

Nicky knew how Jen would react, but the rest of the unit were unknown. Even Jack was still relatively unknown as she'd gone through a lot less front doors with him than she had with Jen. You become a different person. The situation, the energy. It morphs you. Nicky knew some placid guys who turned into the Hulk with a dawn raid in front of them, and vice versa.

Jen would like to be as close to the front as possible, adrenalin-fuelled, wanting in on the action, but her DS status required a different level of responsibility . Her youth still provided a feisty edge, a fiery nature. She wanted to shout her way in and ride the wave. The rush. Something Nicky used to enjoy herself, but she was now happy to let those with the desire and drive to go charging in. Happy to wander in afterwards and gently clamber over a shattered door, shortly after anyone from within the property has been dragged out in cuffs. Usually in their underpants and half asleep. Always a treat.

The time had come. The convoy of vans and cars quietly rolled out of the station adjacent to the Albert Dock, and in the shadows of Liverpool ONE. A Thursday morning, the streets near-deserted at this hour with the exception of a few night workers making their way home. The odd taxi was still lurking, waiting to pick up a committed clubber who had overdone it and wandered away from Mathew Street. Often a young woman carrying her shoes.

Nicky and Jen were travelling the short distance in an unmarked car, an Audi S3 Sportback saloon, driven by DS Alison Smith. Nicky liked it, and was switching her gaze between the Audi's interior and the shiny surroundings of an area she recalled to be less glamorous.

Inhaling the still-new car smell of the Audi was awakening her senses. The aroma of the fabric of the seats and the still-clean carpets and foot-wells. Nicky decided she needed to upgrade.

Alison Smith was in a buoyant mood. She had an energy similar to Nicky's and was smartly dressed with her hair up. Professional and ready to go, but with the aura of a woman who, like Nicky, was used to this side of the job and was equally happy to hang back and oversee the raid. She had earned the position she held and enjoyed the fact it didn't demand she be front and centre.

The journey was quiet. The radio's digital display showed Radio Two, but the sound was turned down. Nicky sat reflectively, and could sense a different energy in Jen, who she knew would prefer to be three or four cars in front. Enjoying the coalface. Relishing it.

Jack was in the car in front, the convoy reflecting the hierarchy in visual form, with a number of marked police vehicles and several vans leading the way. The local boys would be going in first.

Rob remained in the station with DCI James Croft to oversee the arrest; standard procedure with two experienced detective sergeants at the helm and en route to the scene. Rob would listen in over the radio and have access to the body-cams of the lead officers, who would carry out the raid and execute the arrest. He was already comfy in James' office, surrounded by monitors and tech that were considerably savvier than those in his office at Lodge House. Rob had his own tinge of envy, but like Nicky was comfortable with the fact that his rank didn't require him to leave the station this morning, exceptional circumstances aside.

The route to Field Street had been predetermined last night, and had been recommended by James Croft. A loop through the centre, past the large frontage of Liverpool's Lime Street Station, before heading up St Anne Street, a wide promenade of beautiful Edwardian architecture. The cars leading the way had turned off, and were heading towards St Anne Street police station, a small community station and one whose officers had been watching the house since the discovery of Johnathan Alexander several days ago.

Nicky knew the house was close and the journey was short. The roads and route had been clearly displayed last night during the brief, providing those from the Midlands with a mental note of the timings. Only another mile or so, with a small maze of red brick terraces the 'tell' that the scene was close.

A radio crackled and broke the silence in Alison Smith's Audi. The lead units disclosing that they were one minute away and had relieved the officers of duty who had been watching the house for the previous twelve hours. They would now be driving away from Field Street to the north side, with the raid team turning into the narrow Field Street from the south, another detail that had been agreed last night.

Alison gestured with her right hand as she slowed the Audi and followed the Lexus of DC Edward Butterfield-Berridge into Field Street. The vehicles were all parked in a straight line, with the lead vehicle around fifty yards from the front door.

The morning was cold but clear, and Nicky climbed out of the car and onto the pavement with Jen next to her. Jen nudged Nicky's arm and offered her chewing gum. She was already chomping hard, trying to channel the energy and keep herself from rushing to the door and smashing it in herself.

The lead officers quickly exited their vans and scurried up the narrow pavement between the houses and the parked cars of the residents, who were still tucked up inside the row of terraces that formed Field Street.

A dozen or so officers formed the lead block, each with a protective black helmet, making them look more military than domestic police.

Alison Smith picked a jacket off the back seat of her car and slipped it on. She leaned against the car, standing a large black radio on the roof so Jen and Nicky could listen to what was happening only yards up the street. They'd positioned themselves so they could see the officers from behind, but the best information they'd be getting would be over the radio, with little in the way of a visual.

Back at the station, Rob had a better view of proceedings than Nicky and Jen had. His eyes fixed on the screen, a picture less grainy than he was expecting showed the street as the commanding officer of the entry team, Sergeant Daniel Letts, ran towards the front door. The camera fixed to his breast was bobbing up and down, the motion accompanied by the sound of heavy boots striking the pavement.

Letts stopped outside Number twelve. The camera swung around as he looked at the rest of his team. The man behind him, Sergeant Matt Haddock, was carrying the enforcer, and the bright red steel bar flashed across an otherwise dull screen. Rob flicked a glance to James Croft, then back to the screen.

In the street, Nicky looked at Jen. She was on tiptoes, straining to get a view. Nicky looked at Alison then moved a few inches closer to the radio, breathing out cold air, her hands tucked tightly into her coat pockets.

Letts looked at Haddock, who had positioned himself against the wooden door, which was old and would offer little resistance. The rest of the team stood behind him, arms on each other's shoulders to space themselves. Dan stood to one side, raised a hand with three fingers and carried out a short and silent countdown.

His closed fist signalled entry. Haddock smashed the door hard with the 'key'. It buckled immediately, splintering in the frame and falling inwards as the officers behind him stormed in. The energy level erupted. The adrenalin poured.

Jen could see the team flood into the house one after another from her viewpoint, as the silence was broken with loud and clear shouts of 'POLICE, STAY WHERE YOU ARE!' The street emptied as officers burst into the house. Several curtains started to twitch from some of the windows across the street. Jen watched Dan Letts become the last member of the unit to enter the house.

The radio crackled. Alison flicked the frequency to clear it.

Rob saw the hallway. Dark and unclear. The screen black and filled with shadows. The staircase was just about visible in the darkness. James Croft had split the screen to show multiple cameras as officers flowed into different rooms of the house.

Nicky and Jen heard the stairs thump as officers ran up them, heading for the bedrooms, expecting to find a sleeping suspect. The thumping slowed down as officers filled a number of rooms within the house. A number of shouts of 'CLEAR' came from those which were empty. The volume subsided temporarily, the motion in the house fell.

One section hadn't reported a clear room. The team who had headed to the back of the house were quiet. Too quiet. Croft enlarged the screen, focusing squarely on the camera of one of the men who had headed into the kitchen. A dark and cramped area. The camera flickered in scarce light as shadows and figures flashed across the screen. The officer stood still as he looked at what was before him. He stared. The camera stared with him.

Rob struggled to get a view in the light but instinctively knew what he was looking at. He mouthed a 'fuck' to James Croft.

The radio crackled. Dan Letts' voice broke the interference, his intonation flat. "Code Black, DS Smith. We need you guys in here."

The three women outside looked at one another, then started to run up the street, reaching the house together. Alison Smith entered first. She was ushered right into the lounge and towards the back of the house, around a corner and into a small kitchen/dining area.

Nicky and Jen followed her. The house had fallen eerily quiet, and there was still very little light in the room. A curtain had been opened in the lounge, but the morning was dull and afforded little light, just enough to allow the body of Daniel Mortimer to come into view on the floor of the kitchen. Beaten. Bloodied.

Dan Letts stood next to Alison Smith and opened another curtain covering a small window, to allow another fraction of early morning light to enter the house.

The light hit Rob's screen in the station, and he could now see clearly what he'd already thought he had seen.

Nicky looked at Jen.

"Fuck."

CHAPTER 47

Rob had a brief conversation with DCI James Croft before leaving the central police station and driving away from the Albert Dock. His mood was sombre for good reason and he was glad to be alone. Thinking. Gathering his thoughts. He'd spoken to Nicky and Jen who would remain at the house with Jack and support Alison Smith. Sort the immediate aftermath. The mess.

The pathology team had been notified and would be at the house imminently. All over it. Rob had requested that Becky Ryan be permitted to carry out the post-mortem in a local facility, a request James Croft was entitled to reject but, given the complexity of the circumstances, had agreed to.

Croft would also be reporting the events of the last hour, and of the last forty-eight hours, to the Merseyside hierarchy, and in turn the Independent Office for Police Conduct. Any death that had occurred either in police custody or of a suspect on or under the watch of an authority was referable. This was also an embarrassment, and Croft knew he'd have to answer a raft of questions from his superiors, mainly around how a murder of an individual could happen with several officers under his command sitting outside the front door. Sitting. Watching.

Rob had shaken Croft's hand and left the station when the situation presented itself, with both knowing that Rob's continued presence at the station could be viewed unfavourably, or even as collusion, by the IOPC. Neither wanted that. Neither needed that.

The murder of Daniel Mortimer would now be investigated in conjunction with the three unsolved murders, a twist Rob hadn't foreseen when he woke up in the early hours of this morning. He'd half expected to close a case that he would now be having a very different discussion with the assistant chief constable about. A conversation he was no longer looking forward to. It was a call he would make shortly, which would eat into the miles as Rob headed back towards the M6 with the early morning roads still clear. Small mercies.

Rob had spoken to Becky. His call had woken her up, but he needed her up and travelling. He thought he may even pass her on the lower section of the M6 later on, all being well, somewhere near Walsall or Villa Park. Becky had told Rob she'd be about four hours before hitting Merseyside. Leighton Buzzard to Liverpool was a good distance to cover, especially as she'd been rudely awoken and hadn't had the benefit of the early start.

He'd spoken to Nicky too. She knew what needed doing. Knew that Rob would head back to Leicester. Knew he couldn't interfere with a secondary investigation outside of their jurisdiction, especially given the inevitable involvement of the IOPC. The investigation was causing enough of a shitstorm, and the Merseyside team would need to account for their own house.

Comfortable that his house was in order, or as in order as it would get today, Rob sat back in the seat of his car and let out a deep sigh. He wasn't one to procrastinate, but he was in the moment.

He used his voice control to dial Assistant Chief Constable Laura Mathers, a highly political operator. A slick, classy and highly articulate woman, she had climbed the ladder quickly. She was well respected amongst her peers and had always been fair with Rob, had never knowingly stitched him up, but she was ACC for a reason and it wasn't her ability to make friends that had got her there. She was political. She had been earmarked for ACC for years, a rank that Rob had stopped aspiring to.

The phone hit the third ring as the call was answered.

"Good morning, Chief Inspector Rhone," came a very formal answer.

"Good morning, Ma'am," replied Rob, mirroring the standard set. This call warranted that. "I need to report a section 140 outside of my jurisdiction and pertaining to an investigation under my command." He continued before the questions and the rest of the fallout started, the formalities remained heavy in his tone. "The suspect, known to us as Daniel Mortimer, was found deceased at his home address shortly after 0600 hours in Field Street, Liverpool, this morning. He'd been murdered, with the initial signs indicating the murder was carried out by the same individual responsible for the three unsolved deaths in Leicestershire."

"Rob…" came the inevitable interjection. "What the fuck happened?"

The mood dropped and the formality was washed away in a sentence.

"Somebody got to him, Ma'am." Rob sighed inside, the weight of the case sitting squarely on his shoulders.

"Who got to him, Rob?"

"An unknown suspect managed to access Mortimer in his own home, undetected, and past a police surveillance unit sitting across the street. Nobody moved, nobody batted an eyelid. Nobody heard anything."

"Who's dealing with the fallout?"

"DCI James Croft is escalating at his end."

Laura Mathers knew full well there'd be a significant shit-storm from this. Detectives had idly sat thirty yards from where a suspect had walked through his own front door, and in the time in between his entry and the raid had sat dormant. Waiting. Regardless of the details, which would be lost amongst the politics, the police had sat by while a murder was carried out under their noses. The press would add their spin. Embarrassing. Incompetent. Blundering. The tabloids might even drag out a cartoon artist to knock up a graphic. Obese coppers laughing and eating doughnuts while a crook sneaks out behind them with a swag bag.

ACC Mathers would no doubt 'co-operate fully' in any internal review, but would very much play her own political game. Rob knew she was more than capable. She was ACC for a reason. It was a position reserved for the astute, the savvy and the politically aware. Leicestershire wouldn't directly get the flack for this, it wasn't on their watch, so that storm would rain over Merseyside, but to the media the police are the police, and she'd be playing that game. Had probably already started.

The part of the conversation that remained unsaid was how a murder suspect had himself been murdered.

The information that he was a suspect had been passed by Leicestershire to Merseyside. A suspect. Not a target. Polarity at its most extreme.

Mathers knew her counterpart would be playing the game too. The sheer inaccuracy of the information supplied by Leicestershire. How they'd have responded immediately and secured a target, how they'd have made an arrest had the correct information been given, or been given more promptly.

Rob didn't care much for the bureaucracy. He had a fourth dead body on his hands and still didn't have an answer. The most recent body being the prime suspect made the weight even heavier. The prime suspect now being on a slab had really fucked up his morning.

"So what's *your* plan, Rob?" The politician in Mathers flooded the question. How will *you* deal with this so it doesn't make *me* look like shit?

Rob chewed on his bottom lip, resenting the question. "We need to escalate the conversation we had previously, Ma'am. Either the perp clocked a police presence, or the perp knew there was a police presence and was able to plan for it."

Rob spoke as bluntly as he dared to. He was referring to a conversation he'd last had with Mathers not forty-eight hours ago. An unease had festered within, and was now continuing to pulse given the events of the morning. Rob had shared a conversation with Nicky, and subsequently with Laura Mathers, as to the possibility of an insider. A mole. Either directly or through collusion. Parts of the killer's behaviour showed exceptional levels of planning and more than a slice of good fortune, to the point of being suspicious.

"Agreed," came the response. "Come and see me this afternoon when you're back. I've set an internal review and will flag your concern to the IOPC at our end immediately so it doesn't look like we've sat on it."

Rob was comfortable with the position, but heard the emphasis on '*your* concern' in the question. If there was police involvement and the email trails showed that Rob had raised a concern, a delay of any length before a report was filed with the IOPC would look poor. The longer the delay, the worse the optics got. It would look like a hatchet job, like Rob and Mathers had buried it. There would be no winners there.

Mathers hung up the call and Rob turned his radio down to silent as it cut back in. Radio Two. Zoe Ball was on holiday and some DJ he'd never heard of was filling in. He needed time to think.

Rob felt the access that the killer had, and the way in which the victims had been targeted showed an individual with great resource and knowledge. Maybe too much. That suspicion had not been quashed by the murder of Daniel Mortimer, under the noses of two police forces shortly before his scheduled 'arrest' this morning.

It was far too fortuitous, far too slick an operation for anybody to have carried it out on the fly. Even remotely ad hoc. There was far too much skill involved, and the murderer had gone about their business in the way a military operation would have approached it. Subtle, under the radar and with great proficiency, and if not military or medically trained, the killer knew how to detect and avoid a police operation. Or they *were* police. The thought had occurred to Rob. A horrible thought. An unease that a murderer seemed just a bit too well informed. Was a bit too lucky.

He was glad he'd had the conversation with Mathers. He'd covered his own arse and just wanted a clear focus on catching the killer. The task still at hand. For him, anyway. He'd call Nicky later and schedule a session with his senior team, but for now he needed the head space.

He'd wait for Becky's official report, but the killing had the same MO. It hadn't looked as identical as the other three, the body was lying face down on the floor for a start, but the hallmarks all looked to have been there.

Nobody heard a thing.

There was blood. A lot of blood. Rob couldn't see it fully on the screen, it was a dark mix of blood and shadows barely visible in poor light, but Nicky's account had been descriptive. His initial text once he'd seen the body said 'Ear? Fingers?'

He got 'Yes, both' back.

The hunter had become the hunted, only it was now evident that Daniel Mortimer may never have been the hunter.

Rob tapped the steering wheel, laid his head back onto the head rest and sighed loudly to himself.

Despite the proliferation of the murders, there was no longer a suspect, let alone a prime one.

Rob took a piece of chewing gum from a pack he had in his door pocket and started to chew hard, realising immediately he'd bought the strong minty type as the wave ripped through his sinuses. Harsh without having a cold.

Alan Reynolds was coming back in. No doubt about it. There was something in that man's brain. That poisoned and abused brain. Something in there he probably didn't even know was critical that could unlock the case. Maybe hypnotherapy would help to revive the past, but would he agree to it?

Paul Harris was still a niggle in Rob's mind, without him knowing why. He'd questioned his death, which was proven beyond doubt to be from natural causes, and they'd questioned

Elizabeth under caution. Rob hadn't warmed to her remotely, but she had a frailty and vulnerability that simply wasn't congruent with the violence and beatings. She wasn't strong enough. Was she?

The thought that Rob was juggling was that the killer wasn't even on the radar. A name that hadn't yet shown itself as a suspect, witness or passer-by. The scary thought that the killer was so well buried, and not even close to being apprehended, was on par with the suggestion that the killer had police knowledge. Operational knowledge.

Rob needed to shake some trees. The investigation was stalling and there was a level of complacency that he wasn't happy with. Everybody had become *comfy*, and Rob was pissed off with himself for allowing it to happen.

He'd spend the rest of the day getting his thoughts in a row, and throw some fucks into the team who weren't pulling their weight tomorrow morning. Those who weren't now about to come under a secondary internal investigation. Bernie Copp was front and centre, he'd ducked out of the raid and spent two days on the sick, which had seemed flimsy at the time. Now it just looked suspicious.

Alan Reynolds. Elizabeth Harris. Bernie Copp. They were all going to have a shit day tomorrow. Rob would make sure of it.

He tossed the new suspect theory about in his head. Thought about anybody who knew all five suspects and was still alive. Who may have a grudge.

Gary Hunt came to mind. The jobs-worth prison officer. Liaison. Whatever he was. Did it fit? He was capable. He wasn't big but he'd have been trained in how to defend himself as a minimum. But why? Did he know where the stash was? Was he in debt? Either financially or to one of the men? To Joe? Rob wasn't ruling it out. He'd have Nicky look into it. She'd enjoy that. New possibilities needed to be considered.

Rob turned the radio back up. *Riptide* by Vance Joy. He turned the volume up further and put his foot down, as he continued to make good progress south towards Wolverhampton.

CHAPTER 48

Rob ran his right hand across his stubble, which had grown longer than he usually allowed it to get. He realised it was bordering on becoming a short beard and made a mental note to trim it later on. It was the result of a busy few days, and a round trip that had been one to remember, for all the wrong reasons.

Becky was in the process of conducting the post-mortem at the Royal Liverpool University Hospital, along with a local team to support her within their jurisdiction. Rob wasn't expecting much in the way of forensics. The killer had proved far too smart to be sloppy thus far, even at a scene that was notably different to the previous three. An individual capable of committing a murder under the noses of a police surveillance unit was not an amateur, and was unlikely to be making common mistakes. Optimism still held a candle, but Rob was working on the assumption that Becky and forensics would largely draw a blank.

He knew the murders would need solving by other means. He needed fresh evidence, he needed to find the link, and it wasn't going to be coughed up on a plate.

Nicky and Jen had travelled back from Merseyside with Jack, and were leading a team session in Lodge House; a review of the still unsolved crimes. The frustration was clear amongst all involved. With the suspect pool now accounted for in full, next steps was a review of each of the four murders, and a re-visit of everything the team knew so far. Or thought they knew. The evidence gathered was significant; the task was to find the key piece that had been missed or overlooked.

Rob had distanced himself from the session. He needed to be clear of it. There was an undertone to the investigation that he didn't like. Didn't trust. And it was now being played out across various media channels, with political stakes increasing by the hour. The melting pot was full, bubbling away, and Rob felt no closer to unmasking the killer now than he did when he had first set foot into William Reynolds' bungalow several weeks ago.

Taking a step away was the right thing to do. Rob needed to look at the investigation, almost from the outside. With fresh eyes and whilst not in the middle of it, where emotions and opinions were raging. It is always easy to be defensive, or even blind, when it's your work, but easier to be objective when you've taken a step back.

Rob was having to play his own political game too. He was well aware of the shit-storm that was shrouding the investigation, and although nothing had been directly received in terms of a taunting letter or a 'catch me if you can' message, it felt as if the killer was mocking the force. Provoking them further with every murder, for their inability to find him.

Rob was playing a political game with ACC Laura Mathers and Chief Constable David Parker, both of whom had assured him 'everything possible' was being done and 'all resources needed' would be available.

Rob didn't doubt it; he knew the public line. He was also aware there'd be a political price to pay for this, and it could well be his career. The one that got away. The one that fucked it up completely.

He'd discussed the possibility of inside knowledge with Laura Mathers previously. Had it recorded, too, and backed up on an Apple Mac at home – non-police issue – and Rob knew he could use it to cover his arse if needed. He was never sure if it was strictly legal, GDPR and all that, but he'd cross that bridge later, when the brown stuff was neck deep and Mathers was 'unable to recall' the conversation.

Rob had Bernie Copp in his sights. He'd pissed him off by not going to Liverpool, and now Rob was actively looking into why that may have been. Or whether he had travelled up separately and was on the wrong side of Daniel Mortimer's front door.

It was a new line of inquiry, even for Rob. He'd had to arrest colleagues before. Thieves. Blackmailers. A rapist. But a police officer murderer had always seemed a stretch, let alone a serial killer. Something that happened in the States, or on the silver screen. Not in Leicester.

Mathers was in agreement and supported the line of inquiry. She'd also approved a search of mobile phone masts for all cellular activity in the Liverpool area before and after the murder, in conjunction with Merseyside and with the approval of the IOPC. Rob was comfortable that the sub-investigation was being conducted appropriately, although the wider investigation remained compromised, and would become subject to full investigation by the IOPC when the dust had settled. Lessons would need to be learned.

Rob's contemplation was broken by his phone vibrating

in his pocket. He slid it out to see Becky Ryan's cheerful face adorning the screen, and he slid the green icon to take the call.

"Miss Ryan."

"Mr Rhone."

The tone was playful, something of a break from a pensive twenty-four hours.

"How's it going, Becky?"

"It's going ok. Nothing to surprise you yet. Sorry. We're not fully complete and have tox tests to run to establish any chemical involvement, but this one looks *simpler*. Less finesse."

There was a pause. Rob hadn't seen Becky at the house; they'd crossed paths somewhere on the M6, but he felt sure the mood at the scene would have been poor.

"You know three of Croft's team were sat outside, right?"

"So I'd heard."

"It's a fucking mess, Becky. A real mess and we need to get a grip of it. I need anything you can give me. Anything at all. Blood spatter, DNA, hair, a fragment of something. I'd take anything."

Rob was desperate and Becky knew it. She knew the magnitude of what was happening, and although Rob was SIO, this was beginning to reflect on the wider force. The whole of it. She suggested a review of the post-mortems as a collective. A discussion of four murders as opposed to individual post-mortems on a timeline. Rob's team were now circling and going back over what they had found. Becky felt the time was right to do the same with her work, and Rob agreed. Look at it again. See something, find something, interpret it differently. He'd arrange a time to go through it with her in the coming forty-eight hours, when both were back in the city and some of the dust had settled. A small amount at least.

"Well, I just wanted to let you know we're making progress here, and to check you're ok."

Rob appreciated the call, and was grateful for a cheerful tone. It had been a few days since he'd heard one.

"Thanks, Becky, I'll talk to you later."

Rob thought about calling Nicky but knew she'd let him know as soon as she knew anything salient. She was desperate for a breakthrough too, but was managing Jen and Jack well. Keeping them focused. Keeping them motivated.

Rob was deciding in his mind how he wanted the next twenty-four hours to play out. He wanted to be in control. Needed to be. The investigation and the killer were humming the tune and everybody, to a man, was dancing to it. The pool of people was small and so were his options.

Alan Reynolds was top of the pile. He was coming back in regardless. Rob still felt strongly that he wasn't the man. He didn't fit. Not smart enough, maybe not strong enough. Needles wouldn't be his thing either, he was a blunt instrument in every way, but Rob needed to mine him, find a way to open up dialogue, help him to recall something, make him want to dig deep into his memory banks, and share something that may open up the case. Of all the people to be reliant on, Alan Reynolds was not the man of choice. But choices were limited.

Elizabeth Harris was coming back in too. Jen and Jack were already looking into where she'd been the previous evening, digitally at least; and although, like Alan Reynolds, she wasn't top of the suspect board, she was fast becoming a survivor amongst a plethora of murder victims. She'd been married to one of the gang and had had an affair with last night's victim. She was too weak, surely? She wasn't a big lady, she had nothing on her, plus she was well into her sixties. Even with the needles, the murders needed some force. They were big men who wouldn't have gone down without a fight.

Rob had even considered a team, or a couple, who were going at the men. He'd considered whether Alan Reynolds could have teamed up with Elizabeth Harris, or somebody else. A pact to free up the cash for mutual gain. But the options just didn't look viable.

Rob wanted Elizabeth Harris to be told of the death of Daniel Mortimer in a controlled environment. See how she reacted. See what she said. How she responded. She was another protagonist who, like Alan Reynolds, might know something. Something seemingly unimportant and from decades ago that was now causing somebody to butcher the gang, one by one.

Bernie Copp was the real thorn. Yes, he'd pissed Rob off, which wouldn't prove to be a strong career move, but with the line of inquiry now almost certainly proving that the killer had more information than they should have, an inside man looked likely. The way they'd navigated Field Street last night was just too slick, and although Joe Davies' murder was similar; it was a regular house on a regular terraced street, Joe's house had a side entry that would have been the natural route to take for the killer. Plus there weren't police officers sitting outside.

Daniel Mortimer's house was a mid-terrace. There was no rear alley, so to even get to the back door meant fence climbing and garden surfing, which should have meant noise. Security lights. Somebody must have seen something.

Rob knew uniforms from Merseyside had been banging on every door, and forensics would be scouring the gardens to trace back to the point of entry. Hopeful of a fibre on a splinter of a fence panel, a shoe print in a border. Blood.

The whole thing just looked like the killer had gone in the way they did because they *knew* there was a police presence to the front of the house. How they'd then got in was still unknown too. There was no sign of forced entry as the door was still in pristine condition, yet the killer clearly hadn't just knocked on a back door. Or had they?

The skill level was evolving. The killer was showing a deftness that concerned Rob massively. The ability to stay undetected. To lay in the shadows. The only way the killer could have known of a police presence last night was if they were operating from inside the force. If they were one of them. An insider showing exceptional levels of skills, and exceptional levels of dedication to find and execute a criminal gang. Ruthlessly. Efficiently. The thought was horrifying but happening. This wasn't just a serial killer; the evidence seemed to be pointing to the killer having a warrant card.

Rob continued to scrawl on the pad in front of him. A list of names, options he felt were credible. Alan Reynolds had motive, so did Elizabeth Harris, but did they really have the opportunity? If there was an inside element it would explain the opportunity, and the way the killer had been able to access Field Street.

Rob wrote 'MOTIVE?' in capital letters on the pad. He was still missing something.

CHAPTER 49

Rob had slept well. A solid six hours, and in his own bed, had prepared him well for today. Feeling energised and with his plan decided in his own mind, he set out early with a strong focus. He was determined to crack some heads during the course of the day, metaphorically at least, and to try to throw some light into the darkness.

Today was big for the team, a co-ordinated effort to break some of the characters still in the game. Still alive.

He'd arrived at the office early. The lights were still off, the office dark, but a dull light from a computer left on was reflecting across the surfaces of the desks, refracting on shiny surfaces. Glasses. Cups.

Rob hit a couple of switches on a long bank of lights, opting to turn enough on to light up the area he wanted, but keep the rest of the office in the dark. Nicer to work in at this time of day. Kinder on the eyes.

He walked over to the board and stared at Paul Harris' death certificate, which was now pinned to the board, along with his certificate of cremation. Dated and time-stamped. In normal circumstances this would be more than definitive enough for him. Enough for proof of death. But Rob still had an inkling of doubt over Paul Harris. He knew he shouldn't have, but it was there. Nagging away.

On paper he wasn't the right character for this sort of crime. Maybe he didn't have the mettle or had too many weaknesses, but then again, on paper he was dead. Had been for a couple of decades. Rob was disappointed at the cremation. Exhumation was always a good option in the DNA age. More definitive. Cleaner.

Alan Reynolds would be re-arrested in the coming hours. He would be back in an interview room with Nicky and Jack before he'd had time to sober up. Jack would walk Alan through his options and play the proverbial good cop. Nicky would be Nicky and see how much she could push it before Alan Reynolds decided what his best option was. Rob was trying to find out which duty solicitor was on call this morning, but was hoping it was the shit one again so they could really push their luck. Alan needed squeezing.

Bernie Copp's whereabouts of the last forty-eight hours were still being assessed, digitally and otherwise. Rob had a call with the team assigned those duties at 8am. Delicate matters. Officers assigned to investigate another officer. Rob would travel to the Marriott Hotel just outside the city, situated near to junction 21 of the M1, for the call, as well as a meeting he had scheduled. Protocol dictated any internal investigations were not permitted to happen within the police station for reasons of professional conduct. Rob had no issue with that, and knew he would need to be whiter than white on all matters from here on in.

Elizabeth Harris would be coming back in too. Her intimate knowledge of her late husband, of Daniel Mortimer and of the men they called friends could be better than some of the knowledge Alan Reynolds held. Fresher. Less polluted. More credible in court, if it ever got to that stage.

Rob was also scheduling a meeting with Becky Ryan and the senior team, eager to review the forensic details and the assessment of the final hours of Daniel Mortimer's life. The investigation had devolved into a quadruple murder, and the method of the fourth murder was only similar to the naked eye. Daniel Mortimer had been treated as indignantly as the three before him, but was this the same killer? Either way, the gang were now fully out of circulation, all five accounted for, one way or another.

Rob's brain was fully awake. He felt as positive as he had recently, which he knew was odd given the situation. The pressure was still on, and although the gang had been accounted for, the team still didn't know the agenda of the killer. A fact that worried him. Rob was determined this case would not go unsolved. A man who had killed four of his contemporaries was strutting about as free as a bird, and without a mistake, without provocation, he was likely to remain unidentified. That didn't sit well.

Nicky had walked quietly into the office, conscious that Rob was in a groove, so she hadn't initially disturbed him. Rob raised a hand as an acknowledgment, but was reading through some of the material before him. Scanning. Thinking.

"We need to go hard at the options we have left, Gov, right?"

"Bang on, Nicky. Do a job on Reynolds this morning, wring him out for everything he's worth. We'll see what else we can get out of Elizabeth Harris, and I'm hoping with Becky's report and a full run around that we'll find a new thread. We have to."

Nicky's phone lit up on the desk. The office was still dark with the hour and the time of year. Nicky knew better than to flick more lights on, leaving Rob to do his own thing, in his own way. She looked at the screen and smirked. It was Jen letting her know that she'd picked up Alan Reynolds. Nicky shared it with Rob. It was a positive start.

"Reynolds is in a patrol car on his way here, Gov, and we've got coffee on the way too."

"That's a good start to the day, Nicky!"

"Oh, and that dipshit brief is the one who'll be covering the morning, too."

"Then it's an excellent start to the day, so don't fuck it up!"

Rob was playful in his tone but he meant what he said, and Nicky knew it.

*

Nicky felt fresh, ready to extract something from the man sitting in front of her. He looked nervous. Looked like he'd been dragged from his bed from a drunken slumber. He'd likely have been pissed off with the interruption to his morning, but with the discussion in the car being of the discovery of Daniel Mortimer's body, his mood had softened quickly as self-preservation had entered his mind. Jack had been in the car, and had made sure their man was fully aware of why he was coming in. He had brought the conversation up quickly and then let it fester. He could feel the cogs going round in the back of the car as the realisation of a fourth body had hit Alan Reynolds hard.

Jack sat, arms folded, opposite the brief, whose name was very forgettable. Even his demeanour was bland. Short-sleeved white shirt. Plain tie.

Nicky opened. "Who's next then, Alan?"

It was an open question, and Nicky didn't know the answer to it any more than Alan did, which was part of the issue for him.

"Can you protect me?"

"Who from, Alan?"

"From whoever's doing this."

"We haven't got a clue who that might be, Alan, that's why you're here."

Nicky's openness wasn't the normal tack when trying to draw out information, but the team didn't have a suspect, and Nicky was more than happy to let Alan Reynolds know it. Maybe it would jog his memory. Sharpen his thinking.

"We don't know who's doing this, and at the minute we don't fully understand why either. You are the only person who can shed any light on this investigation, so we're looking squarely at you."

Alan Reynolds wasn't aware of Elizabeth Harris' inclusion in the investigation, as far as the team knew. He wouldn't have had the nous to put it together in his head either.

"We've got four dead bodies, Alan, and we're hoping you can tell us something we don't already know so we can find who's doing this. If not, you are free to go home and we'll just have to wait to see who number five might be."

Nicky looked across at the solicitor, who was rigid in his chair, trying to avoid eye contact and scribbling on his pad. That last question was as loaded as it got. Alan Reynolds wasn't free to go and he knew it. He also knew that number five could well be him, and he fancied his chances in this chair more than with the maniac who had killed his dad and left his bloodied body strapped to his kitchen chair. As choices went, it was preferable.

Alan Reynolds squirmed in his seat, coughed and sat back.

The duty solicitor reminded him he wasn't obliged to say anything, but that didn't feel like much of an option either.

"I don't know why this is happening, and I don't know who's doing it."

"Ok, so what do you know that we don't, that might help?"

Alan sighed deeply, deciding the thoughts in his mind were now worth sharing. "There was more than just the issue I had with the drugs. Joe Davies ran a loan shark business, and dad got into debt with him. Times were tough and even though Dad was working, he borrowed some money and that was that. I don't know how much. A few hundred, maybe a grand. He owed Joe and he was in. That's how he ended up being their getaway driver; he was forced to do it. What I did didn't help, but if it had just been that, I think Dad could have sorted it. Dad tried to clear the debt but Joe held it against him, just kept coming back for more, and Dad couldn't deal with it. Joe threatened Mum, he threatened me. Once Dad realised he still owed Joe, he tried to squirrel some of the goods away. We had nothing and Joe was will trying to take more."

Nicky and Jack listened intently.

"He had no way of doing it properly, y'know, through work. Paying it back. Joe wouldn't let him. He couldn't earn enough money quickly enough for Joe's liking."

Reynolds showed something approaching emotion for his dad. Empathy. Trapped in a spiral. Unable to get out of it. Indebted to a violent bully. Unable to fully imagine how it must have felt, but knowing his dad did as much as he could have to protect his wife, as well as him. His son. Whatever was needed to survive.

Nicky wrote 'DEBT' on her own pad. A word that was already on the board but in a different context. Alan's mess with drugs was a type of debt, but if the debt was financial it could go a long way in explaining the involvement of Paul Harris and Daniel Mortimer. She wrote 'STUDENT DEBT? DRUGS?' next to Mortimer's name. She considered that Paul Harris could easily have borrowed some money from Davies during one of the employment lulls of the eighties, and that would have been that.

"So the night on the allotment, Alan?"

"I was looking for the loot, I told you. I don't know if there was any there, there might have been. Still might be. Maybe cash, maybe some watches. I don't know. I was high, it made sense to look. Figured somebody else might be looking too, but I don't know who, I honestly don't. Still don't."

He took a long drag on a cigarette, took a swill of black coffee and sighed. He looked up and met Nicky's eye, the gloss of last night gone as the gravity of the situation showed in his face.

"Everybody lost track of what was taken. I thought I was the only one who knew, or thought, there might be something on Dad's allotment. I panicked, went looking for it just in case it was still there. If it's worth killing my dad and the guys for, I thought it might be worth looking for."

"And did you find anything, Alan?"

There was a complete lack of trust in the question. She'd asked him last time if he'd found anything; he'd said that he hadn't, but Nicky had Reynolds down as the sort of bloke who'd rob his own family for fifty quid, which in a roundabout way is what he was trying to do.

"No! You lot pinched me and I haven't been back as I assumed you'd be watching me."

Reynolds was chatting freely and was far from being finished.

CHAPTER 50

The morning was brighter by the time Elizabeth Harris arrived at Lodge House. Her early morning visit was less early and less intrusive than Alan Reynolds' had been.

She'd been 'asked' for her co-operation, but Jen had made it crystal clear that her morning was going to be spent in Lodge House regardless, and the voluntary way was preferable for all parties.

Jen hadn't yet broken the news of Daniel Mortimer's death. Elizabeth Harris hadn't argued at the request to 'help with the police inquiry', and after asking to bring her coat had walked freely out of her house, her head low, before stepping into Jen's car.

Jen would break the news early. Elizabeth hadn't been arrested, hadn't needed to be, so there would likely be no solicitor. Rob had agreed with Nicky and Jen that she'd be told of the death in the interview room so they could gauge her reaction on camera and under the harsh light. Just to see. Just to be sure.

Jen would take her interview alone. She had an incredible ability to empathise, interrogate, reason and provoke in a unique style that Rob felt was perfect for what was needed. She had the ability to be good cop and bad cop in the same room, and seemingly at the same time, with a fluid style and a changeable approach. She was developing well, was becoming a serious player, and was earning the respect of those whose respect needed earning.

She could start slowly, like a chat between friends, but devolve quickly and become harsh, challenging and intrusive, before reverting back seamlessly.

Elizabeth Harris sat nervously in her chair. Jen had offered her a coffee, which sat on the table in front of her, with steam billowing out of the styrene cup. Although it wasn't cold, she sat with arms folded, rubbing her upper arms through her cardigan. Closed. Defensive.

Jen slid into the chair opposite and sat down, hands entwined in front of her. She smiled. Elizabeth managed a half smile back.

"Daniel Mortimer was found dead last night, Elizabeth. He'd been murdered."

The mood crashed immediately. The clock on the wall ticked over the silence. Jen sat perfectly still. Head up. Eyeballing Elizabeth Harris. Jen didn't blink. She looked deep into Elizabeth's eyes, deep into her soul, knowing the cameras were watching.

The lip quivered first. Elizabeth swallowed hard. A tear formed in the corner of her left eye. She wiped it away and pulled out a tissue to wipe her nose. Jen didn't move, didn't react.

"How? Why? Was it the same person?"

"We believe so, Elizabeth." A short pause. "Where were you last night?" The question was asked bluntly.

"I was at home," came the quiet response.

"Can anyone vouch for that?"

Jen already knew the answer. Elizabeth looked closed. Defensive.

"Well, I didn't kill him, if that's what you're asking."

"I didn't ask that, I asked where you were last night."

The two jostled for position. For hierarchy in the room. Jen softened her approach quite deliberately. Her volume too.

"Daniel was killed in a similar way to William, Joe and Charlie. It wasn't a good death, Elizabeth. He didn't die well." Jen stared at Elizabeth again. "He was almost certainly killed because of his links to the gang. What those men did has got all of them killed thirty years on. We don't know why and we want you to help us."

"Why me? What can I do?"

"You're still alive, Elizabeth. You met all of these men. You were married to one of them. Something that happened has triggered all of this. You might not know what it is, or might not think you know, but you're as good a chance as we've got. Only you can help us get justice for Daniel."

Jen was working on the assumption that Elizabeth Harris hadn't killed Daniel Mortimer. Or any of the others. She was smart enough to know that Alan Reynolds would be getting broadly the same set of questions, and equally smart enough to know that she was the better chance of credible and accurate information.

"Tell me something I don't know, Elizabeth," Jen asked. It was a calm, patient request. Jen sipped from her coffee cup and waited.

Elizabeth Harris adjusted in her seat. She was thinking about something. She had something in her mind and was deciding if she should share it. Some of it. All of it. Edited parts of it.

Jen leaned forward calmly. "That thing that's in your mind right now, Elizabeth, it could really help. I don't know what you're thinking, but whatever it is is more than we have. We need you to share that with us."

"Paul owed money to Joe. Not a lot. He borrowed it when he was between jobs and things were tight. It was the eighties; work was sporadic and times were hard. There weren't things to help like there are now. Charity groups for Paul's illness, food banks, loans. You just suffered until the times changed. Paul borrowed the cash – he didn't ask me, he just did it – and we were in, and couldn't get out."

Jen nodded. Her face was blank, but she was feeling empathetic. She had done for Paul throughout the investigation, and was now feeling a tinge for the woman who had married a man with such complexity, especially at that point in time. She could have married other men. She wouldn't have been unattractive thirty years ago. She wasn't now. She'd aged well. Jen thought that she could have married better, and hated herself immediately for thinking the word *better*.

"I think Daniel did as well," Elizabeth said.

Jen frowned. "Owed Joe money?"

"I think so. I don't know how Daniel met Joe, or Charlie. I think it was while he was studying medicine, so he'd have been a mature student."

It sounded to Jen like 'Wonga', in the days before it existed, when people went to more questionable outlets for money. The picture of Joe Davies lending money to vulnerable men and then exploiting them was ringing out. Even if they had to choose to enter those jewellers and commit the acts they did, it was with one arm behind their backs and with the threat of violence if they didn't do as they were told. More interest on a debt they could never pay.

Jen was almost certain that William, Paul and Daniel were not the only three men that had been manipulated and exploited by Joe Davies. She also wasn't immediately sure how this could help them. If anything, it implicated Alan Reynolds, who would have tried to protect his father and would have been able to deal with Joe's ilk more naturally than his father could have.

"There was another robbery." Elizabeth dropped the words into conversation as casually as if she was in a bar with a friend.

Jen sat and waited. Alan Reynolds had set the team onto a third robbery, but current efforts to dig into the details were proving elusive, and Jack currently hadn't been able to establish a location, or any records of the alleged crime.

"When? Where?" Jen asked broadly.

"I'm not sure I can remember. The group was really devolving by that point. The arguments, the fighting. They weren't all involved, but Joe and Charlie wanted more. Paul didn't go; he couldn't as it turned out but they weren't happy with him, and thought that if anybody was arrested, Paul would be the easiest to get at. They were right, of course."

Jen looked at Elizabeth, who looked as if she'd transported back into the mid-eighties. The glaze in her eyes was as bright as the memories flooding back; as if they were playing out before her in the present. Like a film on a screen. She didn't look back at Jen as her flashback continued.

"I'm not sure William was involved in the other robbery either. Maybe he was. Paul wasn't and I have the feeling only three of them took part in the last robbery. Maybe four if they just left Paul out. I think Daniel was there. I said at the time that he was with me, only he wasn't"

Jen sat. Waited.

"It didn't go to plan. Paul found out from Daniel, I think, but it went wrong. There was a fight, somebody got hurt and they fled before they'd got much."

"What do you mean, there was a fight?"

It was evident that Elizabeth still wanted to protect Daniel. She was hanging on to some misplaced loyalty, but the simple fact was he'd been there. It could be the reason for the events that had unfolded in Liverpool. She still couldn't understand how the third robbery hadn't yet featured in the investigation, but she was in the here and now, and trying to draw as much as possible from their witness. Her witness.

"There was resistance from the shopkeeper, I think. He didn't just roll over or lie down and they went for him. They hurt him. I think it was bad. I remember Daniel struggling to talk about it; he was really shook up, and he wasn't squeamish."

Jen was buzzing inside. She felt importance radiate through Elizabeth's words. The missing piece of the jigsaw was potentially being spilled in her lap, calmly, peacefully, and with Elizabeth Harris seemingly unaware of the importance of her words. Or just using a tone that allowed her to distance herself from the events. From crimes committed by two men she loved, or lusted after, once upon a time.

"The man survived, or he did initially, anyway. I remember how Daniel was for a good period after. Quiet. Withdrawn. He didn't want to talk about what had happened. I asked, I wanted to be there for him, but he just didn't want to talk. He got angry. He got defensive. So I stopped asking after a while."

Jen offered a glass of water, which was accepted.

"Joe and Charlie lost it in the shop, from what I did gather. The guy wouldn't open the safe, didn't have the cash they wanted or was just being difficult. I think they went over the top, they really hurt him. I remember reading it in the paper and never asking again. They were savage and I hated them. Hated them for making Daniel be there."

It was the first time her voice had broken. Showing emotion. Showing anger. She realised immediately and reverted.

"He died. The guy. It was months later but he didn't recover. Never got over it. His injuries I mean. Can I see him please? Daniel."

It wasn't a question Jen had foreseen, but she searched for an appropriate response. "I'll see if I can make that happen, Elizabeth."

Elizabeth had one last question. "Can I go home now?"

Jen managed a half smile.

"Green's."

"I'm sorry?" asked Jen.

"The jewellers. It was called Green's."

CHAPTER 51

It had been an interesting morning so far. Productive. Rob had been pleased with the response to what he had instigated, and he knew there was a more buoyant mood in the station. A mix of tension and energy. Even a sliver of fear was palpable. Bernie Copp had been suspended, and although the investigation into his conduct was ongoing, the initial view was that his conduct was insubordinate rather than criminal. There was little to suggest he'd been in Merseyside in the last forty-eight hours.

The suspension now seemed well known throughout the office, with the rumour mill rotating at speed. Some of the junior officers had seemed shocked that an officer of Bernie's experience had been suspended midway through the biggest murder investigation in force history, but Rob quite liked the juniors knowing that the force wasn't too big for anybody. It may even keep a few of them on the straight and narrow.

It seemed to have a perversely positive effect. More effort seemed to be being made amongst the ranks. Shirts ironed just that little bit sharper. Shoes polished, punctuation better. And nothing seemed too much effort.

Rob was raking over some earlier notes, trying to find any

reference to Green's. Still trying to find out why there was no immediate or obvious reference to a third crime, let alone a reason as to why the men were never prosecuted for it. Alan Reynolds had confessed to knowing about it without having anything salient to add, other than that it happened at some point after the raid on Laxmi, and with the men comfortable that the police weren't hot on their heels.

Rob knew he hadn't seen anything. Not a snippet. He knew what he'd read. Knew what he'd seen. Knew what he hadn't. Green's hadn't been mentioned. It wasn't on the board, it wasn't in any of the files. He picked up the phone on his desk and dialled.

Laura Mathers answered her phone on the first ring, uncharacteristically. The energy sweeping the station seeming to have made its way upstairs too.

"Yes, Rob?"

"Ma'am, there's a third robbery to the case that has managed to stay peripheral in the investigation. It's now becoming central to our focus. The challenge we're having is a lack of information or records surrounding that robbery."

Rob explained the morning's events, and how the interviews with Elizabeth Harris, and Alan Reynolds had unfolded.

"Is she full of shit?"

It was a blunt question. Rob had already considered it. One witness sharing something didn't make it true. Maybe she'd imagined it. Some of it. Maybe it didn't happen, or the name was wrong, or maybe it was completely irrelevant. Maybe she was protecting somebody else, if not herself, or Daniel.

"No, I don't think she is. I think there's something in it."

Rob's gut had been twitching away. He felt uncomfortable about it. Somebody saying something is one thing, but without evidence of it, a record, a court document or a witness in the present day, it never existed as far as he was concerned. Or a court.

So what if it did happen? If it did exist? Rob had a nagging doubt that it must have happened, and an even bigger nag that it was not only relevant, but the pivotal reason why four people had been brutally murdered. The two people with knowledge of it can't have conspired over it. Or could they? Do either of them have any reason to lie about it? But even if it is important, the combined recollection of the two accounts is close to non-existent.

"So you've nothing to prove this has actually taken place?"

The question was typical of an ACC nervous about the integrity of the unit, even if that wasn't a direct thought she had shared with Rob.

But it fitted. It fitted his theory; that of an officer being involved. Somebody responsible for the murders and with access and the power to alter records. Or make them disappear altogether.

"Nothing at all, it's pure conjecture, but it warrants investigation, Laura. We've no forensics still, nothing on the drugs used in terms of source, missing documentation or missing evidence, and nothing remotely solid to look at since Daniel Mortimer's murder."

"And the plan?"

Rob already had one. Wouldn't have picked up the phone otherwise. It was three-fold. Nicky and Jen would be heading back to Gartree. He'd wanted Gary Hunt's cage rattling again, and the time was now, along with Ben Miller, the old guard who'd been on the sick but was part of Gartree's furniture. What did those minds hold? What was in there and what could they remember once pushed?

Jack would be re-checking court documents. He'd already done it once but he was now in the position of having to check his own work. Check it wasn't there, confirm it didn't exist. He'd also be doing the critical work of finding Green's. It's existence, or past existence. Who owned it, who ran it and where it was. It sounded like a family business. Jack would have the high-profile thread of finding the secrets of a jewellers that had remained unknown until now. Rob was highly conscious of the level of risk. If Jack found a line of inquiry, it was possible it would unmask the killer, or shake some trees at the very least.

Rob's part of the plan was also part of the reason for the phone call. He'd identified and located eighty-seven-year-old Eric McCann, the Crown Court judge responsible for sentencing each of the five men, including Paul Harris, nearly thirty-five years ago.

David Parker would block it. Simple as that. Approaching a retired judge for information, to a traditional and conservative chief constable and a man of his generation, would be a flat no. Laura Mathers was younger and less risk-averse, smart and ambitious but with a glint in her eye and a willingness to roll the dice. Even if it didn't go to plan, asking questions of anybody whose memories could contribute to the case seemed worthwhile. Bypassing the chief constable was a risk for both of them, but Rob had sensed cracks in a relationship and sensed that change was on the horizon, one way or another.

"Where is he, Rob?"

"He's in North Devon. Living out his retirement in a barn conversion. The sort of thing that appeared on Grand Designs in the nineties, according to Google maps."

"I'll make some calls to pave the way. Do it, Rob, but keep me posted every step of the way."

*

It was lunchtime before Nicky and Jen had made the short trip back up the A6, the regular routine of searches and signatories had been completed, and they were making themselves comfy in the small room they'd sat in several weeks earlier, on the day Joe Davies had been murdered.

Gary Hunt and Ben Miller shuffled in promptly, the formalities following before the four sat down. The room was cold. Nicky and Jen kept their coats on.

Jen opened. "Do you guys recall any conversations about a third robbery? The gang are alleged to have committed another robbery on top of the two they were convicted for."

Gary Hunt sat blank, folded his arms and looked at Ben. Ben looked at Jen.

"Yes, I think I do. The prison talk was rife in those days. The boasting, the bragging. It was all part of the chest puffing, the hierarchy and the status of the men here. There was no social media and limited TV, so the stories became the reputation." Ben looked across at Nicky. His simple demeanour was unflattering. "I remember talk of it. The bragging was mostly that they'd got away with it."

"As in hadn't been prosecuted for it? Who was this, Ben?"

"Joe and Charlie, mainly. It was all part of their bravado. They wanted to be known as criminals. Wanted the reputation. I don't recall Paul Harris or William Reynolds shouting off about it; it wasn't their way. They were quiet men."

"How about Daniel Mortimer?"

"Not sure. He may have done but if he did, it would have been in the right circles, to either inflate his self-importance or elevate his status amongst the right crowd. Daniel was smart like that. Not flash. He could judge his environment or microenvironment and adapt to it, so if he did brag it wouldn't have been within my earshot."

"Why do you think you recall it, Ben? What makes you remember this, given the number of people who would have been bragging about all manner of things? Some true, mostly not, I imagine."

"With Charlie and Joe, it was always the violence. Plus they wanted to think they'd got one over on the police. I recall them being pleased with their sentence for the two robberies, and I think the talk was of the level of violence they'd used in the third robbery. They were happy with themselves; it was good for their image in here and if they had been convicted, it would have meant significantly longer sentences for them. They were lucky."

"So getting away with one gave them status. Do you remember anything else, Ben?"

"Yes. I think it may just have been the two of them. The details were always patchy, which I think was part of the issue for you guys, but whatever they did to the guy was savage. I'm not sure he made it. It made the other robberies look like a light touch."

Nicky and Jen absorbed a testimony that was corroborating the recollections of both Elizabeth Harris and Alan Reynolds.

"They brutalised that jeweller, if the talk was to be believed. They were proud of themselves for it, too. They really were bastards, detectives, and I'm glad they're both dead."

Nicky and Jen could sense real progress.

CHAPTER 52

Becky Ryan's last forty-eight hours had been interesting. A family occasion and a day off had turned into a rush hour drive to Liverpool, a speeding ticket, and the post-mortem in the Royal Liverpool Hospital of the man the team had been so eager to question. To arrest.

Her initial work in Liverpool had now concluded, and she'd been able to enjoy a more sedate journey back down the M6 to Leicester, cutting out Catthorpe via the M69 and a near certain half-hour delay in the process.

Back in familiar surroundings, she'd scheduled a session with Nicky and Jen, but was half expecting Jack and Rob as well, given the evolving pace of the investigation. Critical new elements had continued to crawl from the woodwork, and with only Rob aware of every last detail collected by the team, it needed to be shared.

Nicky and Jen arrived in a timely fashion, and after a brief catch-up with Becky they wanted to get down to business. The investigation was unfolding and the girls felt that a few final pieces could blow the case wide open.

"Cause of death?" asked Nicky.

"Easier one, this. Blunt force trauma. This one looks to be *simpler*, although to be fair it would have been hard to match the previous crimes."

Becky was alluding to the fact that the police had been outside at the time of the murder, an elephant in the room that wasn't about to go away. Not even the most audacious of murderers would spend hours torturing a man while the police sat idly outside. This had been a smash and grab; a successful one.

"It's the same perp, I'm almost certain of that. The base elements are there. The beating, mainly. There is blood but nowhere near what we've seen on previous occasions. There wasn't a 'chair' factor to this crime either, it's the first murder without one, but the injury pattern, the nature of the beating and the weapons used are all consistent with the other three murders."

Daniel Mortimer had been found face down, unceremoniously dumped in his own home. Beaten to death, but with the minor consolation that he'd endured much less torture than his former colleagues had been subjected to.

Becky added an opinion. "Maybe he was perceived as being less culpable than the others. Or maybe it was just a time thing."

The Liverpool team were still investigating the specifics of the break-in; when, and how the house had been accessed both from the rear of the property and in more literal terms of getting inside, without any visual damage or evidence of a break in, and clearly without the knowledge of the victim. Or had he just opened the door? It seemed unlikely.

"It was real skilful work just gaining access to the victim." Becky acknowledged, and admired the work of their man; not for the first time in the investigation. "There's a significant trauma to the back of the head, which looks to have started the assault. It's a larger single trauma than we've seen before, and there was no use of any drugs to subdue the victim."

"So he just broke in silently, crept up on Mortimer and battered him round the back of the head?" The simplicity of Jen's words poured out beautifully.

"In a word, yes. Without the charm offensive, the skilled break-in or any drugs to incapacitate, this murder started with a blow to the head. It may have knocked him out, but at the very least it would have rendered him close to unconscious. He'd have been unable to defend himself."

"So it was all over before it started?"

"Largely, yes. The assault that followed was relatively short compared to the duration of the other attacks. There are some slash type wounds that match with the blade used previously, but they look to be minimal, or even a token, in this case. There was an implement used that would have struck the first blow; I'm guessing a bat or a club. Something short and round. Like a rounders bat or an old style police baton."

Jen looked at Becky, but didn't need to speak.

Becky immediately realised the literalness of her suggestion. It was just an example, but she would now have Daniel Mortimer's injuries tested against old police weapons. Just to be on the safe side. Just to be sure. Given the suspicions around the killer's knowledge of this case, the thought that he could be taunting Rob's team further by using a police issue weapon was a frightening one.

"How long do you think the assault would have taken, Becky?"

"Ten minutes, fifteen at most. He was beaten heavily. I think where he was found was also the source of the attack. He was attacked and beaten to death on the same spot. There's no blood spatter or forensics to suggest he was moved, under his own steam or by the assailant. It's likely he fell from the first blow where you found him and was then beaten heavily about the body, head and face, and assaulted until he died."

"And the other *bits*, Becky? They were similar too?" Nicky was referring to what had become the signature of the crimes. She'd seem them first hand, but there had been a difference.

"It's definitely the same signature, and yes it's almost certainly the same person who did it, just with a slight variance. His ear was only partially severed, it was still attached by several tendons. And after the progressive nature of the finger removals of the other victims, you'd be forgiven for thinking this guy shouldn't have a hand left."

There had been blood pooled around the left hand of Daniel Mortimer, but Nicky and Jen had noted from the scene that only two of Daniel Mortimer's fingers had been removed, and left clumsily on the floor just a foot or so away from his body. Not as neat as the other scenes. Not as well *presented*.

"Was it rushed?" Nicky asked. "And if the ear was still there but attached could the attack have been disturbed? Did somebody pass the house and spook him? Even if it was a passer-by with a Chinese?"

"It's possible." Becky replied. "The killer must have been on heightened alert. Must have been hypersensitive to what was going on outside. It was a huge risk to go in, but the killer must have weighed that up. We should be able to check who did walk past the house from the records of the Merseyside team who sat outside."

The killer was smarter than that. Better informed too, and certainly hadn't been anywhere near the front door, let alone walk through it. Jen looked perplexed as she shared her thoughts:

"Given that only the killer knew that Daniel wasn't our man, why not leave him in play? That's what happened with Charles Worth. We lifted him, searched his house and established that he wasn't our man, so we cut him loose and the killer was waiting for him. Patiently. Killed him after we'd been. Why not let us take Mortimer, and get to him in a few days?"

"Could he be, though?" asked Nicky, challenging the view. Just to be sure. "Could Mortimer have been our man? But now somebody has taken him out to tie up the loose ends. How convinced are you that this is the same person, Becky? And not just a copycat hatchet job of the other three killings, with Mortimer responsible for the first three?"

"It's not impossible that it's a different protagonist, but the nature of the injuries and the removal of the finger and attempt to remove the ear are just so similar, it looks highly improbable that it's a different killer. We're still analysing forensics, but from the injuries, I'd state comfortably that it's the same person. The gash wounds are the 'tell' in their depth, angle and number. They're consistent with each of the other attacks. They're like handwriting or a signature, and the evidence indicates that they were imparted by the same hand."

Nicky nodded. Considering the implications. Considering what would cause a change of MO. "So working on the basis that it is the same killer, why the variances? Why the sloppiness against the other three kills?"

Becky responded with another opinion. The investigation was in live time with facts and forensics still being established; "It could just be down to time. It might be a burning desire to execute Mortimer, but if that's the case, it could suggest Mortimer may have told us something, or may have known something that the killer didn't want us to find out. It seems irrational to have murdered in those circumstances, so maybe it was forced upon the killer. Maybe he had to kill Mortimer."

"Do you think he knew something, Jen?" Nicky asked. "Could he have known who was doing this, but buried his head? Hoping his cover was good enough or that his door would be left alone?"

"I don't think the murder was rushed due to lack of planning. It was rushed because it had to be." Jen's view agreed with Becky's. "The killer knew time was tight, and seemed to know what was happening outside, but chose that night anyway."

Nicky was playing devil's advocate. "So if it was just time, why take the risk and not stay consistent with the MO? The other crimes were less risk-averse. The use of drugs neatralised Joe and Charlie quickly, meaning the assaults could be carried out more safely, and ultimately leading to the kill. So why not use drugs again and keep it easy? And why less injuries? Why was the number of blows lower than the other kills?"

Becky interjected pensively. "I have a new theory on this."

Nicky and Jen listened intently.

"We've been working to the theory that the attacker is one of the convicted men from the original robberies, and even with the intent to inflict suffering, our belief was that the higher number of blows that we've seen throughout the murders is simply due to their age. That is the theory that Charles Worth hitting you as a seventy year old would do slightly less damage than him hitting you as a forty year old, and it would therefore take longer for the beating to cause death."

She let it hang. Nicky's head was in the moment as she spoke; "So because the evidence has been pointing to one of the other men throughout, we've worked on the basis that age alone made the need for a higher number of less forceful blows to cause the fatality. An old hand needing to strike more to inflict the same amount of damage. Either as straight revenge or to extract a location from the victim. Money, goods."

"Right," confirmed Becky.

"But they're dead. Our pool of suspects are all dead."

Jen was listening, absorbing the details before adding her view. "These are angry crimes. Revenge crimes. You don't torture and execute somebody you don't know or don't have a pure ingrained hatred for. Evidentially, and on the assumption that the killer isn't another pensioner who we're yet to come across, which seems unlikely, I think we could be missing a relative of one of the victims."

Nicky was in complete agreement. Mortimer's death had shone a fresh light on who could be responsible for the murders, and why.

"A child." Nicky added, "We're missing a child."

CHAPTER 53

Rob had travelled down the evening before the meeting, wanting to avoid the bulk of the traffic that he knew he'd hit at some point. The long drive down was one Rob knew would allow him to focus. To think.

Rare isolated time. Time that used to aggravate him. Sitting in traffic, going nowhere. He'd mellowed in recent years, and now actively enjoyed the time alone with no distractions, affording him time to process information. Quietly. Reflectively.

He'd made good time around Birmingham on the M42 before the long slog south down the M5 that allowed Rob to tune in to his own thoughts. The things that still didn't sit pretty. The things that he wanted to ask Eric McCann in the morning.

He'd made good progress, and arrived at his hotel at a reasonable hour. It was dusky, but there was still time for a beer and some food. Rob had booked into a local guesthouse, preferring the charm of a North Devon B&B to the consistency of a Premier Inn or a Travelodge. A home-cooked breakfast in the morning had also helped to swing the decision.

Spending the night in a guest house seemingly in the middle of nowhere hadn't looked ideal, but on paper the house was only a few miles from the rural home of Eric McCann, making an early start possible. It suited Rob, who was optimistic of a productive day and an equally fluent return journey.

The owner of the guesthouse seemed pleasant. She noticed that Rob had clearly had a long drive, and seemed to be carrying a weight over and above that levied by the journey. She offered him a couple of options for tea. Both sounded nice. She told Rob it'd be ready by the time he'd had a shower. He smiled and opted for shepherd's pie as he headed upstairs to get changed, before taking advantage of the local hospitality.

*

Rob had enjoyed his evening meal and had slept well. Maybe not the perfect night Lenny Henry would have promised in a Premier Inn, but the bed was clean and comfy. The breakfast was everything he'd hoped for too. Fried eggs, crispy bacon, two huge hash browns and thickly sliced toast covered in local butter was a good start to the morning. Along with a large pot of tea. The biggest challenge was proving to be phone signal and WiFi. Or the lack of it. Rob had lost his signal at some point on the drive south of Exmoor, and had become unattached from the wider world. He'd got copies of some of the case files in his car boot, so had spent the back end of his evening studying; thumbing documents he'd thumbed countless times already, manipulating the details in his head to find a theory, or construct a new one.

He decided he'd come back. This place would be perfect for a weekend. For long walks where the world couldn't get hold of him. Perfect. Just not ideal now when a call to Nicky was overdue, and he hadn't spoken to Jack since yesterday morning.

Rob keyed the postcode for Eric McCann's house into his sat nav, and headed up the gravel drive to the main road, making the short fifteen-minute journey to a secluded property at Bratton Fleming, to the south west side of Exmoor and with little else in the vicinity. Still no signal.

He arrived at 9am, the agreed time. Not early. Not late. He'd had a good conversation yesterday with Laura Mathers, so he knew roughly what to expect in terms of Eric's character, but still wasn't sure if David Parker knew where he was or what he was doing. He was leaving the ACC to broach that subject. He'd had clearance and was good to go. He needed information, and the number of people with primary memories of the times were literally being killed off. McCann was a rare commodity, and Rob needed his help. Needed his mind.

The house was beautiful. Not huge, but a sturdy stone house of a certain age. Oozing with character and with ornate sash windows and a slate roof, it sat beautifully and was fitting of its surroundings. Rob felt this was a retirement well lived, following a long and successful career.

The front door was traditional and solid, with a large brass knocker that Rob rapped twice.

Eric McCann opened the door and smiled. He was taller than Rob had expected, with a look of wisdom and a real aura of authority. His smart grey hair sat to one side, he was wearing a pale blue sweater with a white shirt and a tie underneath, which Rob guessed was his standard apparel. He offered his hand and invited Rob in. He was bright and chirpy. It was a positive start.

"So you'd like to talk about the Leicester robberies, Mr Rhone."

It wasn't a real question but kicked proceedings off following several minutes of small talk, as Rob took a sip from the cup of tea he'd been offered, which had arrived in a china cup and saucer.

"I do, Your Honour." Rob was formal, respectful.

A hand was raised to bat the formalities away. "Please call me Eric, Mr Rhone."

"I'd like to understand what you can recall from the case you presided over, Eric. The people involved, how the trial played out, and your memories of the five men and their families from the time."

Laura Mathers had spoken to Eric McCann directly several days earlier. She had primed him for the case, and reminded him of the names in question. The protagonists. He'd had the last few days to pick his brain.

"They were a real mixed bunch. Charlie and Joe led the gang, from memory. Decided on the details. Ruled with fear. They were men accustomed to a life against the law, and the likes of you and I were a way of life and an occupational hazard, Inspector."

"Did the trials play out normally, from what you can remember? Were there any interruptions or controversy that you recall?"

"The odd outburst. They were aggressive men. Two of them were, anyway. The other three were quite timid in comparison, almost seemed intimidated by the courtroom and took their medicine to some degree. I sentenced them all in accordance with the guidelines of the time and there were no threats. The three were quiet and looked remorseful. I remember Joe Davies and Charles Worth looking vengeful, but there was no drama. I don't recall anything from the gallery either."

"What about the details around the trial, Eric? Evidence that was inadmissible or deals done with the prosecution. Things the jury didn't see."

Eric McCann sighed, he looked frustrated. It showed in the deep frown lines between his eyes. Laura Mathers had explained the issues around the investigation, the sensitive nature of recent developments, and how the team were battling questionable records and missing files. Eric's age had given him a certain belligerence, a contempt for what in his mind shouldn't need to be asked of him. Rob knew what he was asking but wanted to go fishing, hoping the grey cells could recount something salient.

Eric took his time, took a sip of his tea and pondered. His expression tempered.

"The CPS had only been established for a couple of years before I tried the men. It was new and finding its feet. The police were desperate to prosecute the men for three robberies, but the evidence was patchy and the CPS didn't go for it. The belief was that the gang had committed a third robbery, and on balance, they probably did. The issue they had was that the MO was different, and not all five of the gang had been involved. There was no CCTV, and the circumstances were different enough for the prosecution to struggle to make a case for the third robbery."

Rob nodded, acknowledging a statement he largely knew.

"There was a lot of debate in chambers. Arguing. The prosecution really wanted to go for it. To have them for all three. Nobody disputed that it wasn't a five-man attack, there just wasn't the evidence to progress with it."

Rob sat silently, listening to every word.

"An agreement was reached that the gang would plead guilty to the two robberies and any charges for the third crime would be dropped. It wasn't broadly palatable but it guaranteed a conviction."

"Who wasn't it palatable to, Eric?"

"Everybody really. Joe and Charlie were involved, that was clear to see, and by pleading guilty they saved themselves a lot of time in prison. They had the most to lose. Paul Harris couldn't have been involved, and Daniel Mortimer was alibied, although that was challenged heavily."

"What was the issue with his alibi?"

"His alibi came from Paul Harris's wife. Elizabeth. The third robbery was only three men, I think. Paul couldn't have been there and Daniel was cleared by Elizabeth Harris. There just wasn't enough evidence to proceed for all three robberies; it would have compromised the whole case, and they could have been acquitted on all charges and walked. The CPS were not happy at all, from memory, but this was the best way to secure a conviction. It was viewed as a win."

"Who didn't win? Who lost out? Or who didn't think that was the best way?"

"The third robbery was hard. The jeweller was attacked. Badly hurt. He was very badly beaten, I recall. It was similar to the first robbery, but I recall the shopkeeper was on his own. It was his shop and he was the only one there, and he stood up for himself."

Rob was silent. The untouched ground was appearing beneath his feet. Its relevance was crystal clear as Eric McCann continued to reveal his memories.

"I don't think the third robbery was lucrative, but they almost forgot about the robbery part and took it upon themselves to turn it into a beating. The police pursued it as attempted murder initially, it was that strong. The guy only just made it. He spent a lot of time in hospital and I think he ended up taking his own life. He never did recover and he lost his business. He had a wife and a young daughter and life would have been very tough for them after that."

Rob sat dumbfounded. He could barely believe what he was hearing, the criticality of the information screaming.

"What happened during the attack, Eric? Can you remember?"

"I'll never forget. I saw a lot as a trial judge, even in those days, you understand. They were armed. Bats and a sawn-off shotgun. There was a lot of shrapnel from the broken cabinets and the guy tried to fight back, even after they'd hit him a few times. He didn't desist. He fell on a lot of glass and was kicked and dragged across it. He was badly cut. He still tried to fight. His left hand was stamped on or struck with clubs. The glass and the impact severed two of the fingers on one of his hands. He lost them. The surgeon couldn't save them. He did well to save his life."

Rob swallowed hard, gobsmacked by what he'd just heard.

"Was that the full extent of his injuries?"

"No, he lost an ear as well. Or most of it, anyway." Eric McCann dropped it into the conversation like a bomb. "He was battered to one side of his head. A lot of his injuries were due to that. His ear was nigh on ripped from the side of his head. They tried to sew it back on but they couldn't. They might have been able to save it today, better surgery and methods, but back then there was too much damage. It was a disgusting crime, Inspector Rhone. They left that poor man for dead."

Eric recoiled in his chair, the horrors of the memory spilling back into his mind decades after being laid to rest. Filed away but not forgotten.

"Can you recall his name, Eric?"

"Terry Morley. His name was Terry Morley."

CHAPTER 54

Fucking bitch. How she's got the nerve to float around like Little Miss Innocent… It just feels like a fresh kick in the teeth, and after everything I've been through. Years in the planning, years in the making… And now I'm so fucking close. I'm about to lose everything one way or another and it's like a final taunt. An insult on top of an insult.

It'll just make the final piece that little bit more enjoyable. Pleasurable.

At least now she's exposed. Out in the open. Rob and the team seem to be slowly cottoning on to what's unfolding, if just a little too slowly. Too slowly for her, anyway. My God, they're close.

The last few weeks have gone to plan, though. They've been very, very satisfying. Killing Daniel Mortimer was a different experience. Navigating those terrace gardens, the thrill of executing him with the police sat outside, yards from where I smashed his head in.

Of course he was there. Lying bitch.

That was exhilarating. I was buzzing for hours that night. It was electric.

I was expecting to have to wait until long after dark, until he was tucked up in bed. But it was wide open, and all the while he just sat in his chair with his Beats on after a day at work. It was so perfect I simply couldn't have planned it.

Killing him was a bit like Joe Davies, only I didn't get to see the look on his face. There was simply no time. That was a shame, but I wasn't sure I'd get this far. Dad would be proud of my determination, if not my methods. I made it to Mortimer. Undetected.

Smashing him around the head was such a relief, so enjoyable. It was also long overdue. He had it coming, and hearing the crack of his skull was immense. Over and over. It felt good to see his life ebb away while he lay there, defenseless, his body twitching. I hope the last thing that went through his mind was what he did that day and what he did to my family. I whispered my name to him.

I whispered my name to each of them. Told them who I was. Told Charlie Worth before I got going whose daughter I was. Made them look me in the eye so they knew why they had to die. And then I took their lives. They all knew why. Decades-old vengeance was finally being served.

And so it comes to her. To why she must die too. She is still guilty, despite not being in Dad's shop that day. She's just guilty in a different way. Her way. Ultimately, I'm still not sure who was in the shop that day and who wasn't, and neither were the police, but if you live by the sword, you'll fucking die by it.

Maybe they didn't all have to die, but they still did it. One way or another, they did it. They were responsible. They robbed those jewellers. Decent people, decent men and women, just looking to earn a living in the right way.

Dad was never the same again. He couldn't have been. I watched him suffer. I watched my mum suffer. The times weren't kind. There was no compensation for us. For Dad. No support, no victim groups to talk to. Society didn't understand and wasn't compassionate towards those who were different. Times were hard for the disabled, the blind, the deaf. Society looked differently at you. Judged you. Going to the supermarket with Dad with a mutilated ear and missing fingers... They used the word maimed. They talked about him. He hated himself. Hated being looked at like that. Felt like a circus stooge. He became reclusive, more and more withdrawn, and was a shadow of himself until the day he took his own life.

The day he left me and Mum behind.

Those men would never have been released if they'd been convicted of dad's murder, but they couldn't decide who to charge, and she was responsible for that. She lied for him and they all got away with it.

Who was there, who wasn't. Whether it was even the same gang, or another gang operating in a similar way.

It was them. Joe was there, Charlie was definitely there. The rest is just semantics. Detail. But when you cut out cancer, you cut out the whole fucking thing. Which leads me to the final piece.

One to go.

CHAPTER 55

It felt like hours before Rob got through to Nicky, his signal having been threadbare and failing for miles as he'd headed out of North Devon. He'd hit redial on his bluetooth time and time again until the dialling tone connected and Nicky's phone rang.

"Nicky! Can you hear me?" Rob looked at the signal bars on the display of his car.

"Gaffer, we've got a new theory that we need to look at!"

Rob was taken aback. Nicky had got in first and Rob suspected that the importance of the comment must be high. Nicky knew where Rob had been and hadn't bothered to ask; she'd dived in. Rob invited her to continue.

"We've got a view on the perp and why the murders have gone the way they have; with the nature of the early murders everything pointed to the killer being one of the gang, and Mortimer in particular. We'd worked on the basis that the use of drugs and the injury pattern was indicative of an elderly killer. The force of the injuries and the depth versus the amount all making one of the gang highly likely, and consistently so."

She paused. Rob was intrigued. He'd worked out where Nicky was going with it but was eager to hear her spell it out.

Eager to find out how she'd got there. Their paths were aligning, and they both now knew the relationship of their murderer to the victims. Nicky stopped the suspense and spat out what her, Jen and Becky had reached as a conclusion.

"We think the killer is a child of one of the original victims, Rob, almost certainly the third robbery given the lack of evidence around it and the fact that we've had sight of relatives from both the Stefan's and Laxmi raids. They either didn't lose a relative or simply don't have the level of hatred required to commit the crimes we've seen… Rob, are you there?" Nicky asked, thinking she'd just shared her thoughts with Rob unable to hear her.

"I got it, Nicky, and you're right. It's a guy called Terry Morley; we need to find his family, and more importantly his daughter."

Nicky was taken by surprise. She'd expected a challenge. A question. Something to rebuke her idea and make her question her own thinking, make her doubt herself and check over and over again until it was irrefutable. That would come, but for now Nicky's intrigue flipped and she asked Rob why he was so sure, why he'd agreed with her so easily.

"The third robbery holds the key, Nicky. It's all in there. The reason this is happening is all down to a robbery we know very little about."

"What did McCann tell you?"

The conversation looped back to the place Rob had expected it to start.

"The third robbery was savage, more so than the other two. The jeweller was alone, a guy named Terry Morley. He was badly beaten, and although the method was almost identical to the first two robberies, the gang wasn't the full complement.

They were never sure if William Reynolds was there, and there were doubts over Harris and Mortimer too. They all thought Charlie and Joe were there, but the evidence was patchy and the defence team worked on copycat, so they pleaded on the two we've investigated and got to walk for the third. No charges were ever brought."

Nicky knew there was more. Rob had a way with a narrative and she knew she was being led to a point. She couldn't decide what it was and knew better than to second guess.

"The beating, the glass, the violence. He was assaulted so badly, and beaten so severely that they had to remove one of his ears."

"Holy fuck. And Eric McCann just spilled all this out?"

"He did, calm as you like. Like he was recanting a lost memory. Morley lost fingers too, Nicky, they were crushed and severed amongst the melee. He lost two of them at the hospital."

Nicky sat. A pause. The realisation that had struck Rob like a hammer an hour or so earlier was now doing the same to her.

"He had a wife and a daughter, Nicky. I want to check both but I think only the daughter is viable. Its revenge in the most literal form, and the injuries we have mirror those that Terry Morley endured in the attack on his jewellers all those years ago. It has to be her."

"What do you need us to do, Rob?"

"Speak to Jack. I need him to go and ask some firmer questions of Elizabeth Harris. She gave Daniel Mortimer an alibi, I want to know if she's holding anything else back. If she is, it could mean that we're not done. Mortimer has been murdered for his part, whatever that was, so somebody thought he was there. Somebody has held him responsible, and if they think Elizabeth protected a guilty man she could be at risk."

"The records aren't there, Rob, Jack would have found them. There was nothing in the archive."

Her statement was matter of fact, and Rob agreed. The records of the third robbery weren't there. They'd been removed. The 'when' could come later, but both knew this would trigger a line that should allow them to identify the person responsible for removing the records.

"I need you and Jen to find out who she is. Get Becky involved, she might be able to dig at the Royal and save some time. If there are birth and death records it's highly likely they'll still be there. The pool will be small based on age alone."

"I'll get her on it straight away, plus I've got an idea that might help."

*

Nicky drove south down the London Road, passed the train station and had decided to ditch her car in the car park behind the police station, just behind a busy entrance that Royal Mail vans were recklessly piling in and out of. Jen was waiting, and the two made the short walk across the London Road to the Leicester Mercury offices, less than a quarter of a mile from the office where the investigation had been unfolding.

Nicky and Jen walked through the front door of a tired looking building, not dissimilar to Lodge House, only without the high-rise element and the rattle from the train line. Nicky was on the phone to Becky, with the walk providing an injection of fresh, cool air to both the face and brain.

Nicky was on the phone to Becky as they entered the building; she flashed her warrant card to the receptionist and muttered, "Natalie Allen, please" without lowering the iphone.

Her conversation with Becky was happening in conjunction to their line of inquiry. The race to the truth.

The receptionist picked up her desk phone whilst Nicky finished her call with Becky, who would pull anything she could to identify the relationships, records and offspring of Terry Morley.

Natalie appeared promptly, a tall elegant woman, well dressed and with flowing blonde hair, her demeanour smart and professional. One of a number of senior editors who'd worked these floors for as long as Nicky had worked hers. Her and Nicky had collaborated well and clashed in equal measure down the years, the media keen to support local authority, but also to pour scorn whenever it needed it. Keep it on the straight and narrow.

Natalie knew why Nicky and Jen were there following an earlier call, and had an analyst pulling some details and some old paper archives from around the time of the original crimes to help.

Time was now critical.

CHAPTER 56

It had been troubling Jack heavily that he'd been unable to locate any documents relating to the original crime. He knew he hadn't seen them, but he knew he'd been as thorough as he always was with the details. He'd got the files; he must have had the details. It just wasn't there. He knew it must have been taken. Must have been removed.

He'd spoken to both Rob and Nicky. They hadn't doubted him and had asked him to keep looking. Keep digging. Rob was compiling a list of people who'd had access to those files, those who could have accessed them, taken them. It was a short list.

The team were now focusing entirely on the third robbery, a missing and unprosecuted crime that had fuelled an unprecedented killing spree.

Eric McCann had indicated that Paul Harris couldn't have been there. The facts would need checking, but according to McCann he had a perfect alibi. He was in a cell after a night on the piss. Which left four.

He'd also shared that he recalled that Elizabeth Harris had alibied Daniel Mortimer for the crime, so he couldn't have been there either. Which left three, only that alibi turned out to have been false, so it looked more like Mortimer had been there than William Reynolds. Facts that had become lost on the killer, who had held each of the men accountable. Mortimer had been slayed as brutally as his friends. Found just as guilty in somebody's eyes.

Elizabeth Harris was key. A sole survivor and now more central than the team had thought possible. A crime she'd failed to mention, an affair she'd wanted to hide and an alibi that could have triggered the murders. She was involved. She knew more than she'd shared. All roads lead to Rome.

Jack looked up in Lodge House, and was about to shout Bernie's name. He swallowed as soon as he remembered, but saw Emma Sharpe across the office.

"Fancy a drive out, Em? We need to speak to Elizabeth Harris."

"Sure, why not?" She grabbed her bag and the two made the short drive to Enderby, to the modest and visually plain house that Jack had found just a few weeks ago, when Elizabeth Harris was Elizabeth Warren and little had made sense.

Jack rapped at the door, introduced PC Emma Sharpe, as well as unnecessarily introducing himself.

Elizabeth Harris invited them in with a rueful look. A woman carrying a weight.

Walking into the lounge, she offered both a seat and a drink. Jack accepted and walked to a sofa. Emma Sharpe stood in the doorway behind Jack, watching Elizabeth Harris.

Jack sat down in the lounge, and made an admission of their limited knowledge of the third robbery. He reminded her that she'd alibied Daniel Mortimer, and to ask her to recall what she could of the events of 1983. No easy task, but Elizabeth looked like a woman who had memories etched sharply into her conscience.

"Let's start with an easy one. Why did you give a false alibi for Daniel Mortimer?" The question was blunt, but Jack was pressing for an answer and needed to know.

She exhaled loudly. A sigh.

"I alibied him because I didn't want him to go to prison. I loved him, Jack, you must understand. I had so much to lose back then. So much. I needed him, I thought I needed him. I thought he loved me."

Jack proceeded with his line of questioning, with the team still unsure of the details and desperately reliant on what could be found in the coming hours.

"The reason Daniel and his friends were murdered was because of the third robbery, Elizabeth. The robbery you gave Daniel an alibi for. We now know the gang were never prosecuted, because the authorities could never establish who was present, with the exception of Paul."

Elizabeth swallowed hard. The weight sitting on her was getting heavier.

"What do you remember Elizabeth? This is really important."

"They went in armed for the third robbery. It was them. I'm not actually sure if Daniel was amongst them but I think he was. I never asked; he never denied it. Paul was in custody, and I spent the night before the robbery with Daniel at his flat. He disappeared early the following morning and came back late. I knew something had happened. He took a shower, he was pensive, not his normal confident self."

"Did he ever tell you anything?"

"No. I read about the man in the news. What happened. I didn't want to know. I know that sounds really selfish, but I was vulnerable."

She drew breath. Slowly revealing secrets locked away and dormant for thirty years.

"They were all arrested for it, but they all denied any knowledge. Rightly so in Paul's case. But the police were looking for an attempted murder charge, then manslaughter. They never had enough evidence to prosecute. They didn't know who to charge with what so settled on a plea deal. They all went to prison, so in a way, justice was done."

Jack looked her square in the eye. "Do you think Terry Morley's family think justice was done Elizabeth?"

The name resonated. It was one she'd spent a lot of time trying to forget. It was like a slap in the face, and she chose to change the direction of the conversation.

"I don't think William was involved in the third robbery, DC Bowery. I'd almost certain it was Charlie, Joe and Daniel who carried out the third attack, if you're pushing me. That's what I think. William didn't have an alibi like Paul did, and as there were only three of the four who were involved, and there was no direct evidence, it didn't stick."

"Do you think the person who killed William Reynolds cared whether he was involved or not?"

The question was acidic. Jack was annoyed and trying to channel his questions in the right way. Elizabeth had held the key to the murders and had chosen to keep it.

Jack sat back and ran his hands through his coat pocket for his phone but didn't feel it. He was expecting updates from either Nicky or Becky. Perhaps both. He tried his other pocket. Nothing. It must have fallen out in the car.

"Men have died because of this robbery, Elizabeth. Men have died and you knew why."

A tear formed in the corner of her eye, the pressure reaching breaking point as it started to spill out, running down her right cheek.

"But I still don't know what it means or who's doing this."

Raw emotion crackled, she sobbed. Jack glanced back at PC Sharpe, half expecting a tissue to be offered. He offered one of his when none were forthcoming.

The tension in the room was fever pitch. Elizabeth was overcome with a mixture of grief and relief as the memories continued to race through her mind. Through her memory. Painful, emotional memories.

The room fell silent as Jack allowed her some respite. The momentum dropped. He still wasn't satisfied she'd shared everything she knew, and wasn't satisfied he'd learned anything truly significant. No definitive evidence. No identity. William Reynolds may have been killed for little reason, but this was vengeance, and unlike the initial police investigation, the killer had been less bothered about the semantics of who had and who hadn't been there that fateful day.

Jack stood up. He asked if she would like a glass of water and went to fetch it from the kitchen. He was still checking his pockets for his phone, convinced he'd picked it up and wanting to check on progress across the city, and to let Nicky, Jen and Becky know how things were going here. He headed into the small kitchen and quickly found a glass.

Jack ran the cold tap, flicking his hand underneath it until a cold stream emerged. He looked up and caught a glimpse of a reflection in the glossy kitchen doors. A silhouette. He went to turn. Tried to put the glass down. Tried to defend himself.

He felt a sharp prick on his neck as the needle went in. He tried to react. The feeling of inebriation flooded his body immediately. Unable to move. Unable to function.

His eyes rolled and he crashed to the floor.

CHAPTER 57

Nicky and Jen were sitting in a grey room in the Leicester Mercury office, which wasn't dissimilar to their experience at Gartree, only without the invasive and time-consuming searches.

There was an energy in the room, though. Natalie had stayed and was organising boxes. She was part helping, but her journalistic tendencies were hoping she could be a part of something significant in the history of both the paper and the city. Helpful but with an agenda. It was a mutual arrangement that was working for both parties. For now.

Dominic Nolan was her assistant. Nicky had placed him around sixty. He was a man with the complexion of somebody who had lived and breathed these surroundings, worn by the pressures and demands of an environment constantly on a deadline. He was polite and mild-mannered. Nicky had already asked him how long he'd been at the paper, and once he'd revealed he'd been there since 1980, conversation had quickly turned to the robberies and whether he had any memories of them, or of the time in general.

He'd said that he couldn't remember anything significant, and had nervously added that his youth, a break up, and a short battle with alcohol had contributed to his failure to recall what would have been big news in the city. Nicky smiled, wondering how short-lived the battle with alcohol had been, or if indeed it had ever ended.

The four started to look through some old copies of the paper from 1983. There were some originals, and Natalie had also organised some fresh copies of relevant material, which she'd printed on A3 paper. There were also four desktop computers, and some files from the time; notes, papers, and some court transcripts that pleased Nicky greatly. Snippets that could be insignificant or absolutely critical, and which would need a keen eye. She realised that her and Natalie weren't that different, and shared a number of positive traits. She also wondered how Dominic felt about having a female boss twenty years his junior. Maybe he felt nothing. Maybe he hated the fact.

Nicky hated herself for thinking it, but she knew it wouldn't have happened in the eighties. Days of middle-aged men in plain suits, smoking and drinking cultures and boys' clubs for workplaces. The times had changed. Some things had anyway.

Dominic had expeditiously organised a number of documents and headlines that he thought would help. His ability to maintain documents was seemingly better than the central constabulary's across the road.

Jen looked at a headline from just after the first robbery: 'HEIST AT CITY JEWELLERS!'

The language was incongruous with that of the present day, the medium of a printed newspaper almost unrecognisable to someone of Jen's generation, whose consumption was largely through apps, social media and digital channels.

The print was grainy and pixelated. The picture quality of the front of Stefan's, post robbery, was poor, with a moustached officer and tape from outside barely recognisable. Even the language was simple and uncomplicated. Not tabloid level, but still basic.

Jen scanned, reading how the men had 'stormed in' and 'brandished clubs' at the terrified staff. She read the article, fascinated. The first robbery was brought back to life in another form. In somebody else's words. From a different generation.

Nicky and Natalie had picked up a second article, relating to the robbery at Laxmi. The language was similar, the reporter the same. 'SECOND HEIST ON BELGRAVE ROAD!'

The picture quality was equally bad but the shop front was recognisable, and the report was equally detailed in terms of the level of violence used. Smaller photos pictured the victims leaving the scene, the blood visible even amongst low-quality black and white photographs. The report was damning of the police, who had failed to make an arrest following the first robbery, allowing the men to carry out the second raid. The report went so far as to call the men 'masked thugs' and 'cowards'. It even mentioned Charlie Worth as a likely suspect.

Nicky was fascinated with the content, and had started to look at some of the court transcripts from the time. The stark and compelling words of the trial judge, Eric McCann, who Rob had sat in front of just twenty-four hours ago, echoed out from the pages.

Jen picked up a copy of the Leicester Mercury that featured the critical third robbery at Green's Jewellers, dated June 5th, 1983, and reported on the following day. There had been a two-month lag between the first two robberies, and then just another four weeks before the third. Jen imagined the pressures and strain amongst the group as it splintered. The desire for more spoils with less planning leading to this point. The point where Terry Morley was so badly beaten. Left for dead.

Jen read the top part of the article, taking in the details, feeling the pain. She slid the page to one side, and continued to browse through the pile of papers. She found another article from several months later, and from the day of the trial. The day of the convictions. She frowned, initially scanning the article for relevance but not seeing it. The article had elements of congratulation. A conviction had been secured. The paper was doing everything it could to suggest that Charlie's and Joe's sentences were too short, but stopped short of explicitly saying so.

Jen scanned as the article went into a subsection on a lack of justice for Terry Morley, written in the past tense as his suicide had preceded the trial; an added injustice that the men had not been held accountable for, and something the paper was keen to remind its readers of.

There was a picture of the victim. Of Terry Morley. It was the first time Jen had seen him. A smiling picture of a man in a pin-stripe suit. He looked smart, educated. Proud. There was another of his family. Those he left behind. This was a time without impact statements. Where victims were just victims, and widows and orphans were just unlucky. Jen looked at the picture of Terry Morley in happier times, smiling alongside his wife and daughter.

She squinted and looked again. Focused on it. A small and grainy image of a young girl. But Jen knew immediately. Recognised the eyes, the features and the shape of the face she knew well. She swallowed hard as the fact dawned and the realisation hit her like a sledgehammer.

"Holy fuck, Nicky."

Jen laid the article down. Nicky looked at Jen, then looked at the article, the black and white page with the picture that told them who was responsible for the killing spree. A young, innocent face, but instantly recognisable. Jen sat shocked, struggling to process it. She'd roomed with her before.

"You never truly know anybody, do you?"

*

Across town, Becky Ryan had been reviewing material following Rob's discoveries in Devon. She'd been able to locate genetic material from the third crime, which she had found at the central crime lab, and had expedited a sample to her office for analysis. The DNA of the victim had been stored and sat dormant for thirty years. There was no purpose for the DNA in the mid-eighties, with the storage of the evidence largely for posterity, but seemingly safer than articles that had disappeared, and had been made to disappear, making the third robbery completely invisible until now.

Becky ran a sample of Terry Morley's DNA through the system. She waited, tapping her long fingernails on top of the machine, subconsciously trying to hurry it up. It processed quickly, part of the screen showing the genetic profile in skyscraper form.

She hacked a command into the keyboard, asking for the data to be manipulated, and looked at the screen as the egg timer on it spun. Results appeared. No DNA matches for Terry Morley in any other capacity. His DNA didn't match any other records. But it did trigger one match.

Becky looked at it and frowned. She hit 'repeat' on the system to re-run it and check it again. The result appeared and she sat and stared at it. At what it meant. She sent a copy of the base graphic to a printer, so she could run her naked eye over the DNA patterns, and sense check what the result was telling her.

She held it up to the light, immediately picking out the matches. She knew, but the frown stayed. Perplexion grew. It didn't make sense. It couldn't be right.

There was a familial match, but to somebody she knew to be a serving police officer.

She picked up her phone and called Nicky, unaware that both her and Jen had just made the same discovery, with the DNA merely confirming and supporting the fact.

She spat out what the three of them now knew.

"Nicky, it's Emma Sharpe. She's Terry Morley's daughter."

CHAPTER 58

Jen called Jack to pass on the news, conscious he could be sitting in the station with PC Emma Sharpe within spitting distance.

Nicky was making the same call to Rob, aware that he wasn't at the station without knowing exactly where he was. The arrest should now be a formality. The fallout would take considerably longer. Natalie Allen and the Mercury would give the story their spin, but Nicky's immediate concern was for Rob, who would need to manage proceedings with Laura Mathers and David Parker. Police recruitment and protocol would be called into question, and the national tabloid press would love the notion of a police revenge killer. The controversy, the narrative and the death count would make the story international news, not just a local scandal.

Jen got Jack's voicemail a couple of times. She didn't leave a message due to the sensitivity, cutting the call before the beep.

Nicky got through to Rob and started the conversation, the explanation of how one of their own was responsible for the murders, of how the killer of four men had sat in briefings just yards from Nicky, listening to the details of the murders she had carried out the evening before. How she'd carried out a murder in Liverpool under the guise of taking some time off. Traumatised and exhausted by the experience and granted annual leave, and taking advantage of a focus that had fallen on Bernie Copp, allowing her to access and murder Daniel Mortimer while the team sat outside.

She knew who was where, and when. She knew the direction of the investigation and had access to every file, every document. She'd carried a load of them in with Jack, had uploaded some key documents into the central file for the investigation, allowing her to filter and remove documents that could have identified the third robbery, Terry Morley and ultimately her, at an earlier point.

The conversation continued with a number of points being raised by both Nicky and Rob, as the realisation of the stone-cold facts continued to land.

Rob hadn't recruited Emma Sharpe and didn't know who had. He didn't know which police protocol she'd been through upon her successful application, and crucially didn't know at which point she'd concocted a plan to murder the men responsible for her father's death. In her eyes, at least.

When did she go rogue, and when did she change her name? Who carried out her mandatory employment checks, under which version of it, and when? Questions that would all come under significant scrutiny, both internally and externally over the coming days and weeks, as the policing and political fallout would unfold.

Jen had got through to the station and had reached one of the team who had supported the investigation. She hadn't wanted to raise the alarm until an arrest could be made, and had stayed perfectly calm when she was told that Jack had headed to Elizabeth Warren's house with Emma Sharpe to question her.

Jen started to wave a hand frantically at Nicky, who moved her own mobile away from her face to listen, as Jen told her of the whereabouts of their killer and their colleague.

"Rob, I need to go. Jack's in trouble. He's in Enderby with Emma Sharpe."

The two rushed to Jen's car with Nicky still trying to contact Jack, still to no avail. With Jen driving, Nicky arranged for uniform to dispatch a number of vehicles and officers, who would meet them in Alexander Avenue, a normal residential street in Enderby where Jack had unwittingly travelled to with a murderer.

The journey was short, and the two left the car in the middle of the street with doors open and the blue lights on their unmarked vehicle flashing.

Running to the house both had been to before, they could see the front door ajar. Jen shouted Jack's name as she barged through an open front door, in the style she had wanted to adopt at Charlie Worth's house. Reckless for her own safety and unaware of the inhabitants of the house, she smashed through an internal door into an empty dining room.

Nicky followed her, radio to hand and more cautious of the potential for danger. She continued to report into her radio, now able to hear the sirens of the patrol cars that were less than a mile behind her. Those officers knew the house had been disturbed. They knew Nicky and Jen were inside. She'd requested an ambulance already too, nervous of what lay within the walls of the property.

Jen hammered into another room, and shouted "JACK!" Nicky glanced upstairs then headed after Jen, through another door and into the kitchen. They found Jack, unconscious and on the floor, lying on his side in a foetal position, but alive. Jen put her hands on his shoulders as he slurred a noise without moving his closed eyes.

"There's an ambulance on the way, Jack."

Jen looked for injuries, unable to see any blood or marks on his shirt, skin or head that would indicate a blow or a stabbing.

"I think he's been drugged, Nicky."

"Stay with him. They're close."

Jen took off her jacket, laid Jack's head on it and continued to talk to him as the sirens pulled into the street. He continued to slur back.

Nicky calmly talked into her radio. She was conscious that Emma Sharpe could well be listening, but she gave the clear instruction that she was now wanted for the murders of William Reynolds, Joe Davies, Charlie Worth and Daniel Mortimer, and for the assault of DC Jack Bowery.

She held her radio firmly, and moved her attention to the resident of the house. Whether she was still here was still to be confirmed, but Jack was nothing but collateral. Emma Sharpe was here for the woman who had given an alibi to Daniel Mortimer, which had become an alibi for all of them. A free pass.

Nicky climbed the stairs slowly as uniformed officers and a paramedic entered the front door. She pointed to the lounge door without looking at them, and shouted to Jen to alert her of their presence.

The landing was silent. Four doors were closed. Nicky sensed that Emma Sharpe wasn't there but trod cautiously as she pushed a door open.Nothing.

She pushed a second door. She could sense it immediately. The smell hadn't become offensive yet. Too fresh for that.

Nicky walked slowly into a bedroom. A characterless and pale bedroom. A chair had been pulled into a space, and Nicky could see the side-on profile of Elizabeth Harris's body. A crude injury to her head, and gaffer tape on her wrists.

She felt for a pulse. Nothing.

The body had been beaten. There was blood thick in her hair, glistening in the daylight coming in through a bay window.

There'd been a crude attempt on her fingers and ear, with both still attached but deep cut marks and blood indicating that Emma Sharpe had tried to replicate the other murders, or at least inflict the same levels of violent retribution.

Elizabeth Harris hadn't been in Terry Morley's jewellers that day, but she'd been made to pay the price for her love and loyalty to Daniel Mortimer.

Nicky called Becky, gave her the address and told her she'd be waiting. The cause of Elizabeth Harris' death was almost certainly due to the injuries to her head. She had been battered violently, as had the four men. This one appeared equally as angry. Savage. More so.

PC Emma Sharpe had now murdered five people and Jack was on his way to the LRI.

Nicky walked down the stairs and gave Jen a knowing look in the hall.

"Second door on the left."

CHAPTER 59

Jack was recovering well, having spent a night in the Leicester Royal Infirmary, allowing the drugs to flush through his system, and for any side effects to show themselves.

The staff had insisted. So had Rob.

His pride was also on the mend. The piss-taking would come in due course, but that wasn't for now. The mood in camp was low and would stay that way for a while. Jen would need to come to terms with it. Her friend. Somebody she thought she knew. Five murders and a colleague responsible for it was a loss in anybody's book.

Jack was in good spirits, but hadn't yet had a visitor other than his parents. Rob, Nicky and Jen were desperately trying to trace and apprehend Emma Sharpe. The straightforward arrest hadn't materialised. She'd vanished after leaving the scene in Enderby and was still in the wind.

Her flat had already been raided, and the team were trying to locate and arrest her, with little initial evidence as to her whereabouts, her plan or her escape route, if indeed there is one.

She'd reduced her living footprint to a minimal level, with little excess and scarce possessions in her flat. The kitchen was bare except for a kettle, a smoothie blender, a box of Weetabix and a fruit bowl on a table. She'd been living very cleanly, and was clearly well organised and highly disciplined. A dirty pair of running trainers lying by the front door the only items looking out of place.

There was some physical evidence to hand. A map on the wall identifying who was where, surrounded by countless pictures of the victims in various places, and at various times, all centred around a picture of her dad, her mum and a page with "do it for them" written on it.

The planning had been extensive. Obsessive. Most of the imagery was on the wall around her bed. It would have been the last thing she saw at night and the first thing she saw each morning.

This hadn't been dreamt up overnight. This was years in the making, with the odd piece of flair thrown in, such as the stunt she'd pulled that had brought down Daniel Mortimer.

Outside of the search, the political games were well underway. Rob had spent the morning on the phone, with the hierarchy now more concerned with their own careers than apprehending a police officer who had murdered five people. Perverse priorities.

Rob was aligning himself with Laura Mathers. Primarily because he felt it was the right thing to do, but also because he'd toed her line and felt confident that she'd defend the hill better than David Parker would.

Somebody would pay the price. The smart money was already on him.

CHAPTER 60

It's an odd feeling. I'm not sure I ever expected to get this far. All four of them, plus her for good measure. And I'm still a free woman. For now, anyway.

I've achieved what I set out to achieve, so there's a tinge of satisfaction, but I also feel a little empty. Almost like I wish there was another couple of them. I've become more accomplished at this than I expected.

I've managed to exact revenge on my terms. The justice system of the day failed my dad. It failed my mum. It failed me. The trial didn't even acknowledge him, and those men were never held accountable for what they did to my dad and my family. To his business, which he worked so hard to build. His passion and his love of watches. His love of engineering. His love of time.

I had no choice.

I'm not sure dad would be pleased, let alone proud. Mum neither. They were placid people. Good people. Which is why I needed to avenge their deaths.

Life's monotonous. Boring. I'm happier now having done what I've done than I would be if I'd spent the next thirty years arresting car thieves. Seeing them locked up, then released to do it again. The cyclical nature of life.

I'm content. I did what I needed to do. Wanted to do. It's odd how life can inspire and motivate you in certain directions. I have a picture of my passing out parade for the force in my purse. A young twenty something with the world at her feet. She wasn't a killer. Not yet.

Yet nearly a decade later I'm no longer a police officer and my name will go down in history for what I've done. I can live with that.

My disguise should hold up. I'm confident. The police know one of my aliases but my passport options aren't restricted to Morley and Sharpe. I'm better than that. I have four flights booked in four different names from four different airports. My passports are quality, all genuine. They took a while to obtain but they'll get me through as long as the facial recognition doesn't click. Or some eagle-eyed police officer. Or some passenger who might see me on Facebook in the next couple of hours.

That's all the time I need. Then I'm off to catch a tan in Rio. It was good enough for Ronnie Biggs.

I'll start afresh. I have cash and I have a strong desire to be free.

I'll sleep with one eye open if I have to.

 Matador